Delvyn, instead of laughing, struck an ill-tuned chord on his lute. "What kind of negligent ruler is it, I ask you," the dwarf complained in evident sincerity, "who leaves his fiercest warrior ill-armed, unmounted, and ungirded on the eve of battle?"

"You would have fought valiantly for your king, I'm sure," Conan said.

"And did so!" Delvyn put in sharply.

"Yes, yes, of course. And yet your speeches give him little honor, nor any to his ally, Lord Malvin." King Conan looked up at last from his stack of royal decrees. "If you speak so ill of them in their absence, I wonder, how will you speak of me when my back is turned?"

Delvyn strummed the plaintive air's refrain. "Need you wonder, O King Gut-squeezer" —the pale, close-set eyes glinted at Conan out of the shadows— "keeping in mind that I speak only ill of you to your face?"

Conan guffawed. Once his burst of appreciative laughter had subsided, he swigged from his ale cup and said, "Good then, brave Delvyn! A king learns to cherish frankness above all else—especially from fools, who always flock so thickly around him."

The Adventures of Conan
Published by Tor Books

Conan the Bold by John Maddox Roberts
Conan the Champion by John Maddox Roberts
Conan the Defender by Robert Jordan
Conan the Defiant by Steve Perry
Conan the Destroyer by Robert Jordan
Conan the Fearless by Steve Perry
Conan the Free Lance by Steve Perry
Conan the Great by Leonard Carpenter
Conan the Hero by Leonard Carpenter
Conan the Indomitable by Steve Perry
Conan the Invincible by Robert Jordan
Conan the Magnificent by Robert Jordan
Conan the Marauder by John Maddox Roberts
Conan the Raider by Leonard Carpenter
Conan the Renegade by Leonard Carpenter
Conan the Triumphant by Robert Jordan
Conan the Unconquered by Robert Jordan
Conan the Valiant by Roland Green
Conan the Valorous by John Maddox Roberts
Conan the Victorious by Robert Jordan
Conan the Warlord by Leonard Carpenter

THE GREAT

BY

LEONARD CARPENTER

A TOM DOHERTY ASSOCIATES BOOK
NEW YORK

This book is a work of fiction. All the characters and events portrayed in it are fictional, and any resemblance to real people or incidents is purely coincidental.

CONAN THE GREAT

A Tor Book
Published by Tom Doherty Associates, Inc.
49 West 24th Street
New York, N.Y. 10010

Cover art by Ken Kelly

ISBN: 0-812-50714-2

First edition: April 1989

Printed in the United States of America

0 9 8 7 6 5 4 3 2 1

With thanks, to Tad Williams

Contents

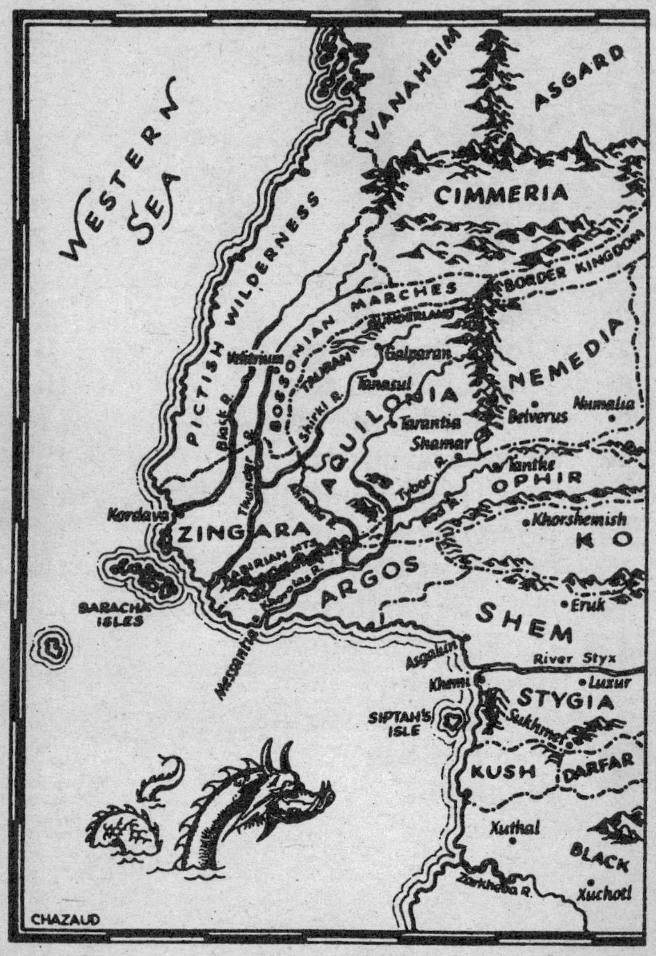

WESTERN SEA
VANAHEIM
ASGARD
CIMMERIA
PICTISH WILDERNESS
BOSSONIAN MARCHES
BORDER KINGDOM
NEMEDIA
Velitrium
Tauran
Galparan
Tanasul
AQUILONIA
Tarantia
Belverus
Numalia
Shamar
Black R.
Thunder R.
Shirki R.
BOSSONIA
Tybor R.
Ianthe
OPHIR
Kordava
ZINGARA
Khorshemish
KO
ARGOS
BARACHA ISLES
Eruk
SHEM
Messantia
Asgalun
River Styx
Khemi
Luxur
STYGIA
SIPTAH'S ISLE
Sukhmet
KUSH
DARFAR
Xuthal
BLACK
Zarkheba R.
Xuchotl
CHAZAUD

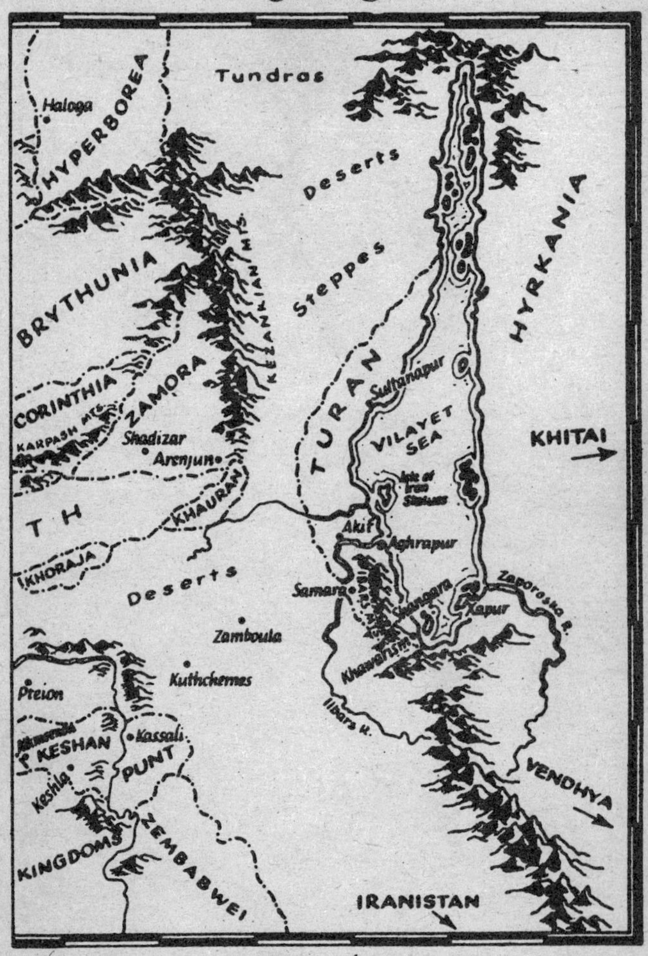

Tundras
Haloga
HYPERBOREA
Deserts
Steppes
BRYTHUNIA
KEZANKIAN MTS.
HYRKANIA
CORINTHIA
ZAMORA
KARPASH MTS.
Shadizar
Arenjun
TURAN
Sultanapur
VILAYET SEA
KHITAI
KHAURAN
T H
KHORAJA
Akif
Aghrapur
Deserts
Samara
Shangara
Kapur
Zaporoska R.
Zamboula
Khawarism
Kuthchemes
Preion
Kassali
KESHAN
PUNT
Ilbars R.
VENDHYA
Keshla
KINGDOMS
ZEMBABWEI
IRANISTAN

Chapter 1
Victory

The Tybor plain stretched level, its grass sheened a dewy, dazzling emerald in the morning sun. Set amid the Hyborian kingdoms of Aquilonia, Nemedia, and Ophir, ever had it made an easy, dangerous route between the three. Now its flatness formed a gentle, open vista broken at intervals by flowering thickets and lone, spreading trees.

The lush greensward made a bright background for the armies that were swiftly deploying across it. Their neat ranks formed gaily colored patterns on its surface, like painted playing-draughts dealt out upon a cloth of tufted green baize.

The masses of troops marching into position, extending their formations and threatening to flank and double one another, were the fighting hosts of mighty nations. The blue-caped legions of imperial Ophir—striding footmen, wheeling chariots, and cantering knights—

comprised the southern half of the line. Their polished spearblades and pointed steel caps made flowing, shimmering constellations of sparks in the early light. Taking their places to the shrilling of reed pipes, they moved close beside allies decked in earthier grays and browns.

These regiments rattled more heavily with armor, and moved in more rigid patterns to the thump and rustle of drums. Crowded beneath the sable banners of Nemedia, the darker armies occupied a place in the battleline matching their kingdom's position on the map, adjoining and to the north of Ophir. They raised serried rows of lances and halberds in a deadly-looking steel fence pointing westward, with the sun warming their backs. At their center, surrounded by a phalanx of armored knights bearing aloft black-draped lances, could be seen the gray-haired, gray-bearded figure of fierce old King Balt.

Stocky in his worn, traditional jerkin of metal-studded leather, Balt bestrode a silver-gray charger, his polished helmet couched beneath one burly arm. At some time in his rise from service as a fighting officer in the Iron Legions of Imperial Nemedia, the gray metal of his helm and his armor-bosses had been reworked with purest gold. A mounted page beside him held aloft his huge shield, its battered old iron likewise leafed over with white and yellow gold. The two contrasting colors were inlaid skillfully in the shape of the royal Nemedian crest: a beaked, taloned gryphon. The shield's polished surface flashed forth a blazing beacon wherever it caught the sun.

King Balt's entourage moved southward through the knee-high grass, centering well behind the foremost ranks of Nemedian spearmen. They moved toward a second plumed, bannered enclave of nobility, hedged in by gleaming knights and flanked by wheeling chariots. This gathering was the elite household guard of young Lord Malvin, mighty Ophir's ablest general and self-declared despot.

Malvin had not yet deigned to crown himself king—uncertain, perhaps, whether kingship might not be a downward step from lordship. But he laid frank claim to the whole vast Ophirean nation; also to sundry neighboring lands, including a portion of these very fields on which the allied armies were massing. In his territorial ambition Malvin enjoyed the zealous support, or grudging acquiescence, of all the various dukes, barons, marchesses, and other Ophirean nobles whose family insignia could be seen adorning the shields and pennons of his host.

Malvin lorded it astride a white stallion draped in silvery chain mail, its reins and harnesses adorned with fluttering blue streamers. The trim young ruler himself gleamed in a costly suit of steel plate; it was crafted well enough to allow him an unequalled range of movement, as his spirited waves and gestures to his massing troops showed. His armor was of pale, unadorned metal, free of any sculpture or embellishment—a costume well-suited to a commander whose force was becoming known as the swiftest and most efficient in the world.

The young lord, in pressing his current territorial claim, had found common cause with his northern neighbor, Balt. Both rulers would enjoy carving off a slice of these western meadowlands as richly carpeted thresholds for their powerful domains. Malvin, now adjusting his visor to shade his eyes, watched the elder monarch approach. As the two noble households drew together he spurred his horse forward through the mob of knights and retainers, greeting his ally with a shout and a brotherly handclasp.

Their meeting made a gala scene, the heraldry of the two great kingdoms converging and mingling like bright confetti. Lusty cheers sounded, weapons flourished in air, and the skirling of pipes and trumpets rose up festive beneath the blue dome of sky. The exuberance spread like a wave to the outer reaches of the horde, raising shouts from the ranks of Shemitish bowmen who marched in the pay of the allies, from mounted Zamoran mercenaries, and from motley crowds of spear-shaking peasants whose masses stretched off into the morning haze.

Bright was their array, glorious their purpose, and there remained but one obstacle to their mission. It lay in the red, black, and green tracings and massings of the army which opposed them.

The force stretched across the plain to westward, their backs to the Tybor River. The assembled host of proud Aquilonia consisted of battle-hard legions from the royal garrisons at Shamar and Tarantia, tall Gundermen mustered at double-time from the chill northern marches, and Bossonians in their forest-green doublets, summoned eastward from the Pictish frontier. Numbering a mere thousand or two horsemen backed by a dozen thousand men afoot, their weapons seemed to add but little to the forests of spears and halberds, the meadows of feathery arrow-fletchings, and the razored thickets of swords which had sprouted overnight on the Tybor plain.

The Aquilonian officers waited in their saddles, well forward in the ranks. Their mounts ranged about a single golden banner beneath which brooded their legendary commander, King Conan. No Aquilonian he by birth; rather, a burly, dark-maned northern savage who made an imposing figure astride Sheol, his coal-black Zamboulan charger. Man and horse alike glistened darkly in the ebon, gold-chased plate armor of the Black Dragons, his elite palace guard.

Conan was not one, sober men said, to let a sizeable chunk of Aquilonian soil be wrested from him by the revival of an ill-remembered territorial claim—not even in the face of treacherous collusion by two eastern neighbors. His army, though smaller than his foemen's, stood ready to fight. This was proven once and for all, as he chose that moment—the meeting of the two enemy kings—to raise high his broadsword and bellow forth the command, "Attack!"

The trumpets' angry blatting echoed his words and heralded the first stroke of war: a flight of arrows from the front of the Aquilonian line. The projectiles rose steeply together, flashing in unison as they arched beneath the sun, and stooped hungrily toward the foremost ranks of Ophirean and Nemedian pikemen.

Some of the shafts may have fallen short, or glanced harmlessly from enemy shields; but the fabled, lethal accuracy of the Bossonian longbowmen was proven as ragged gaps opened miraculously in the foemen's ranks. Among the survivors could be seen a backward cringing and a faint, murmured confusion at this sudden rain of feathered death.

A second, less simultaneous volley of arrows flashed skyward, and a third. Then the first wave of Aquilonian knights charged, and the loosing abruptly ceased, lest the bowmen's clothyard shafts strike their armored backs. These warriors—seasoned horsemen from the province of Poitain, bounding and plunging alongside rakish, richly mounted Tarantian nobles—galloped through narrow openings in the archers' line to bear down on the enemy. Heavy in their plate and mail, the horsemen gathered speed with a thunder of hoofbeats that tremored beneath the soles of every watcher.

Now came the chance for the Shemitish archers, from their places in the Nemedian and Ophirean flanks, to strike at the charging Aquilonian cavalry. Their shorter, thicker bows and shafts were plied ably and swiftly, but could do little damage to the fast-moving armored force. Here and there a mount stumbled, or a rider crumpled and fell; but most of the black-clad knights bore the razor-tipped rain without scathe. Shrugging off arrows like tiresome gnats, they hunched lower in their saddles and couched their red-pennoned lances to a deadly horizontal.

They smote the enemy line, the impact echoing down its length like the measured crash of an ocean wave striking a broad, stony beach. The gleaming fence of pikes, already broken and depopulated by arrow flights, cut and jabbed but a few riders out of their saddles. The charging knights, abandoning their lances in the crushed breasts of luckless defenders, quickly drew broad-swords, maces and flails. With these they set about opening paths for the cheering Aquilonian footsoldiers, mostly red-jerkined Gundermen who came swarming and shouting up behind them.

Again it was the turn of the Shemitish mercenaries to loose their arrows. This time their shafts had more effect against the half-armored footmen. But of a sudden, their crossfire was obstructed. The hindrance was their own allied Nemedian and Ophirean cavalry, who spurred forward in the hope of wreaking bloodier revenge.

It so happened that the eastern allies, pressed back against their own ranks by the onslaught of mounted knights and footborne harriers, found their avenues of attack closed. Their bravest riders, desperate to join the fight, tried the only possible expedient: the frenzied cavalry pushed through gaps in either flank to assault the enemy. Their only strategy was to engage Aquilonian foot and horse soldiers by the shortest possible route, from either side.

But their rude plan failed to reckon with their enemies' most murderous weapon, the Bossonian longbow. The lank northern archers, screened now by a row of spearmen crouching low along the Aquilonian line, were provided with tall, bulky targets moving straight across their vision at near range. The cruel-hearted northmen, thanking ice-eyed northern gods for their good luck, found themselves free to loose, and draw, and loose again at will. Their long-practiced skills were put to a leisurely test; in meeting it, their questing shafts sought out every crease in the Ophireans' armor, every slack, forgotten buckle, every Nemedian page-boy's ill-polished, rusty scale. Or else—if the angle was perfect, the shaft well-turned and its tip properly squared and waxed—the arrow would drive straight through a sheet of steel forged thick as a knifeblade, with enough force left to pierce a ribcage and a throbbing, straining heart.

The jesting bowmen called each mark loudly. They wagered together as they fought, gaining or losing a purse or a wench on the twang of a bowstring. Pairing their skills, they let fly in teams; more than one eastern knight, feeling a rap on his hauberk, glanced carelessly aside just in time to see a second well-aimed shaft rushing into his eye through his helmet's visor-slit. Some enemy riders galloped onward bristling arrows like bright-quilled hedgehogs, dead in the saddle; others lived, yet found themselves unable to fight with a hand pinned to a chest, a thigh to a screaming horse, or a tongue to a shattered jawbone.

Of those heroic knights of Nemedia and Ophir who

sallied forth from their embattled line, 'twas doubtful whether any would ultimately have survived the Bossonian barbs. But the next turn of battle freed them from their feathered torment. Fate left a few score of them alive—to face the charge of the elite Aquilonian cavalry reserve, led by the dreaded King Conan himself.

The sullen western monarch, watching for an opening, saw his chance in the rash charge of the enemy horsemen. Now his spendidly mounted Black Dragons thundered out through the line of archers and spearmen and drove straight across the tattered remnants of enemy cavalry. The last few of those died obediently before his knights' hurtling lances; onward then the king and his company galloped, past the rearmost ranks of cheering, ax-waving Gundermen, to exploit the temporary gap the enemy charge had created in the Ophirean right flank. Their goal, clearly, was to drive straight to the heart of the milling host and engage its commanders.

That meant facing, first, regiments of Shemitish bowmen. The lean, sun-browned mercenaries, clad in belted sheepskins and brassbound leather caps, sped a dense flight of arrows at the approaching wave of cavalry. Yet their bows and shafts, cut from brittle, short-limbed oak rather than the pliant yew of the northern forests, lacked force of penetration. On seeing how little effect their first arrows had against Tarantian steel, the Shemites aimed the second flight less truly, even though the range was growing shorter. Their third volley was a mere aimless convulsion, loosed in desperation as the flying cavalry smashed into their ranks.

Men and weapons were ground beneath iron hooves; many an Aquilonian sword sheared away two or three mercenaries' lives in a single, furious swath. Against the steel-clad frenzy, the southerners' short, bronze blades were even more useless than their bows. And so the Shemites—those not slain in the first thundering heartbeats of close battle—turned to flee. Swiftly infecting the ranks behind them with their panic and confusion, they left only vacancy and chaos in the teeth of the Aquilonian onslaught.

It made a noble picture: the wide-drawn sketchings of red and black sending forth a darkly gleaming crescent, a talon curving out to pierce deep into the blue formation. At its needle-like intrusion, the denser body of troops deformed as if in pain—not just the blue segment, but equally the gray-brown mass welded beside it against the grinding battlefront. Along the widening breach some masses of men, blue and brown alike, surged forward to fight; others recoiled more swiftly, their motion causing a swirling disruption of the once neat pattern.

Before long even the central pageant—the cluster of many-colored flags surrounding the eastern commanders—seemed to falter. The bright-hued assemblage drifted aimlessly, jostled and eroded by the rushing currents of fugitives on all sides; then, as the flailing axes and maces of charging Aquilonian horsemen clove nearer, the elite formation began to melt and recede. There remained no longer a bright bubble for the darting steel pinprick to pierce; only gaudy, scattering shreds, the retinues of fleeing nobles and officers.

Their disintegration joined that of the broader formation and became a general, disorderly retreat. Whole sections of the pattern collapsed and flowed rearward, leaving other masses dangerously exposed. These were promptly encircled and obliterated by the lines of red and black which now, to the shriek of trumpets, surged forward all along the front.

Chapter 2
The Stricken Field

At long last the grim priestess Night obscured the Tybor plain. Stealing across it like death's dark nursemaid, she shaded the staring eyes of the dead and trailed her discreet veil across grisly scenes left in battle's wake. From behind her in the east crept forth a swollen, prurient moon, whose prying eye sought to reveal all in lurid brightness. But its gaze had thus far been foiled by clouds; also by the smoke of burning farmsteads low down near the horizon, where its gloating visage cast a fitful yellow gleam.

From the east likewise came a bulky shambling figure, picking its way between the heaped-up remains of men and horses. It was a primal sight: a man, possibly—else a weary god or imp of battle, walking slumped and unsteady from fatigue and wounds. Yet he moved resolutely westward with a hint of unguessed strength held in reserve.

The shambler was mottled and blackened with gore, some of it drily crusted, some still oozing dark wetness. Girdled by the hacked, ragged remnants of a battle-suit with nearly every plate of armor cut or cast away, he bulked otherwise naked under a lank, clotted mane of hair. Helmetless, he bore in one hand a longsword, fine and costly in its manufacture. The sword of a king it was, but notched now, and foul with the blood and excrement of battle. Its point he let drag carelessly behind him in the trampled, gory grass as he trudged doggedly onward, avoiding the more impassable drifts of corpses by the gloom of the half-shrouded moon.

Of a sudden he paused, watchful, at the sound of a human cry from one of corpse piles. It came again: a low, throaty moan, seeming to issue from somewhere in the deep shadow of a fallen horse, the dead beast already bloating in the spring warmth. He shambled near, gazing somberly down to pierce the gloom. At length he distinguished the outline of a dark-caped footman, a soldier of Ophir by his garb.

The man was pinned face-down to earth by a broken cavalry lance. Its point had passed through his vitals into the ground, where it held firm, its long splinters still blossoming palely upward from his back. The man's peaked helm was now cast aside, his hair tousled, the grass within his reach uprooted or pounded flat by his daylong struggles. As he feebly raised his head from the soil to call out yet again, the moonlight showed off his blondish beard and mustache darkly crusted with the blood that had streamed down from his mouth and nostrils.

"God's mercy, please! In Mitra's name, a balm . . . aah-agk!" His throaty plaint was cut short as the warrior's sword hacked deep into his neck near the nape.

It was not a clean blow, yet it did its merciful work. When the body fell slack, the swordsman dragged his weapon free and turned wearily to shamble onward.

He had not gone far when he glimpsed another feeble motion amid the corpses. With steps growing heavy and reluctant, he turned aside once again to investigate. Here lay a giant Gunderman, sorely wounded but alive. His face shone ashen; his eye and tooth gleamed yellowly in a stray shard of moonlight. He made no sound except steady, ragged gasps, and yet he struggled mightily, dragging himself onward through the grass. The wound to his belly was plainly mortal, and must have been agonizing. But the man's blood trail showed that he had crept a long distance, snail-like, greasing his way with his own entrails.

The longsword arched high and made a heavy clank, striking the rim of the wounded man's bronze helm as it chopped into his skull. Its notched edge caught in the bone, and proved devilish hard to withdraw. Tugging at it, murmuring oaths of blood and fire, the lone warrior paused for breath. An ill fancy caused him to eye the windrows of slain around him, and he shuddered with guilty, superstitious dread. He wondered how many more of these, his fallen subjects and butchered foes, might yet live, gasping unseen in darkness, buried alive under mountains of corpses—or whether every one of them might return to life this night, his loyal friends and enemies alike, to come groping after him with vengeful, clawlike hands. . . .

Wrenching his great sword free, he lurched away, stepping over bodies strewn like jumblesticks, even tripping on some in his near panic. Then, as he staggered past the hulk of an overturned chariot, a sharp voice beseeched him:

"Nay, killer of the helpless, slay me not! Spare me in the name of Crom, Manannan, Mitra, or whatever gory god this feast of souls is for!"

The gory shambler peered into the dimness, frozen in feral surprise. A moment later he made out the face and form of the speaker: a stocky, thick-featured man lying supine in the grass a mere half-stride ahead of him. The stranger could pose no threat; the nether part of his body was pinned to earth by an overturned chariot—crushed and crippled, undoubtedly, since the vehicle's heavy bronze rim had gouged deep into the soil. Its centerpole was further weighted to earth by the carcasses of two matched roan geldings slumping dead in their traces.

Yet the voice had rung out bold and firm, and was answered in the same spirit by the swordsman.

"Why, then, should I spare you?—to make you captive? I am a warrior, not a slave-catcher!" Holding his sword level, the speaker forced his breathing to a steadier cadence, lest he be thought afraid. "As an honest soldier, 'tis my part to slay the wounded cleanly, to accept what humble loot they may offer up in payment, and hope some honorable soul will do the same for me when it is my turn." The warrior scowled down at the homely, upturned face. "Should I not extend the same kindness to you? 'Tis no more than my duty!"

"An honest soldier?" the fallen one demanded. "Nay, a liar!—because I know you for a king!" The word rang out harshly over the field of slaughter, seeming to echo accusingly to a hundred dead ears in the moment of stillness that followed. "King Conan the Bloody-handed . . . Conan of the Dripping Ax, royal upstart of Aquilonia!" The speaker, though evidently wounded, showed amazing vitality, his face leering and grimacing froggily beneath the rim of an oversized antique helmet. "As king, you need trouble yourself no more with the petty codes of common soldiers! Has none yet told you that? To you, O King, all things are possible!"

The pause the hulking warrior allowed before answering was judicious. "So say you, stranger, and you seem to know the ways of kings." He did not trouble to deny his identity; strangely, as a result of this grisly banter with a dying man, he found his soul being teased out of its morbid fears. "And yet I may kill you even so—to ease the pangs of your wound, or for better cause."

"My wound? Nay, King Butcher, I have no wound! I fought too fiercely to be wounded, even by your back-shooting archers." The speaker grew animated once again, rolling his eyes up at the king and thrashing both his arms, which looked oddly foreshortened in the moonlight. "I would be fighting still if this chariot had not pinned the skirt of my armor beneath its weight." He gestured down to where the brass rail cut across the metal leaves, crushing them uniformly flat at thigh level. " 'Tis but a cheap, ill-fitting suit, furnished at my insistence on the eve of our march from Ianthe. Such was my frenzy for slaughter that even tight-fisted old King Balt could not deny me! Lord Malvin provided me the chariot—a shame that it lacked an able driver."

"By Crom, I see . . . you are a dwarf!" Lowering his sword and easing its grimy point between the chest-plate and skirtwaist of the mashed armor suit, King Conan sawed at the leather strapping he found there, not meanwhile encountering any hips or belly within. At last the upper segment of the armor loosened and twisted free; two booted feet emerged, tentative and turtle-like, from the bottom of the hauberk.

"There, you are unpinned."

"Yes, at last!" Clambering to his feet, the dwarf stretched out his stocky frame to a height near equal to the midpoint of Conan's thigh. "And here is my noble sword, Hearts-pang. It has lain just out of reach, and tantalized me since morn." Stooping, he picked up a somewhat oversized dagger and held it above his head, twisting it to catch the glint of moonlight. He thrust his face up at Conan from beneath his skewed, ungainly helmet and cried out spiritedly, "Which way the fight?"

"The fight is over, little man. Your side lost."

"What? I feared as much—a bitter shame!" He cocked his head aside, frowning and looking crestfallen. "And yet," he added philosophically, " 'tis possible to be over-hasty in proclaiming that a war is over, and who the victor is!" He shrugged his shoulders, making the helmet joggle loosely on his head. "But say, O King—if you do not have the pluck left to fight me, and settle matters once and for all—would it be too great a lapse of your royal dignity to help me remove this breastplate? It bangs against my shins when I walk."

"Why, certainly, fellow—if you swear not to try any tricks!" Reaching down and catching the dwarf's knife-fist in his own burly hand, Conan plucked the dagger from it, then knelt to ply its point in the vulnerable seams at the sides of the obsolete battle-dress. Before its razored steel, old leather parted, and the armor plates soon clanked free. "What is your name, little man?"

"Ow! Careful, King Jabber, I am no lobster for you to gouge the meat out of!" Tugging away from Conan's grasp, the dwarf shucked the breast and scapular plates off over his head to clatter on the ground. The helmet he retained, straightening it so that it rested more on his shoulders than his brow. "Delvyn is my name. I am, or was, imperial jester to King Balt's court in Belverus—depending, I suppose, on whether the old gas-bladder still lives and spouts drivel."

Beneath the armor the dwarf wore a jerkin and pantaloons, well-fitting yet scallop-fringed and clownishly adorned. Their sheen of silk in the moonlight seemed to confirm his boast of high office. "Balt?" the king's voice rumbled ruefully. "Yes, he lives, in spite of my best efforts. As does his fellow traitor Malvin, as far as I know. I gave orders that none of my troops were to slay them, since I hoped to reserve that pleasure for myself."

"Then the two of them must have cravenly fled the field! I would have guessed as much." Delvyn's grotesque face, canted habitually upward and now facing the moon, creased in a sneer of scorn. "Balt is but a withered hangnail of the warrior he used to be, and Malvin was never anything but a fop. Ah, it pains me to serve such weaklings!" He shook his head in disappointment. " 'Tis a rare king nowadays who craves to die at the forefront of his troops—who courts death as a maiden, and so becomes her husband! Though I have heard that you, Conan the Butcher, are one such." Squaring his shoulders, he strutted up to Conan's shadow and extended a stubby hand. "Return my noble sword Hearts-pang, I beg you, O King!"

"Nay, little one, not so fast!" Conan slipped the knife into his crusty girdle and turned to grasp the hilt of his own sword, where it stood thrust into the earth. "I fear to return your cutlass to you so soon, and risk being stabbed in the knee. But come along with me, brave Delvyn, you are now my prisoner!'' Choosing a path between corpse drifts, he resumed walking, using his own moon shadow as a pointer. ''Mayhap I will barter you back to your kingdom for thrice your weight in gold.''

'' 'Twould be a poor bargain at that rate. I venture to say I am worth thrice your own unwieldy weight and more, O King!'' Delvyn shrugged and scuttled along, catching up to his captor with an air of resignation. ''Not that the crotchety, bilious old Balt would ever admit my worth or pay it! More likely he would say I bedeviled him, and blame me for his miserable defeat. Just because I counselled him to settle his territorial claims in the only honorable way!''

''King Balt is old and addled indeed, if he heeds the advice of his professional fool.'' Conan led the way around an oak tree, its lower branches broken and pruned by flailing weapons, the west side of its trunk furred by a blizzard of arrows. ''But ho,'' he grunted, ''here come riders! If they are my enemies, you may yet win your freedom.'' He raised his sword and moved to place his back against the tree. A moment later he lowered the weapon as it became clear that the three horsemen's mail was black not only with night and soil, but with the glossy lacquer of the Black Dragon guard.

''Glory be unto Mitra!'' a familiar voice hailed. ''It is the king—he lives!'' The armored man, wheeling his galloping destrier to a halt, swung elegantly down from the saddle. Gracefully and silently he caught the weight of his steel suit on the ground, then sank smoothly to one knee at Conan's feet. There, devoutly, he bowed his head and raised one mailed hand to be clasped in his ruler's. The other two horsemen, meanwhile, reined up and dismounted less expertly, clanking forward to assume indentical postures just behind and to either side of the first rider.

"Come, Trocero! By Crom's bunions, you know I hate such obeisances!" Reaching down and clasping the armored man's shoulder, he hauled him up to his feet.

"Aye, Your Majesty!" Count Trocero reached up to loosen his helmet, lifted it off his head, and lowered it into the crook of his arm with a heavy clank. The face thus exposed was broad and handsome, its nose and cheekbones arching firm above a black mustache shot with gray, its hawklike dark eyes taking in Conan's figure intently. "Are you well? Sire, you cannot imagine the agony of doubt we have been through!—searching the whole vast wake of the routed armies, not knowing whether you might be slain or captured, whether Aquilonia still had a king, or whether half the empire would be demanded as your ransom. . . . Forgive me, Sire, but 'tis well you are here!" Bowing again swiftly, the nobleman seized Conan's hand and pressed his mustached lips against his king's blood-grimed knuckles.

"Faugh, enough now! Trocero, I warn you!" With his free hand Conan dealt his friend an ill-tempered buffet to his armored shoulder, making the solemn knight stagger as he stood upright.

"Aha, a king well-beloved by his army," Delvyn observed from behind Conan. "Such a one can go far."

"Nonsense!" Conan muttered over his shoulder. "And blast your impudence, dwarf, I already have gone far!"

"But Trocero speaks true, O King," affirmed one of the other two knights, rising stiffly to his feet. "We missed you sorely." He paid no more heed to the watching dwarf than he would have to a child. "Our fears were greatest after we found Lord Elgin, cut down with three of your bodyguards a league and more from here. All were dead, and so there was none left to tell us whither you had gone."

"Alas, Elgin too!" Conan answered glumly. "The staunch fellows were struck down escorting me through an ambush laid by Ophirean knights. That was our closest approach to the fugitive kings, and still the scoundrels would not turn and fight! By Baalok's bloody furnace!" His foreign oath was accompanied by a toss of his head and a fierce grimace. "Brave Sheol carried me through, only to be slain a half-mile further on by skulking spearmen. Bless his noble fetlocks, there never was such a horse!" The monarch shook his head in genuine regret. "By then I was the last rider still in pursuit, with any surviving horseflesh too well prized by our fleeing enemies to be found! So I had to walk back, killing a slinking invader when I could. I saw some good men fallen, and other grievous wounded. . . ." His voice rasped away to silence.

"What of your armor, Sire?" Trocero asked attentively. "And your crown?"

"Bah! Cavalry armor only hampers a man afoot! 'Twas but a drag on my sword-arm. As for the crown"—the king scowled tempestuously—"why, 'tis nothing but a damned nuisance! At first glimpse of a crown, a man's enemies scamper fecklessly away—or else they'll try to maim and capture you, rather than killing you fairly! It makes it too hard to chase down an honest fight." Conan shook his shaggy mane, disgruntled. "I cast the thing off into a pile of bodies, somewhere near Sheol's noble carcass."

"Your Majesty, if I may suggest . . ." Trocero's tone was respectful, his expression grave. "Before we rejoin the other officers, Sire, I want to say to you as a friend . . . might it not be more prudent, Conan, if you did not press so hard in an attack as to endanger yourself, and outrun your army? We have fought together for many years, and I know your ways. But now things have changed, and it might be wiser to preserve yourself—''

"What, Trocero? You mean hang back from a fight, like those cowardly hens Malvin and Balt? I'll pretend I didn't hear you say it!'' As Conan flared at the remark, his bearing grew stiffer and more energetic than it had seemed at any time since the battle. "What, man, are you trying to tell me? That I'm too old, too frail, to fight alongside my troops? I am still an able warrior, remember, Trocero—until some better man takes it into his head to disprove it!''

"Nay, nay, Sire, I did not mean any offense!'' The count shook his head, holding his ground broad-shouldered and firm before his commander. "Conan, I did not mean you were unable! Rather, too important—too well-loved, and too vital to the Aquilonian nation to risk throwing your life away in battle! If you would but be content to direct our campaigns and give your officers the full, measured benefit of your judgment, without galloping forth to win every fight yourself—''

"No, Trocero, you ask too much.'' Conan's scowl was less tempestuous. "After languishing so long in the boredom of the court, busying myself with a pallid round of domestic trifles, I require action, risk! It makes me young.'' Still scowling, he shook his crusted mane. "Battered and weary as I am, I have not in months felt as alive as I do now! Just because a man's brow glints with gray—or with gem-crusted gold, for that matter—it doesn't mean his manhood is past. I am more than a king, I tell you—I am still a warrior! When that ends, so does my reign."

"Yes, Sire. My apologies. I should have known you would see it as a point of honor." The count bowed deeply and turned to grasp the reins of his waiting mount. "Take my horse, Sire, so that you can hasten back to ease the minds of your staff."

"Nay, Trocero, I want you to ride along with me." The king's nod to his friend was grudgingly accepting. "Let me take Stavro's mount, here—if he does not mind the walk." The knight he had named dropped graciously again to one knee and proffered Conan the reins of his steed. "Though I am heavier than you, Sir Knight, I lack armor, so your beast will not be sorely overburdened." Conan swung himself stiffly up into the saddle.

"And what of me, O King?" Delvyn called from far below, waving his arms to get attention. "My legs will hardly keep pace with a hulking, lumbering knight, much less a troop of horses. And you leave me here disarmed! Am I to find my own way back to Belverus?"

"Nay, fool, of course not," Conan rumbled, his smudged features cracking to a white-toothed laugh at the pathetic sight of the dwarf. "You are my sole plunder from this day's noble affray! Come, ride along with us. Trocero, you would not mind carrying him on your saddle hump, as you would a sack of turnips? Aye, Sir Stavro, that's the way! Fling him aboard and we're off!"

The figures moving about the campfire looked glum and weary. Pale glints of moon and firelight on armor plate, surmounted by pale, downcast faces—all was strangely subdued for the camp of a victorious army. At the sound of hoofbeats, faces looked up and brightened, first with firelight, then with elation as the sentry's hail rang forth.

"It is Count Trocero . . . and the king!"

"Praise Mitra and Crom," voices buzzed around the campfire, "the king returns!"

"Huzzah! Conan lives, and so our victory is complete!" The first to come dashing around the fire was a tall, slender man in jerkin and pantaloons, his armor removed except for his breastplate. He ran up as the king reined in; but, catching the gleam of firelight on wet blood at the dismounting warrior's rib cage, he halted without laying hands on his ruler. "Sire, you are wounded!"

"Nonsense, loyal Prospero, 'tis but a welt!" Turning from his steed, Conan seized his retainer in both arms and dealt him a friendly clout on the back. "So we have our victory, costly as it is, and our lives—the luckiest of us, anyway!" He addressed the broader, exultant group of faces. "Once again, generous invaders have shed their blood to sweeten Aquilonia's rich soil!"

As Conan turned with Prospero from the onlookers' cheers, he heard the nobleman ask, "And what have you there, Trocero, a child? Or is it a Tybor River troll?" His gaze rested on the small figure being helped down by the count from the warhorse's high saddle.

"Rarer than that," Conan told him. " 'Tis a dwarfish clown of King Balt's court. I caught him on the battlefield, helpless as a mouse with its tail in a snare. If we keep him by, he may afford us some amusement."

"I may as well," Delvyn said, swaggering into the crowd of armored knights as an equal. "My former master will have little use for me in the days to come—resting and rejuvenating as he probably will be among the randy trollops of Lord Malvin's harem, in the palace at Ianthe." The dwarf looked up at them innocently. " 'Twas there they planned to retire, I heard them say, in the unlikely event of a military defeat by a ham-fisted western king."

His joke brought no laughter from his listeners, rather, gruff murmurs. "Silence, rapscallion!" one knight barked.

Another muttered, "Sounds like an ill desert for a pair of treacherous scoundrels!"

It was Trocero who spoke next, bringing up a matter of business. "King Conan, we should recover your crown, methinks. There have been few looters so far, because our army's swiftness outran the camp followers—"

"Aye, and our enemies' shameless rout stampeded theirs." Conan nodded good-naturedly. "But we can easily send troopers after the bauble. Tell them we'll pay the finder a gold talent; that will simplify matters. But no murdering one another for it, or the prize is void!"

The order was passed, causing an immediate, audible stir in the encampment spreading beyond the fire.

Then it was Prospero's turn to raise a practical matter. "By the grace of the gods, and by your generalship, Conan, we were able to defeat both enemy forces. They are weakened, I would guess, beyond any hope of prosecuting their war plans." The Poitanian smiled in the firelight, waving one beringed hand in a gesture of dismissal. "But as you know, my liege, we still have footborne companies marching here from the northern and western frontiers, and fresh levies and supply columns coming from my home province. I can send word to have them halted—"

"Nay, Prospero, do not turn the reinforcements back

yet." Conan's face was pensive as he gazed into the flames. "The country behind us is secure, and our border forts will hold now. But Aquilonia has suffered insult from these eastern kings. I will think on how best to conclude this matter, and secure our land against further trespass."

With the comfort of sour wine, watery forager's stew, and undersized camp chairs, their council lasted late into the night. Meanwhile, spoiling troopers roved the Tybor plain, seeking treasure amid the hacked carcasses. They had no need of torches, for the moon glared down brightly over the field of their ghastly victory.

CHAPTER 3
Homecoming

The royal palace at Tarantia swarmed with torchlit shadows. The vaultings of its banquet hall boomed like a basswood drum, echoing fierce jungle rhythms. At the center of the great room, before King Conan's broad, onyx table, cavorted lithe black dancers of Kush. Lissome females, lovely in their tall headdresses and tight waist-wraps, sat on folded knees with their shapely posteriors toward the feast tables; they watched as intently as did the royal guests, while the men of their troupe danced a mad gavotte of spears and billowing torches.

The black southerners leaped and tumbled like demons, hurling themselves over and beneath scything spearblades and scorching plumes of yellow flame. They brandished high their blazing spears, twirled and exchanged them, and at last crossed their long, wicked points in a razored steel gridwork. Atop this perch the most agile of the dancers leaped to balance himself—barefoot, arms aloft, his dark skin shining with the sweat of exertion and daring. When at last the pounding crescendo of wooden drums ceased, the room's breathless silence filled with shouts and cheers from the audience. They stood applauding at their tables, raising foamy goblets high in sloshing salute.

The lead dancer, to renewed applause, somersaulted nimbly down from his spear trellis. As the lamps were unveiled, King Conan himself arose from his demi-throne at the royal table. "A brave performance, men of Kush! —better than any I recall seeing, even in the days when I myself ruled as king over a part of your distant homeland. But one trick I remember which I did not see tonight."

Laying a hand on the red chalcedony inlay of the ornate table before him, he vaulted lightly over it. His soft-booted feet easily cleared the goblets and wine ewers to land smoothly on the marble paves at the farther side. Adjusting the gold circlet of his imperial crown on his scar-seamed forehead, he strode forward, making an imposing, broad-shouldered figure among the lean dancers.

"Have you forgotten this?" He reached out, seized a pair of the long-bladed assegais from two of the tolerant Kushites, and began twirling them in his big hands, stepping nimbly backward to place any bystanders outside the flaring, slicing arcs. In a moment the blazing wick-ends of the spears, fanned by their swift motion through air, traced bright, interlinking circles of flame in the dim-lit hall. At this, watchers and dancers alike laughed and applauded.

"And furthermore, lest you think the risks these warriors take are mere mummery"—the king deftly halted the spears' flaring orbits and grasped their thick shafts one in either fist, spearblades downward. Then, bunching his mighty shoulders, arching his entire body and taking a great, plunging stride forward, he flung both assegais simultaneously—straight, it seemed, into the faces of the shocked onlookers. The spears raced flat across the hall, to embed themselves with a *chunking* double impact in the leather-finished back of the ornate chair the king had recently vacated. One flaming, oscillating spearbutt knocked over a goblet on the banquet table; the other torch-end sagged lower, its flame sizzling in dregs of spilled wine.

The guests applauded dutifully, amid murmurs of astonishment and relief. There was laughter, too, at the expense of the uneasy courtiers who had been sitting nearest the place targeted by their king—especially white-bearded Chancellor Publius, who had tumbled from his chair to the floor in panic. He arose now with a rueful grimace and dusted himself off, aided by a pair of similarly discomfited servants who had dropped their trays in fright.

One seatmate of Conan's appeared scarcely to have noticed—Zenobia, the stately queen sitting in her ivory chair immediately to the left of the throne. She only gave a toss of her long, lustrous black hair and adjusted her posture slightly. Another face that seemed wholly unruffled was that of the dwarf Delvyn, perched just beyond Publius on the king's right hand—and yet a rather different demeanor on his part had been observed when the spears flew. Not only had he ducked beneath the rim of the table—which, in spite of the thick cushions placed in his seat, came up to his chin—but he had dropped from his chair and scuttled beneath its legs for protection, to the merriment of the company.

"Well enough, then, Aquilonians," the king decreed as he waved away the dancers and strode back to his place, "we can continue feasting for the nonce." Vaulting the table once again, he lent assistance to the servants who were trying to unstick the heavy spears from the seatback. At length the still-smoking weapons were carried out; the king, resuming his seat, exerted himself to catch up with any banquet courses he may have missed.

"What think you, Zenobia?" he asked of his queen, between bites from a joint of beef which he plied aloft in one greasy fist. "Is this not a jolly triumph and homecoming feast? Too many months have passed, methinks, since our gloomy palace saw its like."

"Yes, Conan, 'tis a splendid affair—though not as gala as it might have been with more preparation. And not a real homecoming, since so many of our lords and officers remain posted with their troops at the eastern border. But your dancers from Kush were an inspired choice—truly a . . . barbaric spectacle."

"Indeed." The king nodded innocently, reaching for his wine flagon. "And my double spear-cast was almost a success—not quite perfect, by Crom's thorny cudgel! But it pleases me to see that you, my love, did not fear that your king meant to make a flaming kebab out of you—unlike some others I could name."

The last was spoken with a reproachful look at Chancellor Publius, whose thin, silk-clad shoulders stirred in protest. "Your Majesty, I apologize for my lack of faith." A pout ruffled the chancellor's neatly trimmed white beard. "But I remind you, such weapon-play is hardly a custom in the stately court of Aquilonia, and so I was unprepared. I did not fear your intent, Sire, only that you might miss your target—"

"You mean," Conan said irritably, "to suggest that my arms have grown weak and unsteady with age." He barked out a curt laugh. "You think the years have made me as feeble and unsure, perhaps, as your own frail self?" Though the king's questions were made patently in jest, it was clear that he bristled underneath, due perhaps to cloying wine or other distemper. "In that you err, old man—"

"Now, now, Conan, do not rave on so!" Queen Zenobia leaned to her husband's side and placed soothing, restraining hands on his shoulders. "Publius meant no offense, my darling! He knows as well as I do how much you enjoy your strongman tricks, and how of late you feel you must prove to all that your strength is supreme and unfailing."

Under her gentle touch, the monarch eased back against the pierced leather of his chair. He smiled at last and waved his beef haunch forgivingly at his companions. Meanwhile, from beyond Publius, a throaty voice piped up.

"As for my own sudden departure during your athletic display, Noble King"—the dwarf Delvyn arose to his feet upon the seat of his capacious chair—"though some might brand it cowardice, a charge for which I would most assuredly trounce them flat—I assure you, fine sir, 'twas only to fetch my lute from beneath the chair, that I might pluck you a song of tribute."

"A song, then!" Conan proclaimed, sitting up to hail the company. "How fitting for this victory feast! Attend his words and chords, merrymakers, for the little man is a skilled and famous fool!"

At this introduction and the ensuing laughter, Delvyn produced from beside him an oval-bellied instrument. He struck the strings, and sounded a chord that bore an eerie tone to it, like the mournful airs of the western coast. He called out the name of his song in a loud, squeaky voice, strummed a less plaintive chord, and then launched in with a comically bouncy rhythm.

The Ox-Bone Scepter

A reaver there came from the blustering north
Who throttled a monarch to fatten his worth.
Now he rules Aquilonia, a royal brigand
More suited to Kush than a civilized land.

Brave Conan the Clouter he's called through the realm
For the play of his scepter 'gainst enemy helm.
He clouts them with bronze and he clouts them with steel.
Better, give him an ox-bone, his full strength to feel.

His reign shall prevail in a wide, gruesome swath
So remember to duck when the king waxes wroth.
If you're wishing his statecraft and skill to reveal,
Why, give him an ox-bone, nor mutton nor veal.

As the verses ended and the last chord was strummed, there came a moment of breathless doubt as to how the listeners would respond. Then a guffaw of mirth from the king himself decided them all, precipitating an avalanche of titters, hoots, and table thumps. It was clear that Conan had decided not to take offense, at least not for the moment. The scurrilous ditty had not, after all, pushed beyond propriety, and so the tension was released. The applause was too scattered to drown out critical comments, such as:

"A truly execrable rhyme, that!"

"Yes, but not bad for the prong of the moment. And it took gall!"

Publius's judgment was delivered over the undersized minstrel's head to his seatmates at large. "Hardly in keeping with the dignity of the crown, I would say. And scarcely a fit tribute to our recent victory on the field of battle! I would have expected a more inspirational sort of ballad or anthem celebrating our triumph."

"But is the victory yet certain?" put in Count Trocero, leaning toward Conan and his chancellor from his chair beyond Delvyn's. "We have received no pledge of armistice from the offending kings, nor any offer of terms."

"Terms!" Conan snorted from his half-throne, making Publius flinch. "I know what terms I'd offer them: the term of a pike through their rotty gizzards—"

"Now, Your Majesty," the chancellor chided dutifully, "in diplomacy, 'tis not always wise to press quarrels to the death. 'Tis better to allow your adversary some means of escape, the better to profit yourself by reducing his will to fight." The elder counsellor shook his long, lustrous gray locks. "Our recent enemy Lord Malvin, for instance, was probably driven to attack Aquilonia by the increasing pressure he felt on his kingdom from the east."

"The east?" Conan queried. "You mean from Koth?"

"Yes, truly, my king." Publius nodded patiently. "If you wouldst but recall, we spoke of it a fortnight ago, before the hue and cry of the invasion. Young Prince Armiro, Koth's new satrap out of Khoraja, has for some time now been whittling away at Malvin's eastern lands in a deft series of campaigns."

"Aye, 'tis so," slim-mustached Prospero put in,

craning into the conversation across Queen Zenobia's shapely bosom. "Young Armiro is a deft intriguer, and a military commander of considerable grasp. Not content to rule Khoraja, he jockeyed himself into control of the entire Kothian Empire. Now he strains even at those vast borders to badger Ophir. A real firebrand, he!"

"I know of Armiro." Conan nodded thoughtfully. "But I assumed, Publius, that your talk of border skirmishes between Ophir and Koth was exaggerated." The regent frowned in perplexity. "For can it make any sense that Lord Malvin, embattled on his eastern border, would open up a second battlefront to the west with an enemy as powerful as ourselves?"

"That," a sharp voice proclaimed, "was my former master's doing." Delvyn's words, rising up fife-pitched in their midst, came as an evident surprise to most of the speakers. "King Balt, Regent of High Nemedia and the Subject Domains, said he desired a further partition of western territories as a buffer to guard the vulnerable lowlands of the Tybor Gap." The dwarf gazed placidly around at the eyebrows his intelligences raised.

"As you know," he went on authoritatively, "Nemedia is protected by mountain ranges to the west and south, but not toward the Tybor Valley. 'Rectifying his borders,' the old scoundrel called it. Balt made it a condition of his alliance, in undertaking to aid Ophir against Koth, that Lord Malvin would help him first in an incursion against your kingdom. Ophir was to share in the spoils, of course, but crusty old Balt was the instigator."

"Aha, so that's how it stood!" Conan's fist smote the table a blow that rippled the wine, even in its heavy crystal vessels on the massive tabletop. "Curse that vile curmudgeon Balt and the spineless dandy Malvin! 'Tis well that we bloodied their prying noses!"

"The Kothian Armiro thinks so, Sire," Publius answered levelly. "His armies are even now engaged in hounding the Ophirean stag that was crippled by our Bossonian archers."

"Already? You know this?" Conan turned a gimlet gaze on his chancellor. "I know, Publius, you receive news here in the capital sooner than our spies on the eastern border!"

The chancellor shrugged. " 'Tis nothing, Your Majesty. The Corinthian legatee receives dispatches via carrier pigeon; his messengers occasionally find their way into my stew-pot instead. The brief we intercepted this morning states that Kothian troops are on the march in southern Ophir, extending a flank toward the capital at Ianthe. The Nemedian king's force remains in the southern realm, but the allied kings do not seem very active in the field."

"Stalled at Ianthe, most likely." Delvyn's laugh was shrilly vindictive. "Unsure whether to flee east or west, or sit and wait for a siege! That would be just like the two of them, simpering Malvin and my fuddled old master."

"By Crom," Conan exclaimed, "slow down, all of you! Am I to understand that even as we sit here, Ophir, the kingdom we bested in the field, is being gobbled up from its farther side? —and largely as a result of our victory, but by another invader? —and this a greedy, energetic princeling who bodes to become an even worse neighbor than the present king of Ophir?"

Faced with slow, reticent nods from his counsellors, Conan frowned and shook his regally maned head. "If true, 'tis a sobering thought . . . more sobering, I fear, than Queen Zenobia and I would wish to entertain on this night of gaiety and mirth. Therefore I shall wait until tomorrow midday before considering a plan. Winebearers!"

The king snapped his fingers to hurry the servants, and so the feasting proceeded. As the flow of banquet courses from the kitchen gradually trickled to an end, a new troupe of dancers and musicians was summoned forth. These were more familiar to the courtiers, being all female, recruited by the king as public entertainers from what, before the advent of Queen Zenobia, had been his harem. Their skills were well-practiced, their dances and adornments painstakingly selected for freshness and originality.

In the course of the entertainment, however, their costumes tended to dwindle and fall away, while the repertoire inevitably narrowed to certain favorite, earthy steps. Before long, to the thumping of timbrels and tweeting of pipes, they performed independently about the hall, some dancing on tables, others almost in the laps of their enthusiastic admirers.

The king himself sat hemmed into his demi-throne by two of the most energetic dancers. They pranced and whirled, trailing shawls across his face and through his playfully grasping fingers. They flounced their skirts and ruffled their loose bodices before him, the better to commend the marvels of their supple, undulating bodies to the royal sight. The king watched dry-lipped, patting or clutching at elusive, flying forms where he might, otherwise lounging in his chair and praising their skills aloud to the company.

"Splendid, Mora, wherever did you learn that trick? You are keeping yourself in fine feather, girl! But Lilith, do not overwork yourself so—come here, wench, and rest on my lap! It has been long since we had an intimate talk."

But the pale-haired temptresses, with a glance aside to the patiently watching queen, continued spinning and writhing just beyond their monarch's reach. Not long afterward, at the discreet wave of a red-nailed hand, both dancers flitted off to tantalize other lingerers at the emptying tables. It was Zenobia who at last hoisted the wine-bleary king up from his gilded chair—as it was her silk-gowned body his greedy fingers finally closed on, and her kisses and coaxings that drew him away across the banquet hall, toward the winding stairway to the bedchambers above.

As the intensity of the dances heightened, many of the revellers had departed—in pairs, mostly, for the sake of greater propriety or greater ardor. Conan's high counsellors had gone their way some time before. That left the feast tables in the possession of a few hardy guests, bachelors or lone travellers, whom the entertainers lingered late to tease and console. One of the dancers, the shortest and plumpest of them all, rested near Delvyn where he sat dwarfed in his chair. But when she made cautious overtures of friendship, he hopped down from his seat with a look of loathing, shaking his lute at her as if it were a weapon. He retreated to the shadows of the chimney corner, whence his green eyes could be seen glinting throughout the remainder of the night.

"The folk of the court are saying that we are an unlikely pair, little man."

Conan sat at his writing-table in the east tower, listening to Delvyn strum his lute. A casement window, standing open on a vista of blue sky and leaf-shimmering treetops, threw morning sunlight onto the scrolls and parchments arrayed before the king. As he worked, writing and signing proclamations and military orders with a black-dipped ostrich plume and sealing them with drops of red beeswax from a candle-heated urn, chords of eerie melody drifted from the shadows where his companion sat.

"Tongues will wag," the dwarf replied, "the envious ones most loosely. As is fitting, perhaps, since our meeting was such a lucky chance." With a melancholy flourish of strings, the minstrel launched into the refrain of a languid western air. "If not for a clumsy charioteer," he complained, "an ill-fitting suit of armor, and a barbar-king's mad whim to rove the field of carnage alone, why, I would now be dead. Or in Ianthe, or Belverus, playing to a more jaded audience of besotted nobles and their fancy tarts."

"Hmm. And yet, my friend," Conan equably remarked, "I smell the taint of destiny in our meeting. We have much in common, you and I. For one thing, I betimes have had my own problems finding armor that fits."

Delvyn, instead of laughing, struck an ill-tuned chord on his lute. "Chalk that up to Malvin's miserliness as a host," he said, resuming his melody, "and to my master Balt's loutish inattention in not getting me properly outfitted before we left Nemedia. What kind of negligent ruler is it, I ask you," the dwarf complained in evident sincerity, "who leaves his fiercest warrior ill-armed, unmounted, and ungirded on the eve of battle?"

"You would have fought valiantly for your king, I'm sure," Conan said.

"And did so!" Delvyn put in sharply.

"Yes, yes, of course. And yet your speeches give him little honor, nor any to his ally, Lord Malvin." The king looked up at last from his stack of royal decrees.

"If you speak so ill of them in their absence, I wonder, how will you speak of me when my back is turned?"

Delvyn strummed the plaintive air's refrain. "Need you wonder, O King Gut-squeezer"—the pale, close-set eyes glinted at Conan out of the shadows—"keeping in mind that I speak only ill of you to your face?"

Conan guffawed. Once his burst of laughter had subsided, he swigged from his ale cup and said, "Good, then, brave Delvyn! A king learns to cherish frankness above all else—especially from fools, who always flock so thickly around him. I can accept your acid tongue, as long as you'll warrant that I need not fear spying by you, nor outright treachery." His speech ended with a direct, somber look to Delvyn in his seat atop a heavy brassbound chest.

"No spying, O King. And no treachery, outright or otherwise." Delvyn's strumming shifted subtly in key, although his gaze did not drop. "I have no need of such devious tricks, I assure you. And I pledge no further loyalty or fealty to King Balt and his jackal Malvin." Without interrupting his melody's soulful conclusion, the little man rearranged his stubby legs beneath him. "To be frank with you, Sire, I have seen more than enough of their half-handed misrule. And I know friends in Ianthe and in the Nemedian officer corps who feel the same way."

"Indeed, little man. You know much about the ways of kings, 'tis clear." After gazing thoughtfully another moment at the dwarf, Conan turned back to his desk-work. "And with your vast trove of experience, what think you of this, my kingdom?"

"Aquilonia? Yours is a passable realm, Conan the Neck-cruncher." Now Delvyn plied his lute tunelessly, wandering into an eerie thicket of notes lost or abandoned between melodies. " 'Tis a wealthy land, to be sure. Worldly and many-striped to my eye, and yet docile enough to let itself be yoked and tamed by a belching, brawling savage from its barren northern hinterlands. A strange combination, that: the nation which gives rise to perhaps the highest flower of Hyborian art and culture, cowering under the knotted fist of an unschooled, unlettered foreigner! A clear case of the dominance of brute, barbarian force over decadent, civilized maunderings—"

"I respect the arts, little man," Conan interrupted him, "your own plinkings and plunkings included. Since becoming king, know you, I have learned to write and have even set my hand to bardic verse."

"A great achievement for you, doubtless. Many monarchs and generals turn to such pastimes in retirement, after they have reached the compass of their powers and ambitions." The dwarf strummed idly on, his chords making a shifting background to his words. "Once a man forsakes the work for which he is best suited, he may find it equally challenging to perform less well in a less notable pursuit. Such tasks can lighten the burden of indolence and sated hopes."

"Rapscallion, you call me indolent?" Conan was provoked once again to look up from his work. "Why, man, I am galloping just as hard as I can, and barely keeping apace, what with sorceries and uprisings here at home, and rapacious kings at my border!" He shook his black mane. "Long ago I learned that a throne is a slumbering tiger, easier to mount than to ride!" He shook his head angrily, his dark locks framing a darker scowl. "And sated—well I deserve to be sated, after spending my life scrabbling and searching for treasure and ease. Now, by dint of the harshest and most gruelling efforts of my days, I command power and treasure enough to satisfy any man!''

''Interesting, King Purse-grabber. To each his own.'' Delvyn shrugged. ''And yet, from the viewpoint of the greater world, your kingdom is by no means unique. It is no richer than mighty Turan, for instance, and no vaster than far-flung Khitai—or so at least the travelling adepts tell me. How much greater, I wonder, are the needs and cravings of the rulers of those lands, that they should have attained more than you in all your barbaric rapacity?'' He struck an idle chord on his lute. ''And tell me, O King, all this power and treasure you possess—does it indeed satisfy you?''

Conan set his pen into his inkpot with an air of barely restrained exasperation. ''Crom's curse on you, little man! What is it you are prying and probing at?''

From his shadowy perch, the dwarf shrugged. ''Merely to sound you out, King Gold-filcher; to learn whether you are a truly exceptional king, or just an ordinary one.'' His small hand scattered a handful of notes from his lute-strings. ''For you know, although the world abounds with bold generals, clever court intriguers, and brilliant priests and magicians, kings are not an especially able lot, as kings go. They inherit or usurp their power, and keep it or lose it as the case may be, generally without doing anything remarkable after they become king. By then their greatest exploits are usually far behind them. Often their kingship is but a retreat from life—a dotage, as with sour old Balt, or a morass of vanity and fleshy abandon, as with Malvin. They are surrounded by comforts which imprison a man, and by loyal, solicitous friends, counsellors, and family who do what no enemy or hardship could ever have done: that is, they tame and disarm the ravening self-seeker who made himself king." Delvyn shook his head musingly. " 'Tis true, perhaps, that most men crave ease and security. But for a king to surrender to them—that, O King, is a death worse than death."

All through Delvyn's speech, Conan sat with his brow knit, listening to the blending of words and tuneless, haunting lute notes, remaining idle and pensive.

"Now in you, King Sword-slinger, I thought I perceived one whose spirit could not be so easily tamed. Are you not after all, besides being such a vast brute of a fellow, a sly and ruthless fighter, free of all the moral qualms and crotchets the weak call 'civilized'?"

During Delvyn's brief pause, Conan could feel the dwarf peering at him inscrutably from the shadows.

"And, from what I have been told of your escapades and luck, one would suspect a further influence at work, some hint of an unseen power. Since you are no spell-caster, and your rustic aversion to magic of all kinds is well known, it implies something even more mysterious, be it witting to you or not—the touch of the gods, no less. A strange thought, that; and yet it seems impossible otherwise to explain the swift, astonishing rise of one so ill-suited to grandeur and high estate.

"If indeed you enjoy the gods' favor—that elusive gift so many kings lay claim to, based on far less convincing evidence—why, then it raises the inevitable question: to what end? Were you raised from barbarous obscurity to idle here amid callow, womanly comforts, to fret over vulgar daily concerns and cling to what wealth and sway you have? Truly, O King, were you fated to come only so far, and then cease? Or does it lie in your destiny to achieve something more—something, perhaps, which no monarch on earth has yet achieved?

"For it is a small world, O King—the stretch of it we know, at least. 'Tis little more than a hamlet, really, a sleepy village of tired, passable kings. There never yet lived the man who mastered more than a small part of it—a measured, circumscribed tract, no greater than a hand's-breadth on the sheepskin maps you kings are so fond of drawing and redrawing in bright ink and brighter blood." Delvyn ceased his strumming and gestured with his lute to one such map, which was pinned to the wall beside the casement.

"Get on with it, dwarf! Where are you leading me?" Conan's voice sounded level in the silence, toneless and resigned.

"I am telling Your Majesty that, since 'tis but one paltry world, why should it have more than one ruler? And who better to rule it, King Skull-basher, than you? Is that not your obvious, unalterable destiny, for which the gods have been saving you so diligently from your own bloodthirsty folly?"

The interval before Conan answered was a silent, lengthy one. He sat motionless before his writing-table, half-turned toward Delvyn sitting against the tower room's rounded wall; even in his gray cloth jerkin, dagger-belted kilt, and plain leather sandals he was every inch a king. At last he spoke once again with the same air of weary resignation.

"And what part of the world does that leave for you, little man? What is to be your share of my divine destiny?"

Delvyn riffled the lute strings once more. "Is it not plain to you, Sire? I am but a jester. The only way for a jester to be great is to be the jester of a great king. And I intend to be the greatest jester who ever lived."

CHAPTER 4
Leavetaking

"The king is preoccupied of late, Trocero."

"Aye, Prospero. He is not as jovial in the flush of victory as I would expect him to be."

"True. One would look for it to cheer him, and yet he seems glummer than ever. What, I wonder, is eating at him?"

The two noblemen, taking their noon wine on the terrace overlooking the palace entry, pondered in silence a moment. Trocero sat on a weathered wooden chair, his shoulders hunched forward, his elbows braced on his knees, letting the sun warm his broad back. Prospero assumed a more courtly posture, standing with one foot propped in a crenellation of the battlement as he surveyed the leisurely bustle of the palace yard below.

"Perhaps," Trocero declared, "it is the baneful influence of that noxious dwarf he has taken to his bosom. I trust not Delvyn."

"You think him a spy?" Prospero asked, stepping down and shifting around to make a seat of the embrasure.

"A spy?" the count asked. "Yes, to be sure, if listening goggle-eared and spreading outrageous slanders is spying. As to what it may avail him, why—that is hard to say, since he has little commerce with anyone at court except the king."

"He has told us much about our enemies," Prospero said. "None of it is provably false."

"Aye, precisely, the better to insinuate himself into our trust! By now he knows enough about our plans to make him a peril to us if he were freed. That, methinks, is why Conan has ceased to talk of ransoming him back to Nemedia."

"Ah, well." Prospero shifted sidewise to lean back against the warm stone. "He is too small and too conspicuous to be an assassin. Mayhap the king is only burdened by the weight of middling years and too-easy triumphs. After all, Trocero, 'tis hardly unusual for a king to enlist the services of a court jester or a fool."

"Yes, but mark me, this one does not jest and he is no fool." The count finished his wine and set the tankard down beside his chair. "He has a treacherous way of ferreting out a man's weaknesses and playing on them. Who can know what part he played in his former king's downfall in battle? And the way he treats Conan with open contempt . . . I, for one, find it revolting!"

"Come, fellow! Such is the value of a jester, as well you know. A king, especially one as great as Conan, needs relief from constant flattery. He enjoys being taken down a notch or two! He craves laughter at his own expense, which full-sized men like us can ill afford to offer him."

"That were well spoken, if the midget really cheered the king. But he seems to do the opposite, over the long haul at least. Do you remember how we would hear that damnable twanging and plunking from Conan's vicinity every moment—in his tent at Tybor, and on the march home? Just listen!" Trocero glanced up toward the window of the east tower, whence even then the faint, eerie strains of a lute could be heard. "Mitra knows what devilment he is whispering in the king's ear, and what sorcerous spells his foreign music is weaving!"

"Now, now, my good count," Prospero laughed, "have a little faith in our king! No man is leerier of sorcery than Conan. And what weakness can he possibly have for such an ill-favored little imp to play on, as the victorious king of a thriving realm, and head of a devoted court and family? Let us observe Conan in our meeting today, and see if his judgment of military and diplomatic affairs is weak or spiritless. If so, we can speak to him; otherwise let him enjoy his dwarf. There are great issues afoot which will serve as a test of his kingship."

It was late dusk by the look of the sky—or else pale night. But not Aquilonian night; something about the wan color of the heavens low down near the horizon, and the mournful soughing of the wind through the stones, seemed to preclude that. Halfway up toward the zenith, a watery disc of moon glared down. Framed by looming black pillars, it cast faint shadows of ruined cyclopean stonework across the cracked pavement of the courtyard.

The wind was gusty and piercing, but there was no vegetation to be vexed by it—not even grass stalks to wave, or dry husks of leaves to be frighted about the enclosure. The restlessness of the air was visible only in the changing traceries of pale dust blowing over the fractured stones, and in the rippling of dark water in a low-curbed pool at the center of the court.

The lone figure walked slowly forward, looking timid and small in the vastness of the ruins. He was undersized, frail and stunted even for a puny mortal in this abode of forgotten gods.

"Kthantos?" the thin voice called out, squeaking in its essay at boldness. "Elder One, why am I brought here? I have not conjured you, Kthantos!"

The answer to his question was not spoken. Rather, it bubbled up, surfacing in oily splatters from the center of the black pool that spread before the questioner.

"Conjured, you say?" The cracked glottal sounds were punctuated by laughter, which gushed forth in a thick-bubbled geyser. "Men conjure demons, mortal! Gods conjure men."

"Always before this I have invoked you." The small, hunched figure halted at a judicious distance from the pool's rim. The breeze had abated, yet the pond's dark waters stirred restlessly from the bubbling. "Can it be that your strength waxes greater already, Kthantos?"

"As a god's strength should," the low-pitched accents burbled, "who has more followers than he formerly had."

"One more follower, at least," the mortal visitor mused aloud with a note of skepticism in his voice. "Hmm, from zero to one is an immeasurably large increase. So you should feel infinitely stronger—for the time, at least."

"For your lifetime, at least," the black water gurgled back mockingly in reply, "pathetically short as it will be, compared to mine." And yet, on more careful inspection, the pool might not have been filled with water after all. Its bubbles and ripples seemed to have a thicker, oilier quality, like that of molten pitch. "After all," the voice spoke on, "I possess your unalterable belief."

"Perhaps, Elder One," the visitor added disputatiously. "Even so, my devotion to you might falter someday."

"If not through devotion, then through simple fear I own you. Having once believed, mortal, can you cease to do so by an act of will?" The pool's contents roiled, forming black wavelets that lapped the stone rim with a hint of menace. "Remember, a weak god is a jealous one. One who punishes his forswearers harshly. A fat, complacent deity like Tarim or Mitra can afford to let a few followers lapse, but not I! And even in my former supremacy, I was no god of mercy. . . ."

"Yes, yes, Kthantos," the mortal said with a valiant show of boredom. "You told me already of your vast powers and cruelties of old. Pray, do not exert yourself so greatly to frighten me, lest I begin to regret that I ever resurrected your name and rite . . . out of a crumbling, scarcely legible scroll, which had lain forgotten in a catacomb for countless centuries."

"Indeed, mortal," the disembodied voice said, "well may you taunt me with memories of my lost glory." The pond bubbled idly, tossing a reflection of the pale moon hither and back across its surface like a child's plaything. "Yet I caution you: even in my present state I retain more than enough power to slay any mortal, swiftly or slowly, as I may choose. Short of that, I could withdraw the boon I have already bestowed upon you—''

''Enough of this idiotic sparring!'' The listener spoke with sudden, daring vehemence. ''Tell me, why have you called me here? Or have your forgotten, in your doddering ancientness?''

''Why else, but to hear of your schemes and successes?'' The voice in the pool bubbled awkwardly to a stop, as if embarrassed to request any favor of a mortal, or to admit any lack of omniscience. ''What of this new king?'' it asked finally in a reluctant, oily spurt.

''He is promising, most promising indeed, and receptive to my influence.'' The human crossed his arms with an air of relaxed certainty. ''Even so, there are other possibilities—younger ones who may be more energetic and malleable. Shortly I will begin to test this one's strength and resolve.'' The visitor laughed. ''I have already told him the gods are on his side.''

''So they are,'' the pool blurted, ''one god at least. Though I am an ancient god, a mere shade of my former self. That will soon change. I shall take my place among these upstart Hyborian deities and in time supplant them—''

''Yes, yes,'' the visitor agreed. ''But only through my efforts, remember. For now, instead of reminiscing, try to bring your full, senile strength to bear on my behalf. Let there be no more talk of divine punishments. If I fail or die, remember, so will you.''

''Speak not of failure, 'tis heresy!'' Kthantos proclaimed from his bubbling pit. Beyond the pond, above jagged stumps of pillars, a new disc was rising into the sky. A second moon—or could it be a sun? 'Twas hard to think it one, it seemed so wan and blighted, its glow barely paling the clear, starless dome of sky. Meanwhile, the submerged voice continued its gurgling.

"Have faith in me, mortal! Serve me as my loyal minion, and divine justice will ultimately triumph. Fret yourself not about this puny king; if he fails, he will but lead us to a stronger one!"

"This border war appears to have been one of the lesser threats our dynasty has faced, O King."

Queen Zenobia sat at ease on the alabaster garden bench, the late afternoon sun picking out the bluish luster in her long black hair. The white stone of the bench and the frothy, flowing whiteness of her gown contrasted sharply with her raven tresses, making her fair limbs look dusky tan.

"Though you were gone less than a fortnight, Conan, we missed you sorely."

"You could have ridden along with me, Zenobia, if you so wished." Conan sat poised on an alabaster seat opposite his wife. In contrast to her languor, his posture seemed alert and vigilant, his sandalled feet braced firmly underneath his backless bench. A jeweled dagger-belt, donned as ornament for his meeting with his counsellors, bound a shirt and kilt of kingly purple about his torso, and a gleaming gold circlet crowned his black-maned head. "Conn might have come along with me, in any case. He is getting to be of an age. . . ."

"Milord, I hardly think so. He is but an infant!" Zenobia's tone was gently disbelieving.

"Well, mayhap not." He watched their son playing idly by the splashing, lotus-carved fountain that served the sunny southwest wing of the palace. "And yet, by his growth," Conan said, "if memory plays me true, I was hunting and fishing alone in mountain glades.'' The king shook his crowned head. ''Needless to say, I knew little of scribery, counting, and the other civilized arts he is learning—except to count the number of man-tracks left by a Vanir raiding party, and to notch my spearhaft once for each rabbit I killed.''

Young Conn's interest in the water was, quite evidently, only secondary; he seemed more fascinated by the hunched figure of the dwarf Delvyn, who sat brooding at the far side of the fountain, staring into its crystalline depths. At length, craftily, the boy launched an emerald-bright oak leaf into the rippling pool. Prodding and blowing it slowly and tentatively toward the object of his interest, he edged after it along the circular marble curb.

''A spirited life, it was! I know, Zenobia,'' Conan resumed, ''that your best strength lies in running the palace and certain domestic affairs of the kingdom. It takes up much of your time—but 'tis a good thing, perhaps, since I have so little patience with those matters.'' He laughed and shifted restlessly on his stone seat. ''At times, there almost seems no use for me here. Petty daily concerns weigh me down worse than any crisis, and too much lazing about the court only makes me feel the ache of my past wounds.''

''Conan,'' the queen replied softly, ''I am aware that you pine for battle. Sometimes I think you love adventuring better than you love me. Even a great hunt or a fighting tourney seems only to whet your cravings.''

Conan nodded. ''In some ways, Zenobia, this attack from the east has been a boon to us. It proved the value of my recent shake-up of the army, and that I still command the respect to lead it.''

''Two things I never doubted,'' the queen said. ''Nor

anyone else in the kingdom but yourself, I would guess.'' She heaved a small sigh and smiled tenderly, leaning closer to her husband. ''Conan, you need not fear ruling a land at peace, or dealing with the courtiers, or just . . . growing old here. Your judgment is as sound as theirs or mine, Mitra knows. Your friends and subjects do not love you only for your wealth and power, darling, or out of fear of your fighting prowess! They revere you as a good king, a man of mirth and charity, with so many joys and accomplishments ahead of you—But oh, my poor child, what is the matter?''

Her attention was distracted; for young Conn, having finally ventured near the brooding Delvyn, had not stayed in his vicinity long. Now he came scuffing up to his mother, teary-eyed and pouting. Plumping down on the bench beside the queen, he buried his head in the soft fabric of her billowing gown. She enfolded him in her arms and pressed his face to her bosom.

''Always crying—perhaps he is a babe yet, after all,'' Conan said resignedly. ''Old enough to cast a spear, and still he wants to cuddle his mama! Such conduct would have been thought unseemly in my home clan.'' The king shook his head. ''But then, who can say what is right in a civilized land?''

''Milord, he is only a child!'' The queen spoke with quiet, offended dignity. ''You too have sought refuge in these arms at times, sir, against this same breast. It ill befits a grown man, king or not, to be jealous of a boy!''

''Aye, perhaps 'tis so.'' Conan nodded again, looking up to meet her sternly protective gaze. ''Zenobia, I must tell you, this war with Ophir and Nemedia . . . it is not over yet.'' He shook his head decisively. ''The doings to eastward are too turbulent, and far too perilous, for Aquilonia not to take a hand. So at least my agents tell me. I may be gone longer this time—and it must be soon. We shall move swiftly.''

''Aye, milord, I feared as much.'' The queen shook her head and hugged Conn, who looked large-eyed from her to his father. ''By your agents, Conan, do you mean the turncoat Delvyn?'' Her gaze shot to where the dwarf's limber form squatted, having moved into the shade of one of the orchard trees.

''Yes, among others. Publius and the rest are in agreement. The jester's information has been most useful to us.'' Conan digested her remark soberly. ''But Zenobia, Delvyn has been nothing but a pawn or slave until now, with little choice of masters. I think he is ready to be of greater service to me.''

''Perhaps.'' The queen nodded, fondling Conn's hair, which was as black as that of either of his parents. ''But please, Conan, when you go adventuring, take your dwarf with you. I do not trust him here with us.''

CHAPTER 5
The Feast of Steel

The next morning the king departed Tarantia. Resplendent in a new set of black and gold armor, he spurred his new black charger Shalmaneser at the head of a sizeable body of troops—an escort fully as large, in fact, as the force which had marched from the capital to secure the border a fortnight before. Most of the survivors of that army had remained in the southeast, but here the royal legion was joined by masses of Gunder and Bossonian footsoldiers slow in arriving from the northern and western borders. Additionally came new levies on horse and foot alike, out of the farms and forests of central Aquilonia, to be commanded by sleek knights freshly outfitted from among the city nobles and rural squires.

The people of Tarantia, though uncertain as to the threat this new legion was to counter, made a brave showing at their departure. They furnished flower-petals to rain down from the rooftops, and copious tears to stain the breasts and gauntlets of departing lovers. There rang forth cheers, too, and laughter, especially at the sight of the dwarfish armored man astride a shaggy-maned, undersized swamp pony. He struggled to stay in the saddle beside the heroic figure of the mounted King Conan.

High above the melee presided Queen Zenobia, standing on a flower-decked parapet of the palace with young Prince Conn at her side. Gravely she watched Conan canter down the Road of Kings, as she had first watched him so long ago, years before her queenship.

The march southeastward was swift, favored by fine spring weather. Local landholders, though surprised at the size of the force, provisioned it liberally out of respect for the king. All along the way the army waxed stronger with new companies of horsemen and battalions of footborne volunteers from the rich southern provinces.

By the night of their arrival at the Tybor camp, the legions guarding the border had already launched new attacks against Ophir. On orders sent ahead by courier, Aquilonian detachments had driven deep into ill-defended territory. The news gleaned from scouts and prisoners was sobering.

"King Balt rests for now with Malvin at Ianthe, but his departure northward seems imminent." So spake the field courier Egilrude, newly returned from the front. "Both the Ophirean and Nemedian troops are demoralized and falling back toward the capital. Our prisoners tell us the city is in more imminent danger from the east, where the Kothian Prince Armiro is advancing swiftly and wreaking great carnage. The prisoners seem eager to cooperate, being more afraid of

Armiro than of Aquilonians. Our scouts estimate that it will take the Kothian force two or three days to reach the city gate.''

''So,'' Conan declared to his assembled counsellors, ''it appears that we are now in a race for Ianthe, with time yapping at our heels. I was a great fool not to follow up at once on our initial victory.''

''You would take the capital, then, Your Majesty?'' General Ottobrand asked. ''And likely, most of Ophir to boot? That would be splendid, Sire! But I must tell you, we can scarce move an army to Ianthe in less than seven days, even with only scattered enemy resistance.'' The general, a gray-maned Gunderman in steel armor and a cloak of stitched furs, leaned forward over a folding table and poked a scarred forefinger at a map of Ophir. ''The Kothians, our scouts tell us, enjoy a broad front. They may hurl their cavalry through gaps and weak areas and outpace the enemy. But we are forced to send everything we have straight up the Road of Kings, where it can be stalled by even half-spirited defense at the castles and bridges, or by a spoiling cavalry assault or two. Why, the mere logistics of moving our entire force—''

''And that is not the worst of it, Conan,'' Prospero added from close beside the king. ''Once there, we shall certainly face a siege. City walls, unlike troops, are not routed and do not suffer from flagging spirits. Quite likely, too, we will meet the Kothians outside Ianthe. Lord Malvin may be in a position to watch from the battlement as his enemies cut each other to pieces.''

''We could send forth envoys to treat with Armiro, Sire,'' Ottobrand suggested. ''With any luck they could slip through enemy lines to the Kothian front and get the prince to agree to a fair partition of Ophir.'' He drew his forefinger knifelike across the parchment map, dividing Ophir on a rough northeast-southwest axis.

"Nay," Conan growled, "for it would still boil down to one thing: who controls Ianthe. I would rather take the city first, then deal with Armiro." He looked around the officers assembled in the lamplit tent. "You, young Egilrude—can you get me four seasoned riders? Men who will keep their nerve and obey me unquestioningly?"

"Certainly, my king!" The officer, a blond-haired, broad-faced Bossonian, touched the visor of his red-plumed helmet in readiness.

"Good. Get them nondescript clothing, strong mounts, and several days' rations. Equip yourself similarly and meet here by first dawn." He turned from Egilrude to the others as the Bossonian disappeared out the tent flap. "Sometimes a handful of men can accomplish what an army cannot."

"What is your plan, O King?" Count Trocero asked. "I stand ready to ride at your bidding."

"Nay, Trocero, what I have in mind would not be . . . the highest use of your skills. I need you and the rest of my officers to muster your troops and drive them along the road to Ianthe at all possible speed. Do not burden yourself with prisoners, and bypass the best-defended strongholds if you must. If I get my way, the city will be awaiting your relief." He turned to a dwarfish, brassbound figure sitting stiffly on a camp stool in a corner of the tent. "Delvyn, do you still vouch for your friends within the walls?"

"In sooth, O King." The dwarf, clad in his new armor suit, nodded cockily with a rasping of bronze. "If you present yourself to Duke Lionnard at his estate in the town, he will gain you entry to the citadel. He is the first and bitterest of Malvin's foes. Our hardest task, my king, will be entering the city."

"It should be no great matter in this season of panic and hasty troop deployments. Here, Prospero, help me with these buckles." Conan began sloughing off his polished black and gold plate. "I will need foreign armor," he told General Ottobrand, "mayhap from one of your larger prisoners."

"What, Sire?" Trocero demanded. "Are you planning to ride to the city yourself? And on the word of this . . . this mountebank of your enemy Balt?" Pointing a gauntleted finger at Delvyn, the count obviously found it difficult to restrain his anger. "How can you trust him, Your Majesty? How do you know he is not going to lead you into the hands of his former master?"

Shrugging free of his cuirass, Conan hung it from a peg on the tent post. "I trust Delvyn because he will remain behind with you, my loyal officers. If I fail or die, his life is forfeit."

The ride to Ianthe required two full days and the more arduous part of a night. In late afternoon of the first day, from Aquilonian cavalry lodged in a captured village, Egilrude obtained fresh mounts in trade for their lathered, half-dead ones, using the anonymous authority of the king's signet ring. There too the six riders, Conan hulking among them, lay themselves down briefly and slept, awaiting nightfall to slip past enemy sentries in the forested lands beyond.

The next dawn found them deep within Ophir, cantering past refugees on the broad highway and swinging wide through the trees to avoid formations of fast-marching troops. That evening, at long last, the lights of Ianthe spread out before them. Torches flared atop the city walls, and lanterns of moored vessels drifted restlessly on the Red River, doubled by their own wavering reflections. By luck, the riders reached the West Gate before curfew. Under the guise of Nemedian irregular troops seeking to rejoin their cavalry unit, they were passed directly through.

The atmosphere of the doomed city was oddly feverish, almost festive. The streets thronged with idle soldiers, and with citizens trying to sell their property for cash they might hoard or carry off to the countryside. Sharp-eyed speculators and thieves stood ready, alert for quick profits, while civil guards and military units trooped past, too preoccupied to enforce the peace. As a result, there was lively uncertainty whether the city would be sacked first by the enemy or by its own rowdies.

A pub-crawling roisterer was located, and his aid purchased with a jug of ale and few prods from a knifepoint. He led the six invaders to Duke Lionnard's estate, a high-walled palazzo near the river. The eye at the peephole in the gate narrowed suspiciously, at first. But after lengthy debate and the payment of a substantial bribe, the grizzled, hooded King Conan was admitted for a private audience with the duke.

"This way, quietly!" The nighted avenues through which Duke Lionnard and his man guided the Aquilonians were all but unguarded. Those few sentries whom the duke's squint-eyed servant encountered, he approached confidently. Invariably his low mutter, punctuated by the clink of coin, caused them to ground their pikes and turn discreetly away, letting the motley band file past.

Exactly where the disreputable series of littered alleyways, rusted gates, and foul-smelling tunnels merged into the citadel of Ianthe, Conan could not say. But he was confident he had reached their destination when a carved wooden door admitted them into a broad, shadowy corridor lined with murky tapestries and pallid marble statues of long-dead nobles. This, recognizably, was the interior of a royal palace.

"You swear to me, then," Lionnard asked for the seventh time, "that you will make no treaty with Malvin himself?" He walked with Conan near the head of the party, following the candle-bearing servant. Close behind them trod Egilrude and his quiet, competent troop of four, hands propped on their sword-hilts. Their looks were discreetly watchful and their motions all but silent, fitted as they were with scant enough armor to avoid clanking as they walked.

"I would not object, mind you," the duke continued, "if you dealt with King Balt against Malvin. I have little influence with the Nemedian myself, since I have been excluded from the high councils. But I can sway the other lords." He brooded a moment, then declared, "I give you notice, my country will bear no more of the lordly upstart's rash deeds and pusillanimous judgments."

Lionnard was a small, spidery man a good deal older than his lordly nemesis was reputed to be. Clad in a doublet thrown hastily over the loose silks he wore lounging at home, the duke scarcely made an aristocratic figure, even with his nobly waxed mustaches and goatee, and the finely turned rapier slung from his gemmed belt. Yet he pursued his vendetta with the spite of an unmistakable aristocrat.

"Truly, O King—if indeed you are King Conan of

Aquilonia—I urge you to do your neighboring country a favor, and write Lord Malvin out of any bargains you may strike tonight."

"Aye, Duke," Conan affirmed in a low voice as he strode down the hallway. "No deals with Malvin. Fear not, the rapscallion is no friend of mine."

"As you suggested," Lionnard said, "I have already summoned my bodyguard. A half-score men is all the ruling cadre have left me, but I bade my lieutenant march them here before the main entry."

"Good," Conan grunted. "They may be of help to us when the time comes. Which way here?" he added curtly, halting at a T juncture.

"To the right," Lionnard said. "This corridor leads to the vestibule of the grand hall, where Malvin and his sycophants assemble each night. There will be guards outside, household troops whom I cannot buy or cozen. Most likely they'll be facing the other way, toward the front entrance."

"Good, then," Conan said, "time for the play of steel!" The hiss of his sword drawn out of its scabbard was echoed by similar sounds from his retainers, so that for an instant the corridor sibilated like a viper's den.

"Nay, Duke!" Conan whispered then, restraining Lionnard's hand on his elegant hilt. "You would do better to play the part of rescuer than rebel." The king withdrew his weaponless hand from Lionnard's and used it to unlimber a double-headed ax from his belt and heft it. "Remain here now with your serving-man, and go join your troops when you can."

The duke nodded and stood against the tapestried wall with his servant, both men looking more relieved than reluctant. Conan turned to Egilrude and nodded once, sharply. The officer told his band, "Come along, men! Swift and silent!"

The rush of soft boots in the carpeted hall was scarcely louder than the drawing of swords had been. An eerie darkness closed on them as they left the candle behind; then a lighted archway came into sight ahead. Beyond it could be seen the figures of four helmeted guardsmen, standing with arms akimbo or leaning on pikes, watching an ironbound door that opened on a torchlit outer court.

The guards did not expect trouble, clearly—least of all from within the castle. But at the last moment one of them heard or felt heavy footfalls and spun in alarm. Conan's sword whizzed through the air and sheared in under the edge of his helm. It bit deep, thunking against metal or bone. When it wrenched free, its steel was oiled a thick, bright red. The man toppled, gargling blood, even as Conan raised his ax to parry a blow of the neighboring guardsman's pike.

Two more guards appeared, lunging from unnoticed places beside an inner double door. Even so, the fight was short and one-sided. Conan met the second man with an ax-blow that fractured the nosepiece of his helm, stopping him long enough for the officer Egilrude to deal him a killing thrust beneath his backplate. The other defenders fought futilely against worsening odds, the last one cut down by four different swords striking in rapid succession. None escaped to spread the alarm, though the din of weapons and death cries could scarcely have gone unnoticed in the near vicinity.

As the last defender writhed and gasped to stillness on the stone floor, Duke Lionnard and his servant crept forth from the corridor. Following Conan's wave, they passed on through the exit to the courtyard.

"Shut that door and bolt it," Conan ordered, giving two of his troopers a shove toward the portal. "Admit only Lionnard's men, when and if they show. You two, come with me." Returning his bloodied ax to the hook on his belt, he beckoned his remaining two troopers and Egilrude to the inner double door. "Here, stand ready," he said, laying hold of one of the heavy ring handles. He hauled the thick oaken panel open partway and peered in through the hand's-breadth-wide crack.

Inside was a banquet hall, thronged with richly dressed men seated on stone benches at heavy stone tables. In the open area beyond the door stood a tapped, dripping ale keg on a wheeled trestle. Beside it, a brazier threw shimmering heat waves up around the hacked, drying carcass of a spitted pig. The nobles, some thirty or forty in number, appeared to have finished their meat if not their drink. Now they carried on a many-sided, boisterous discussion of some political or military subject. At the jarring of the door, a few of them glanced across at Conan, not evidently alarmed by his sullen face or by any sounds of strife that had filtered through the thick oaken panels.

After only the briefest look, the king let the door fall shut and turned to the men around him. "Once I enter, bar this door behind me—use the pikes of the dead guards, there." Conan's voice rasped deeply, like the keel of a ship launched from a stony northern beach. "Let none but me pass through," he told them. "Do not abandon your posts unless you are sure that I am dead."

Egilrude frowned at the king's words. "Sire, if you are dead, our lives are nothing. What can we do to keep you from danger?"

"Do as I command! I do not shirk danger." He gave

Egilrude a level look. "All I ever craved, before I was king or since, was sharp steel and a straight path to my enemies!"

So saying, Conan turned to the double door. He grasped both rings of worn bronze, hauled both doors wide—though one would have been sufficient even for his kingly size—and stepped into the banquet hall. As the thick portals fell shut behind him he armed himself fully, drawing his ax from his belt with his swordless hand. He held both weapons wide and high as he strode forward.

This time, at the unannounced entry of a large, heavily armed man, the discussion in the room faltered. A pair of burly, competent-looking underlings arose from a nearby table to head the intruder off.

"And so, milord," a speaker resumed, "without a doubt the citadel will hold. 'Tis clear our enemies are overextended. With aid of our Nemedian allies, we can sweep them from the field—but who is this, a messenger from our generals?" The speaker, a portly noble in a yellow silk cloak and cap, turned to gawk as Conan strode past the ale butt. "His weapons are red-rimmed! Is the war at our very gate, then?"

"Probably another battle deserter with calamitous news from the east," a second, skeptical voice chimed in. "Why don't you ask him how many Kothian foes he has swept from the field?"

Further jibes were lost in an outcry of astonishment as Conan met the two guardians. The first he brained with his ax; the second, caught tardily drawing his sword, tried in vain to duck away. His head was struck cleanly from his shoulders by Conan's lashing blade.

"What, murder! Vile mutiny, 'tis a foul assassin! Stop him at once!" The cries rang out sharply as nobles sprang up from their tables, reaching for weapons. Yet fewer actually sought vengeance than cried out for it. Just three men darted toward Conan with alacrity, brandishing their rapiers high. The rest managed to stumble over their scabbards and each other's feet, or otherwise found cause to hang back and watch.

As the fighters met, steel clashed deafeningly overhead. The attackers rained slashes and thrusts at Conan, fanning out widely to gain access to their quarry. But his ax and broadsword danced through air with effortless swiftness, striking aside the lighter weapons and returning threat for threat, blow for blow. Amid the flurry of flashing steel a sword broke, sending a bright splinter whirling high overhead. Then a second sword fell clattering to the stone floor. A bloody scream rang out; then came an angry shout, silenced suddenly by a crunching ax-stroke.

That left Conan facing a single adversary, stalking him swiftly and darting onto him as the man stumbled over the still-thrashing legs of one of his fallen comrades. A final, deadly sweep of Conan's ax sent the man spinning away in a shower of red droplets. There was an appalled silence in the room, then the other nobles moving to confront the stranger slowed in their tracks.

" 'Tis a fighting demon!" someone was heard to whisper.

"Here, berserker," a more gravelly voice proclaimed, "come hither to me and let me soothe your gnawing madness! For know you, I have cured many such as you before."

The speaker, a stocky, white-haired man, was none other than King Balt, the battle-hardened monarch of Nemedia. He also happened to be the most heavily armored man in the hall, clad from neck to knees in the thick leather hauberk that had enfolded him since his days as a line infantryman. Adorned now with bosses and lozenges of bright gold, it had through long use become his mantle of royal rank. Where his suit of mail ended, studded leather boots sheathed him. The monarch wore plated gauntlets as well, wrapped now around the hilt of a two-handed sword longer and broader than the one Conan plied in his right fist.

Balt's crown, though not a war helm, could almost serve as one, since its gold filigree overlaid a dinted, pitted steel cap. The old king was as broad-shouldered as a plow horse, and sturdy-limbed beneath his stoutness. He looked formidable even as he patiently waited, letting the unknown attacker come to him.

"Nay, courtiers, keep back," the old king shouted. "This reaver is mine! Your tricks will only play into his mad wiles." Balt's rebuke was addressed to his own seneschals, sporting the gray and brown livery of Nemedia. But it was spoken too late as, swinging their rapiers, the two came pelting impetuously around their king to head off his enemy.

The first, meeting Conan in a blinding flurry of sword-strokes, halted abruptly in his tracks. He shuddered, sank down to one knee, then slipped aside to the floor, leaving his heart's blood sleeting brightly from the tip of the Aquilonian's withdrawn sword.

The second, before he could even close in, toppled on his face senseless—felled by the flat of his own king's blade as it struck his soft-hatted pate from behind.

"Back, I say!" the old one roared. "This is my fight! I cannot promise to spare the next disobedient whelp who comes scampering to show me up!"

Before Balt had finished his diatribe, Conan was upon him, his sword and ax swinging in swift, lusty arcs.

And yet the old warrior stood his ground, taking the strokes solidly on his broadsword with a din of steel, or else spryly dodging them without lifting his booted feet from the floor. In so doing he used a stock of deft, confident tricks learned in an unnaturally long lifetime on the battlefield. Time and again Conan's weapons slid aside off his heavy blade or scraped harmlessly down his padded armor.

In return, the Aquilonian king felt the tip of the Nemedian's heavier broadsword strike and gouge his breastplate with impacts that hammered breath out of his lungs, and came near to piercing or splintering the inferior steel. So the two kings struggled within the circle of watchers, who had evidently come to believe that no other hand was necessary to save hoary old Balt from his assailant.

And yet the Nemedian's deadliest trick came unexpectedly. Conan felt his sword trapped in an unseen crevice, a sword-breaking spur forged near the base of King Balt's heavier blade. To the elder king's snarl of exultation, Conan's hilt began to twist aside out of his grip with hard-levered, wrist-snapping force.

A desperate sweep of the Aquilonian's ax struck the juncture of the two blades, knocking them apart. The release of tension interrupted the old butcher's practiced motions, throwing him momentarily off balance. It was fierce, agile improvisation that made Conan's ax plummet heavily on the backswing, striking his adversary's steel helmet-crown. The force split the headpiece in two, doing equal damage to the white-haired skull beneath. The gruesome spectacle of cloven brains was wrenched swiftly out of the victor's sight as King Balt plunged lifeless to the floor.

"By Erlik!" a voice cried from the watching throng,

frozen now with horror. "It is Conan, the enemy king! Conan of Aquilonia has felled the King of Nemedia!"

"Aye," a second watcher marvelled, "I recognize him from the coins—he comes to slaughter us in our very fortress!" The realization was accompanied by an indecisive slowing in the rush of the crowd toward Conan, who stood panting with a half-dozen bodies at his feet.

"King or knave, he is a villain, a monster!" another voice cried. "But hold, brothers, keep back from him, I have him now! Just give me a clear shot—" These exhortations came from a bearded, broad-shouldered man who stood beyond a table at the back wall of the chamber. He had just finished stringing a darkly varnished wooden bow, probably taken down from the mantlepiece behind him. Now the noble was carefully nocking an arrow from a quiver at his side. "Here, miscreant, I offer you payment for your black sins of murther this day. . . ." His voice trailed off in massive effort as he drew back the bowstring, his clenched hand trembling visibly from the force needed to bend the heavy stave.

And yet when released, the flight was obscured by a metallic flicker. The arrow went untrue, skittering low into the crowd at one side, and producing howls of pain from one of the watchers. The archer himself lowered his arm, the bow turning slackly in his grasp. He twisted slowly and tottered backward against the wall, where he slumped open-mouthed—his chest cloven by the ax that had flown a dozen paces across the room from Conan's lashing, thick-muscled arm.

An eye-blink afterward the thrower himself came bounding in his ax's wake, striking down a first, then a second interloper with his whistling sword. He cleared the table in a bound, to hack down a third rival with vicious cuts before turning to snatch the bow from the slack fingers of its dying owner.

The quiver stood ready; on the instant, an arrow was plucked from it, nocked, drawn, and released. The smooth, disciplined motion left the shaft lodged in the throat of a nobleman, an Ophirean lord who had stepped forward with his straight-sword raised. Almost before the eye could follow back to the archer, a second shaft shivered in the breastbone of the man just behind him. A third attacker turned to run; instead he took Conan's arrow below his shoulderblade and lunged forward against his comrades, grunting less with pain than with the force of the strike.

Pandemonium gripped the hall as men strove to save themselves at the expense of all others. They shrieked and collided, hurling themselves over and beneath tables to avoid death's whimsical, airborne touch. Some huddled behind furniture, others behind corpses. All cringed from the black-haired slayer's inferno-eyed gaze as he stalked the head of the room, quiver at his shoulder, choosing his victims with silent efficiency. Only a desperate few tired of their coy flirtation with death and laid hands on weapons, to charge forward and meet extinction head on.

There was no third choice, for the banquet hall had but one entry: the great double door, where a crowd of men now battered and clamored in vain. A second smaller door existed in a rear corner of the room, leading presumably to a closet or pantry; early in the fight, servants had scuttled inside and barred it. Now their masters begged, pounded, and rattled the latch in vain, stumbling over bodies of former supplicants who had grovelled there too long.

At the main doors the half-score fugitives reached a frenzy, pressing the door panels apart and outward with their massed weight, meanwhile sawing and chopping at the makeshift bars with knives and swords, against the half-visible efforts of the guards posted outside. Several captives hefted a heavy stone bench and ran with it to batter the doors wide. But even as they did so, Conan was picking targets among them. Pluck, nock, draw, release—in a few fatal moments, the numbers before the door were thinned. The battering ram fell abandoned, its surviving bearers sprawling for cover behind tables, benches, the dead and one another—

—none too soon for Conan to turn and meet a nearer threat, as a half-dozen desperate men combined to lift one of the heavy stone tabletops from its massy pedestal. They tilted it up protectively before them and advanced behind its shield against the murderous archer, seeking to pen him into a corner and crush him with it.

They came forward at a rush, but Conan backed coolly away, feathering first an exposed leg, then the shoulder of a second man. The wounded fell aside and the advance slowed, the circular slab thudding and scraping against the paves. Drawing the last arrow from his quiver, Conan sent it at short range through the shin of one of the remaining carriers. Then, nearly trapped, he sprang forward from the wall and drove his full weight in a kick high against the faltering tabletop. It paused, canted over backward, and slid to the floor, its weight cushioned by the nether limbs of two or three men unable to escape from beneath it. Instead of a thunderous crash, its fall produced only their bleating gasps and the sound of cracking bones.

"O horror, the demon yet lives!" one of them wailed.

"Spare us, please, O terrible one! We are few, we are beaten! We crave only life!"

"He is king!" others cried. "Hail him, our conqueror! Praise and fealty to Conan, King of Aquilonia and Ophir!" The salute was a travesty, piped from three or four dry, quavering throats.

"Where is Malvin?" Drawing his sword, Conan slashed the string of the bow and cast it aside. On the arm which had held it, the thick sleeve of his travelling coat was frayed and blood-fringed from repeated, ill-protected lashings by the bowstring. "Lead me to Lord Malvin!" he rasped hoarsely. "I have him yet to slay!"

He strode the room, sword in hand, kicking bodies onto their backs and squinting at faces pale with death, pain, or fear. The place was not awash in blood, for the arrows had pinned only thin scarlet love-ribbons upon their chosen favorites. When he passed hiding places of the living and peered in at them, feeble voices croaked, "Hail, Conan the Great!"

Uninterested in killing these last pathetic few, he went to the only place in the room where there was any independent stirring—an oval table larger than the rest. Beneath and near it, survivors huddled. A short, seam-faced man in commoner's garb crept out from underneath it and stood resolutely, raising a long knife to protect others still hidden.

"Fight him, I say! Save your kingdom!" This voice was high, but not with fear: female, though it came from a mannishly clad, leather-caped figure. She crouched beside the table and expostulated with someone under it. "Kill him! Or at least face him and prove you were a man! I promise to die beside you." Glancing up as Conan approached, she dragged a rapier out of a scabbard at her belt. Her figure was trim and leather-sheathed, her dark red hair cropped just long enough to tremble with agitation as she stood there. Her cloak was open down the front, exposing the half-contained fullness of her bosom.

A voice murmured from beneath the table, too faint for Conan to hear the sense of it. The woman cocked her red-maned head down attentively, then tossed it back in outrage. "Bargain, you say? Offer him . . . what? Nay, Malvin, cowardly wretch, I offer you death!" With a sudden, diving thrust she drove her sword into the shadows beneath the table, then released hold, abandoning it there. In reply came a gasping, scraping flurry of limbs. A figure stirred and dragged itself halfway clear of the table—a nobleman, devoid now of his bright steel battle-armor. Her saber protruded upward from his neck, its hilt standing out just behind his ear.

"Amlunia . . ." Lord Malvin gasped, reaching weakly to her booted ankle. Then he collapsed, a red froth drooling from his lips. The male retainer before the table gaped down at the noble death. He tossed aside his knife to clatter on the tabletop and stood open-handed in surrender.

The woman Amlunia ignored all this. She strode forward to meet Conan, stepping boldly into reach of his sword. "Kill me if you must, marauder . . . or else spare me! What Malvin would have asked a kingdom for, I give you freely!" She pressed closer to Conan, her bosom flattening against his hauberk as she craned up on her toes to plant a hot, moist kiss on his lips. "He was no man—but you are a man, and a king! King of Ophir, and of me, if you can hold what you have won by slaughter!"

CHAPTER 6
Siege

"We hold Ianthe, so let Armiro pound at our gates until his fists are broken and bloodied."

Thus decreeing, King Conan strode the citadel's broad battlement. He gazed out over the red-tiled roofs of the city and the winding river, its currents sheened silver by noon sun. "The capital is ours," he declared, "along with the remnant of the Ophirean army and half the kingdom, to the line of the Red River in the east and the Arond to westward." He turned back to his handful of advisors with easy confidence. "The Kothians ride fast and fight hard, 'tis true! But there is little they can do against city walls and closely watched river lines."

"Aye, milord, and yet . . ." Count Trocero moved nearer his king, though he stayed a little farther back from the low stone curb, which dropped straight away to the black shale of the river cliff. "Prince Armiro will lay a siege. Our watchers on the wall report the Kothians already building breastworks and assault engines."

"A siege, to be sure." Conan sniffed, his broad nostrils flaring, then laughed outright. "But to the prince's misfortune, the city of Ianthe straddles the river. We control both halves, and with them, both bridges! With our line of supply unbroken, his badgering can scarcely be a siege. There will be no starvation within these walls, no plague, no civil strife! We Aquilonians are the country's liberators, remember—its heroes, with the full welcome of its new and rightful governor, Lord Lionnard." Conan nodded to the diminutive nobleman, who bowed deeply, his mustaches twitching nervously.

"It is Armiro's enemies who hold a bridgehead against him," Conan continued with a sweep of his hand over the grand prospect. "He is the one to fear a siege, so long as he continues to squat on my rightful holdings—your holdings too, of course, good Lionnard."

"Ours to a common purpose, my liege." Lionnard flushed deeply and bowed again to Conan.

The view the king commended to his followers was indeed a splendid one. The Red River was a broad, swift stream having its source in the Karpash Mountains, whose foothills were hazily visible to the northeast. Swollen and muddy with spring rains, the torrent wound in a red-tinged swath through lush meadow and woodland to the city.

The high stone promontory on which they stood, and around whose base the river bent, served to narrow the channel to a bridgable width. It was also the highest point to which the river was navigable by sea-going ships year-round. It was on that outcrop, dim eons past, that some bandit or river pirate had chosen to raise his stronghold; and there, under his descendants' feudal protection, that ferrymen, tolltakers and merchants had set up business. There, too, the city had slowly grown, around its succession of ever grander forts and bridges.

Now beneath the cliff spread a view of stately domes, towers, and the huddled roofs of humbler shops and dwellings, threaded by narrow streets whose windings would have been impossible to trace even from this high vantage. Two bridges spanned the river, one upstream and one down; the upper one was a straight, many-arched viaduct, the other a broader, angular span piled high with shops and garrets. Boats, too, lay at anchor in the river, though the largest ones were restricted to the downstream side of the bridges. The whole was girdled by a strong, crenellated wall, proceeding in straight segments between towers set a hundred paces or so apart. The wall ended at the river in sturdy buttresses whose bases foamed in the river currents, two upstream and two down.

Near the center of it all, on the high knoll half-eroded by the river, reared the citadel. And on its highest, southernmost parapet stood the king, surrounded by his retainers. These included Trocero, Lord Lionnard, the officer Egilrude, who now wore an eagle-crested helm signifying captain's rank, and a handful of other Aquilonian and Ophirean officers. A little apart from the rest, lounging against the chocked wheels of a catapult, the armored dwarf Delvyn and the leather-girdled warrioress Amlunia listened. Evidently the two were acquaintances from past days at court. Though Delvyn generally had been seen to avoid women, he now exchanged occasional low-voiced comments with the king's new favorite.

"We are lucky," Conan mused aloud, "that this fortress lies on the Aquilonian side. Otherwise the Kothian might send log rams or sappers downstream to break the bridges and cut us off. As it is, he will want the bridges intact to reach us." He waved at the row of sturdy ballistae facing outward along the parapet. "We command the river traffic. These engines can throw stones or fire into any unfriendly vessels that try to pass. The bridges, too, lie within their range, as does a good part of the city." This last remark the king added with the briefest glance to Lionnard; it made the satrap stir in acknowledgment. "With Aquilonian troops manning the citadel and acting as advisors, I think we can rely on Ophirean forces to defend the walls of their capital."

Lionnard concurred promptly. "Never doubt it, Your Majesty! No true citizen of Ianthe would let our gates be opened to the ravages of Armiro the Koth!" He cleared his throat. "Even so, Sire, can it be wise to send the bulk of the army off to other campaigns so soon after your . . . rescue of Ianthe?" He ceased speaking, obviously reluctant to question the king, and looked to the others for aid.

"Indeed, Sire," Trocero agreed. "Armiro is an energetic commander. He could still cross the river and wreak havoc in the countryside, even encircle the city to complete his siege—"

"Let him try," Conan interrupted. "The water is high, he would lose half his force in the crossing." He nodded again to the river, where it coursed swollen through lush green meadows beyond the walls. "The nearest safe ford lies a dozen leagues upstream, in the foothills. And there is no ford downstream, even to the Khorotas River and the sea. When we beat the Kothians in the race to the river, I gave my generals the order to tow all boats and ferries to our side, and burn the docks and boatyards on the far bank. I myself would not risk crossing in Armiro's teeth, except by these bridges. He will not risk it in ours, unless he is a greater fool than I think him."

The monarch shook his head resolutely. "Nay, Trocero, 'tis best that we send every unneeded trooper northward to fight in Nemedia. With their king slain, the northern barons will not wait long to name a new one and mount a troublesome war against Aquilonia. My error last time was failing to follow up swiftly and ruthlessly on a victory. I will not err so again."

Trocero nodded, impressed. "If we succeed, a mighty empire will be born."

"Do not question our success. We can hardly fail!" Conan smote Trocero heartily on the shoulder, making the count stagger uneasily on the brink of the sheer precipice. "General Ottobrand's march has outpaced the very rumor of King Balt's death. The Nemedian nobles will be caught off guard and ill-prepared. I told Prospero to seek out some patriot who, like noble Lionnard here, can offer a wiser rulership to his country. I myself shall ride north in a few days, swear him personally to fealty, and then deal with the more warlike barons." He laid a hand on his retainer's shoulder. "You, Trocero, I will entrust with the defense of Ianthe—and, until our northern front is subdued, with keeping Armiro at bay."

"To be dealt with later, no doubt." Trocero's gaze roved eastward.

"Aye." The king nodded. "Driving him out of Ophir can be but a step to the conquest of Koth itself."

"I see heavy smoke at the south wall, Sire," Trocero said, giving voice to a fact which had become more evident over the course of a few moments.

"Aye. Armiro is burning the suburbs." The king

watched the gray-brown billows rising beyond the distant battlement, without undue concern. "Let him, I say! 'Tis folly to let hovels and tenements grow up outside a city wall."

"Yes, but, my noble liege," Lionnard put in, "and Count Trocero, permit me, please! I have been reading the semaphores." The bearded satrap pointed to a gleam of reflected sunlight that could be seen winking from atop one of the nearby towers. "The Kothians are mounting an attack under cover of the smoke. Our troops are calling on the garrison for reinforcements."

"Are they?" Conan asked, turning to shade his eyes at the flashes. "Well, make sure they get them! I shall come as well." With his officers at his heels, Conan strode to a hatchway and started down the narrow, spiralling staircase to the stable yard.

The ride across the city was headlong. A pair of Black Dragon guards galloped ahead, ostensibly to part the traffic, yet the king drove his horse Shalmaneser almost on top of them. Trocero and Lionnard rode some way behind, trying to keep the stallion's massive hindquarters in sight. The riders chose the newer, uncluttered bridge to avoid crowds, but inevitably they encountered throngs on the market avenue leading to the Gate of Oxen, the city's south gate nearest the rising smoke.

Citizens, startled by thunderous hoofbeats, scattered out of the roadway before the riders. On looking up to see Ianthe's grim-faced conqueror, they gaped with looks of more than supernatural dread, having heard tales of Conan's sudden appearance in Count Malvin's palace and the awesome butchery that ensued. But as he thundered past, flanked by the familiar if unrespected figure of Lionnard, they gave the band belated and obligatory homage, bowing their dark-tousled heads and knuckling their brows. Perhaps, if this terrible, remorseless warrior was now bent on preserving their city, things would turn out for the best after all.

Near the south wall, more citizens hurried through the streets away from the smoke-darkened sky. Ahead could be heard hoarse shouting and the whizz and crash of projectiles overshooting the wall.

"You two, hold up!" Conan barked to his guardsmen, who reined in obediently. "Keep the street clear! Use swords if you have to! We cannot have refugees blocking the path of our reinforcements." The guards, barking acknowledgment, spurred off to comply.

The commanders left their horses tethered to the gatepost and mounted through one of the flanking towers. Atop the wall, smoke hung thick in the air. It poured up over the wall on a gentle southern breeze, forcing the defending troops to crouch tear-eyed and hoarse at the inner edge of the parapet. A glance over the battlement revealed nothing but a blinding smother of fumes.

"Fetch water to the top of the wall, and more washtubs to store it in!" Conan commanded an Ophirean officer. "Tell off a bucket brigade. Your men may need to douse the gate—till then they can use it to rinse their eyes." As a whizzing sound thrummed in the air, he turned to watch a crenelle struck by a hurtling stone, and a kneeling man knocked from the back of the parapet by its flying splinters. "By Crom's horny hilt!" the king blasphemed, "where did the Kothians find catapults? They've been here but a day and a night!"

Amid the periodic crash of projectiles, poorly aimed in the smoke, Conan and his subordinates paced the wall, goading the sentries to greater courage and readiness. Within moments, however, new masses of smoke were billowing up between the gate towers, this time veined red and gold with living flame. It was clear that some incendiary mass had been brought up against the gate, probably a burning wagon.

By then, fortunately, water had begun to arrive from the aqueduct in the plaza below, raised by means of a pulley existing for the purpose; the buckets were detached and emptied into casks or directly over the battlement, beating down the worst of the flames and smoke.

Conan mistrusted the men on the rampart to watch the wall. Now he strode through one of the gate towers in time to see the head of a boarding ladder clash against the parapet beyond. Up it, through the thinning smoke, Kothian troops came swarming, looking wraithlike and monstrous due to the wet rags draped across the front of their helmets.

"By the Crooked One! To arms, you dogs!" Raising a bellow, the king laid hold of a halberdier who crouched nearby. He dragged both the Ophirean and his weapon to the battlement. Together, as the first attackers reached the top, they used his long, ax-headed pike to thrust the ladder's mortised timbers out and away. It toppled over invisibly into the smoke, yielding back screams and the sound of crashing armor.

Elsewhere along the wall defenders sprang into action, overturning more ladders and knocking Kothians off the battlement with pikes and axes. Meanwhile, from behind the rampart came the clatter of reinforcements, Ophirean and mercenary, under a cadre of Aquilonian officers.

Conan, finding his commands and exhortations no longer needed, sought out Trocero and departed with him. They left the defense of the city to the soldiers who would doubtless be burdened with it for many days to come.

The common kitchen of the citadel at Ianthe had been cleaned, spruced, and lavishly fitted out for use by royalty. The room's coarse wooden tables were gone, replaced by gilded wonders from the apartments above; the rough flagstones were now carpeted and cushioned, and the broad oaken mantlepiece burdened by bric-a-brac of silver, crystal and faience, with a perpetual guard assigned to protect its opulence.

The upper council hall would normally have accommodated the dinners and debauches of high state. But its expanse was too recently sullied by slaughter, the crevices of its inlaid floor too fetid with the blood and bile spewed forth there, to admit of dining and festivity. By the superstitious, it was whispered that the vacant room still echoed with the shrieks and flickered with the shades of the famous and infamous lords butchered in its midst.

And so it was in homier, warmer-lit surroundings that King Conan drank and feasted this night. Before him ranged the new, smaller Ophirean court. In a sable-padded chair, nearly equal in size and lushness to Conan's own, Lord Lionnard sat elevated and vindicated. A handful of his squirely cousins, looking in various degrees awed, rustic, or slack-witted, rested on either hand of sober-faced Count Trocero. Captain Egilrude and two other trim, hard-looking Aquilonian officers muttered together, dicing and drinking more than they ate. In a chimney corner the while, Delvyn strummed tunelessly at his lute.

On a broad seat facing the fire lounged Conan with the woman Amlunia seated close beside him. Since their first charnel meeting, the warrior girl had doffed her cape and sundry outer armaments. She retained her black half-boots, her short, tight-laced trousers of matching black leather, a dagger belt, and a brief leather vest. Though snug at the waist, its laces hung slack about her bosom—a concession, no doubt, to the fire's heat. By its light, her skin shone stark white against the black accoutrements. The only splash of color was her red hair, cropped short for comfort beneath the war helmet she sometimes wore. Her hair, short as it was, nevertheless was lavished on Conan's face and loose-shirted breast with the darting of her limber neck—for Amlunia postured and pouted, whispering in the monarch's ear and pecking his face with her dark-stained lips in the course of their conversation.

As they talked and drank, Delvyn struck up a ballad to the accompaniment of his lute:

Of players and minstrels who wander the East,
The court of Ianthium harked not the least
When Conan the minstrel, of harpists the king,
Played them an air on his harp of one string.

The dwarf seemed to accept the situation at Ianthe, including the passing of his former master King Balt, with equanimity. He showed no unease or jealousy at the intimacy between Conan and Amlunia—unlike Torcero, who seemed abashed at having the murderous wanton, so recently one of their enemies, admitted to dinners and high privy councils. Trocero saw in it further evidence of the change he had sensed recently in Conan. And yet there had been no flagging of the king's vigor and leadership—rather, the opposite, certainly no ground for complaint. Conan seemed able to juggle these obvious risks, and to parlay them into greater glories for himself and Aquilonia. So Trocero held his peace.

He strummed them a ballad so soulful and brave,
'Twould pierce to the heart of the naughtiest knave.
He played of ambition, of hate and mischance.
To liven the party, he led them a dance.

They danced all the evening, they danced the nighttime
To the notes of his harp and his clashing steel chime.
Then softly he played, with strummings so deep,
So sweetly and softly, he lulled them to sleep.

At the conclusion of the jester's song, acclaim and laughter sounded from the company. Amlunia—looking flushed and a little wild-eyed, perhaps from memories of the night memorialized in Delvyn's tune—reached across the complacent king and snatched his ale jack out of his hand where it rested on the chair arm. Raising the flagon high, she cried out shrilly, "A toast to the emperor, everyone! To King Conan, player of the sweetest funeral dirges!"

She gulped lustily from the jack; then, laughing, she turned it against Conan's lips and tilted it, so that he had to swallow mightily to keep from choking. When some of the ale sloshed down his face, she jerked aside the flagon and darted to lick the foam greedily from his neck and chin, ending with a deep, passionate kiss on his mouth.

The other revellers set down their flagons and waited, admiring or abashed, while the seemingly endless kiss endured. When at last Amlunia pried free of the king, gasping for breath and clearly unready to resume love-making at once, Trocero spoke up.

"Aye, a skilled player our king is! The question remains, Your Majesty: what kind of ditty shall we play to Armiro as he scrabbles at our city gate?"

" 'Twill have to be a quick-tempoed one, 'tis clear." Conan sat flushed, recovering his wind with gusty breaths. "The scamp showed us his skill and the zeal of his troops by his attack this noon. He almost carried the wall—thank Crom he will not have slums to burn outside our gate again soon!"

"Armiro the Koth has the reputation of a clever commander," Lionnard said. "Aye, and ruthless! We can thank Mitra—and Crom too, milord—for that part of it." The lordling stirred uneasily at Conan's sudden, suspicious glance. "I mean to say, there are none in Ianthe who would want to open the city gate to him, after the toll he has taken in southern Ophir. Fear of flame and pillage will keep our city's defenders vigilant." Lionnard peered anxiously at Conan across Amlunia's shapely bosom. "After all, O King, your conquest of Ianthe was practically bloodless."

Conan laughed. "Bloodless? Ask your rival Malvin about that! Ask Balt, or gentle Amlunia here." He pulled the girl's wriggling weight against him. "Even so, I misdoubt that my conquest of Armiro will be so bloodless."

"You plan to defeat him in Koth, Sire?" Trocero asked. "Or merely drive him out of Ophir? The gods know, there is considerable difference between the two undertakings."

The king shrugged. "From what I hear of Armiro, he will not take a rebuff lightly. Belike I shall have to hound him into Koth, even back to Khoraja, or destroy him utterly to keep him from being a poor neighbor to us. Ah, but then, 'tis for the best . . ." Conan swigged from his tankard before resuming in an expansive tone. ". . . Because, after all, once Nemedia is secure on our northern flank . . . why, Koth, Khauran, and even fabled Turan may be ours, with all the dozens of kingdoms in between!"

"Is it surprise I see in some of your faces?" Sitting up more regally in his chair before the others' stares, the king shook his black mane. "Know you, my captains, Aquilonian power is ripe to become empire! We would find allies aplenty for such a gambit. In my time I have set kings, queens, and outlaws on half the thrones of the Hyborian lands! It may be time to call in old debts." He spoke in firm accents, glancing at them over Amlunia's worshipful, seductive face. "In Khoraja itself, our adversary's homeland, I'm sung as a national hero for my service as general under the once-queen Yasmela."

"Ah, yes, O King," Delvyn piped from his corner, "the dowager Yasmela, I have heard of her! She was a power in the Khorajan court—until a few years ago, when Armiro's faction seized control. Now, 'tis said, he keeps her prisoned in a rural castle, a safe distance from the intrigues of the palace." The jester gave a strum on his lute. "But that may be just a rumor to lull her former friends. More likely she is dead."

"What . . . Yasmela slain? Or a prisoner? Say no more of this matter, jester!" Wearing a scowl fearsome to behold, Conan slammed his ale jack down on the table beneath the wavering spigot of a startled ale pourer. "Crom's devils!" he muttered dangerously at Delvyn, who in turn regarded him with an insolent, unruffled air. "I will ask you about it later, in private! The wretch Armiro must be dealt with, in any case."

With this shadow cast over the king, his talk of empire waned. Instead he summoned the ale ewer more frequently, while bantering with the wench who squirmed at his side. Their talk was of their established common interests, butchery and lechery.

"You rode into battle against me with your late lord, I was told, Amlunia." The king reached up to trap her delicate chin between his callused thumb and forefinger. " 'Tis said your blade took a red toll among my footmen and carls."

"Aye, 'tis so!" The woman, instead of showing dread of him, laughed with pride as she twisted her jaw free of his grip. "I never troubled learning to joust, or swing a mace against clumsy mounted knights. But riding down men afoot is fine sport! Better than hunting antelope, or wild pigs!"

Conan laughed in his turn. "By Ishtar, I like a girl who rides to battle! Cimmerian women of my home tribe did so. They fought beside their men," he said wistfully, "and avenged them when they fell, even to their own deaths!" He stroked Amlunia's short hair and the lithe, slender neck beneath it. "Of course, some men say the presence of women on the battlefield is immoral . . . a warrant for rape, since rape is a lesser hurt than killing . . . or at least, it may be. And yet, rape does not rule out killing!" The king shook his head in ale-dim puzzlement. "Fah, I am no philosopher! But give me a warrior wench any day, one who scorns such dangers!"

"Thank you, lord." Amlunia stirred pleasurably under Conan's hand. "The hazard of rape is why I wear full armor, and keep it tightly fastened. No warrior has yet unhorsed me, or mounted me himself . . . in battle, that is!"

Conan guffawed at this, laughing long and hard. Then he guzzled ale while recovering his breath. "Doubtless, too, Amlunia, the danger of rape explains your liking for leather underwear!" His hand roved to the waist of her tight black pantaloons, where it idly pinched and pried. "Tell me, girl, does it not get hot and sweaty at times?"

She reached to her midsection, took his hand, and guided it instructively. "And what of you, O King?" she asked him breathily. "Do you want to rape me? I would not let you."

"Is that a challenge?" He set down his flagon, clasped his arms about her, and drew her closer against him. "You have a hatchet concealed in those jodhpurs to fend me off with, perhaps?" He finished his question with a playful nip at her earlobe.

"Nay, my king," she gasped in his ear, "but you cannot rape me! We might swive together, but I—I would not let it be rape!" Her words were followed by squirms and caresses too imperative to allow further conversation.

The dinner's official function had dissolved, in any case. Lord Lionnard had crept away with half-heard apologies, and soon afterward Trocero had gone for a night tour of the south wall. There remained in the king's party only Delvyn, asleep or thoughtful by the fire, and Egilrude and the other officers, who soon trapped the comeliest of the Ophirean serving-maids on their black-kilted knees. These women, though reluctant at first, could scarcely refuse to tarry with their city's conquerors. They let drink be poured down their throats, and thereafter let themselves be pawed by the men as the courtesan Amlunia was pawed by Conan, and even reciprocated.

The company's frolic continued late, with the servants kept scurrying the better part of the night for more ale, sweetmeats, and firewood. At last the revellers sank down drugged or sated; the fire was banked high and blankets were laid over their drowsing bodies. Then the lights were snuffed out, and silence fell.

But in the gray hour of dawn, the king was awakened from his depleted, ale-heavy slumber by clanking footsteps and a firm, insistent prodding at his shoulder. "Conan! Arise, my king! The news is most urgent and requires your orders."

"What is it, Trocero?" Relaxing his grip on the dagger he had instinctively clutched beneath his blanket, Conan heaved Amlunia's stuporous weight aside and sat up on the hearthrug.

"Armiro has bridged the river."

"What? You mean he's attacked the bridge!" Conan jerked the blanket from his kingly undress and began casting about for his kilt. "Has he gained a foothold in the city?"

"Nay, Conan," the count said patiently, "he has bridged the Red River, a league or two north of Ianthe. He built a bridge himself."

"Crom's curses! A ferry, you mean. A bridge of boats, we can easily destroy such—"

"No, Sire! The courier says it is a real bridge, one that horses and chariots are being driven across. His shock troops have already seized territory on our side of the river. I have alerted the city guard, but we must hasten to stop the invasion in our midst!"

CHAPTER 7
Kings and Quarrels

The riders advanced upriver, through scattered trees lining the high western bank. A low ceiling of mist overhung the water, which ran muddy red as the river's name implied. Yet occasional glimpses of sunny white and sky blue through the landward boughs hinted that the fog would soon lift.

The Aquilonian formation was spread wide and deep to frustrate ambushers. Close before King Conan rode Trocero and Ottobrand, with shields raised high on their saddle pommels to screen him from enemy arrows. The king's mood this morning was not such as to make him gallop into battle at the head of his troops.

"Blight this river fog!" he growled. " 'Tis no wonder Armiro could build a bridge under our noses!"

"Aye, 'tis so, Your Majesty!" Ottobrand said. "With the nightly fog and the noise of the river flood—" The general fell silent a moment and let the murmur of rushing waters fill their ears. "But truly, milord, the prince must be wizard or demon himself to have raised the span so quickly, in a single night!"

"Nay, nay," the king said, "to think on it, I have heard tales of the Stygian army using such contrivances against rebel tribes on their rainy southern border." He scowled. "Armiro must have planned it far in advance. His attack on the city was but a distraction." The monarch shook his head ruefully. "We should have known and provided against it. You, Ottobrand, might have thought to—"

"Yonder lies the bridge, Sire!" The burly general, anxious to deflect criticism, raised a gauntleted arm pointing straight upriver.

There, between a low curtain of mist and the river's braided torrent, stout timber piers and cross-braces marched across the wide, shallow reach. At their bases, swift currents could be seen foaming and leaping over abutments that appeared to be made of sticks—withe baskets, Conan guessed, laid into the stream and filled with stones. The bottom edge of the white pall obscured any sight of the span itself; whatever now passed over the bridge was invisible as well, due to the knife-edge of hovering mist. The obscurity almost seemed sorcerous in origin—and yet Conan remembered seeing many such morning fogs hanging over Cimmerian lakes in his youth.

From the forest just ahead came a sudden disturbance. There sounded the din of arrows striking armor, the scream of a horse, and prolonged, fluent curses. A moment later one of the scouts came striding back through the weeds on foot.

"Enemy pickets ahead, sir," he told Ottobrand with a brisk salute. "They have raised a line of timber bastions along the far side of a stream. The posts are manned by skilled archers."

"So. Send one of your fellows with a live horse inland, to alert the rest." Ottobrand waved the formation of riders to a halt and turned to the king. "Defenses lie ahead, Sire. It sounds like a risky position to attack with this scratch force. I sent word south ere dawn, so we should have more troops arriving by noon."

"Aye. But by then Armiro will have the rest of his army across the river." Conan spurred his horse past the general's and forward along the bluff. "Let us have a look at this bridgehead of his."

Just ahead, the course of a forest brook cut into the river bank at right angles. Its bed wound through reeds and tussocks in a shallow gully, to vanish abruptly in the silty wavelets of the Red River. Conan reined up his horse amid a stand of stout tree trunks and gazed across at the brook's far bank. His view was unobstructed by the fog, which hung lowest and thickest over the river.

Ahead, a short distance away, a breastwork had been reared to defend the headland that was the terminus of the bridge. A low, curving palisade of treetrunks already faced out over brook and river, with the brush cleared away down to the waterline. As Conan watched, new timbers were lifted into place by laboring Kothian troops, whose heads and shoulders were visible behind the wall. The soldiers, purple-caped and wearing pointed helmets, swarmed methodically to their task, like ants.

Trocero and Ottobrand reined up beside Conan, shields raised high to protect their king. On seeing the palisade ahead, the general swore softly. "Milord, the prince has guessed we would come this way. Our approach is blocked."

"A formidable bastion," Trocero added, "to be reared so soon—" His words ceased abruptly at the approaching swish of an arrow, and its meaty thunk into a nearby tree. Around its shaft was knotted a broad, trailing streamer of white silk—a heraldic adornment that had undoubtedly slowed the arrow's flight and made it far less deadly. As the ribbon settled to earth, a voice hailed the three from the far bank of the stream.

"Who comes? Is it Conan the Aquilonian, henchman of Ophir in her treacherous assault on Imperial Koth?"

Conan, shouldering his horse forward between his officers' mounts, rode to the very crest of the bank. He halted close beside the beribboned arrow. "Nay," he shouted back. "I am Conan, King of Imperial Aquilonia, and savior of Ophir from the Koth's spoiling attack! Is the princeling Armiro present with his troops?"

"I am Prince Armiro!" A younger, angrier-sounding voice took up the challenge. "Why do you not address me with the respect due a Supreme Tyrant of Khoraja and High Prince Designate of Koth?" At the highest point along the palisade could be seen the plumed helmets and shoulders of two officers, probably the prince and his lieutenant.

"I know nothing of such titles!" Conan bellowed back. "I see only a rash stripling whose greed makes him trespass on the domains of his betters!"

"In you," the prince's sharp-edged voice retorted a moment later, "I see but an uncouth brawler, trampling the robe of kingship under soiled, cloddish feet! What, then, is your business here? Do you come to plead an armistice?"

Trocero spoke softly and urgently at Conan's shoulder. "He wants to bargain, Sire! Offer him southern Ophir, if he will but withdraw across the river."

"Aye, Your Majesty," Ottobrand added earnestly, "or even the nether half of the capital, south of the river. We can take it back later if we choose."

Ignoring them, Conan thundered back at the palisade in the voice he used to move armies across battlefields. "Armistice? Nay, Khorajan whelp, I come for your head! You will rue the day you set about stealing the kingdom I chose to liberate! This," he roared, "is a matter to be settled between men—if you have yet attained enough manhood to face me in single combat!"

"Yes . . . splendid," the sharp, arrogant voice drifted back, "that is also my wish—though I hate to sully proud Kothian steel with the blood and spew of a low ruffian that styles himself king! But since you dare insult me"—there came a moment's silence, as if for consultation—"I have little choice. For a meeting place, what about yon islet?" The figure on the palisade raised an arm and pointed out over the river. "We two can row out alone, each of us, and decide who rules all of Ophir!"

The isle he pointed to was a sparse, barren sandbar lying well outside the fall of a bow from shore. Though low-lying, its surface looked dry and firm, and its position was ideal. On the smooth, naked expanse, a passage of arms between champions could be witnessed by all and hampered by none.

"Good, then," Conan shouted to his rival, "I will meet you there!" Aside to Ottobrand he ordered, "Fetch me a boat."

"Aye, Your Majesty! There is a string of them at Ulm's landing, a short way downstream. But, Sire, would you really hazard everything on the outcome of a duel—?''

''Hazard?'' Conan asked sharply, wheeling his horse back among the trees. ''What hazard? Remember, I have just slain forty rogues of Armiro's ilk single-handed! This will be but a trifle—that is why I provoked him to the fight.'' He laughed scornfully, spurring toward the riverbank. ''The prince is a landsman. He will do well to reach the field of combat without perishing in the toils of the river serpent!''

''Aye, perhaps, Your Majesty,'' Trocero took up the argument, ''but how many times can milord afford to stake your kingship and your country's fate on the strength of your lone hand? Armiro is said to be a skilled fencer, strong and clever even considering his youth—''

''His youth?'' The king twisted in his saddle to glower at the count. ''You mean to say I am too old, that my strength and battle luck have run out? Why do you plague me with it? What must I do to prove otherwise?'' His eyes smoldered a chilly blue at his old friend. ''When I am king of the world, will that be enough?''

As Trocero tried to reassure Conan of his faith and loyalty, a boat was summoned. It came towed by horses at a gallop, a mastless skiff drawn through the river shallows near the bank. Into it were laid an assortment of weapons, including arrows and a stout longbow, unsheathed and strung taut in spite of the river's damp. The king doffed his spurs, armor, and heavy sable jacket, which would have been a foolhardy costume in a boat. Instead he borrowed the wooden buckler and round helmet of a Gunder warrior, which he laid in the bulwarks. Seating himself facing the boat's stern, he grasped the oars and pulled out into the stream.

The current was considerable even on this slow, shallow side of the river. It took most of his effort to hold his place upstream, abreast of his goal—three dips of the oars at least for every dollop of forward motion. At this rate Conan knew that Armiro, coming from upstream, would be less fatigued when he reached the field of honor.

Yet he scarcely minded the labor, and thanked the northern gods for his years of boat-handling experience among the Vilayet pirates. Keeping his eyes on the bearings he had established behind him—a pointed rock in the river shallows against a split tree high on the shore—he toiled onward.

Halfway to the sand bar, he saw the men behind him turn upstream, and glanced that way to see his rival emerging from behind the headland. The prince stood erect and forward-facing, one foot braced on the thwart, driving the boat forward with long, effortless strokes of two oars. Doubtless some quirk of the current favored him greatly; even so, Conan begrudged the haughty youth his evident skill, and the bold figure he cut to the watching troops.

Their audience was by then vastly increased, for the fog had begun to lift. It exposed the far bank of the river, a treeless slope where throngs of men and horses gathered under the drooping standards of the Kothian legions. Likewise, further upstream, the bridge itself was unshrouded—and shown to be laden with men, carts, and horses moving across it in a steady westward flow. The soldiers marched three and four abreast, in broken step to keep from shaking the fragile structure apart.

At the sight of the two kings rowing out to their engagement, the troopers began to slow down and gawk in the middle of the span. This caused their officers and quartermasters to bellow at them, waving flails and whips overhead; but they were hampered from reaching the offenders by the crowd on the viaduct. In moments, all traffic on the bridge trundled to a halt.

Conan, struggling against the river's dimpled currents, could spare little attention for the other boat and the bridge. Pulling smoothly and steadily, he rowed his skiff into the shelter of the islet, and felt its bow ground at last in firm mud. Stepping out into the water, he grasped the painter in both fists, which throbbed from his labor at the oars, and hauled the craft up onto the sand bar.

Its surface was muddy and adhesive, but underlain by hard-packed sand. It would show tracks but not greatly impede a fight. As the water drained from his breeches and boots, Conan paused over the array of weapons in the boat. He chose the Gunder buckler, his own familiar broadsword—which he slid into his dagger-belt—and a long, steel-tipped spear.

He eyed the longbow and quiver thoughtfully, but did not take them up. To feather his enemy with arrows before the man had left his boat, or immediately as he set foot on the sand, might look unkingly to the watching hordes. Furthermore, in Armiro's hot-headed answers and readiness to fight, Conan sensed something he could not entirely bring himself to hate. Perhaps, if the princeling put on a brave show and fought him to a fair impasse, he might spare the lad's life—'twould be victory enough, he told himself, to swear the prince to withdraw from Ophir along with his armies—and, of course, to release the Khorajan Queen Yasmela from captivity.

The welfare of Conan's former lover had been much on his mind during the ride here. That, in truth, had been his main reason for goading Armiro to single combat; he planned to put him to the question on it. If Conan had his way, the Kothian prince's survival would hinge on the good report he could give of her situation. Assuming that Yasmela was unharmed, the lordling might, after all, prove a useful ally on the road to world conquest—if he could be taught to render Conan the respect due a conqueror.

Raising his spear and buckler, the king strode forth onto the sand. Armiro's boat was nearing the upper end of the islet, moving diagonally downstream under smooth forward strokes of the oars. The prince wore gleaming chest armor and a fur-trimmed cape of Kothian purple—a mad costume for a flood-swollen river, and yet Conan knew it made the Koth look more regal than his own motley garb. As he approached the head of the islet, there sounded acclaim from the watching soldiers on the bridge and palisade; fists were raised and weapons shaken, and a cheer drifted faintly to Conan's ears over the river's rushing murmur. By contrast, the salute given the king from the few friendly warriors visible on the downstream bank was a faint, silent pantomime.

But Conan's attention was fixed primarily on Armiro's boat-handling; admirable as it seemed, there was something far too smooth and effortless about it. The low shallop moved steadily onward through the swirling currents; yet the prince's oars swung at a stately, ineffectual pace, barely dimpling the water. Could the craft be propelled by some other force—sorcery, perhaps?

There became visible something dragging from the

boat's sides, from loops of rope girdling the gunnels: dark, wavy masses with long, straight antennae protruding upward and forward. As the craft drew into the shallows near the sand bar, these shapes resolved themselves into the heads and shoulders of men, submerged, a half-score of them walking on the river bottom. As the naked toilers emerged from the water, they cast aside the long reed mouthpieces they had been breathing through, grasped the boat by the loops of its towrope, and lifted it, carrying it up onto the beach.

Armiro had abandoned his stately pretense of rowing; he was already stepping forward out of the boat as it slapped down onto the sand. Smiling cynically, the prince fitted an arrow to the stout Kothian bow he had taken from beside him. Meanwhile his escorts, with water still draining from their silt-reddened hair and beards, reached into the bottom of the boat and drew out crossbows already drawn and primed, one of them for each man.

No vain formalities or words passed between the unequal sides. The prince's arrow arched high and black against the fog and swooped down, to be struck aside by Conan using the stave of his spear. The bolts of the crossbowmen, who fanned out forward in a ragged line and discharged from standing or kneeling positions, were another matter. Those the king dodged more ignominiously, by dropping his spear and diving aside into a head-roll. He became instantly plastered with mud and received a slice on his leg from his own unscabbarded sword. As he slithered on his belly into the river shallows, he felt tardy bolts striking the muck alongside him, felt them lodge in his clothing and even in his flesh, for all he could tell in the desperate press of the moment.

The chill water deepened, and Conan's splashing, scuttling crawl turned to lizardlike swimming. He kicked off his boots and cast away his ungainly sword; yet he retained his helmet and shifted the wooden shield to his landward arm for protection. He gasped and sputtered for breath in the waist-deep water as the second volley of projectiles struck all around him. One clashed against his helmet with brain-jarring force; others drove like timber spikes into the buckler he raised up defensively at the churning, splashing surface of the river.

Hope lay in the twining currents. Fighting into deeper water, he let the river draw him away. He used helm and shield for protection during his brief, choking struggles for air, and alternately as ballast; their sodden weight drew him mercifully beneath the surface as he kicked and clawed out of sight of the enemy marksmen.

His real enemy found him then—or his imagined one. It was the river-haunt—the soul-thirsty red serpent that wrapped him in its tortuous folds and held him down in the chilly depths. Seizing hold of his limbs, his hair, his garments, the evil sprite strove to hide him away from light and air, to roll and tumble him forever in the slimy caress of its weedy bed.

Against the demon Conan fought determinedly, though it was hard to tell in the silty darkness which way was up, and which way to swim for his life. He felt that he was being drowned not in water but in thick, black oil, with the bubbles of his own escaping breath gurgling and chuckling evilly in his ears. And still, when he managed to break the surface, he was the target of mortal huntsmen whose barbs struck and skipped over the water around him.

Providentially, his officers had brought another boat

from the landing. With it they met the king near the friendly bank, downstream and outside crossbow range of the islet. Trocero's sturdy arms helped Conan up over the gunwale, and took from him his dented steel cap and dripping buckler, which bristled like a hedgehog with short, ugly crossbow bolts. Ottobrand and a common trooper rowed the boat back inshore as Conan removed his soaked shirt, revealing more spikes caught in its folds. On shedding his riding breeches, he cursed violently at finding a deep puncture in the flesh of one buttock. Lodged still in his leather trousers was the square-tipped quarrel that had caused it.

"It was the foulest treachery, my king!" Trocero assured him. "Praise be to all the gods that you survived! We could see something strange about the way Armiro was piloting his craft—but by then you were far beyond hail and recall." The count shook his head, watching Conan guardedly. "Such a ruse proves that the prince, though quick and sly, is no honorable foe."

As they rowed in under the eyes of the Aquilonian troops, Conan remained grimly silent. The only sound over the rushing current was the echo of cheers from upriver, as Armiro and his henchmen pulled back from the isle in a pair of boats.

"Well, my king," Ottobrand ventured, "at any rate there is no great gain or loss—save Your Majesty's wounds, which do not seem severe, and a few items of milord's equipage. We can still defeat Armiro the Koth—in fact, I would guess, word of his perfidy will rally the spirit of every good Aquilonian against him. I have sent orders upstream that fire barges be prepared, to send down upon his bridge—"

"Well enough, General!" The king stepped naked from the rowboat onto the river marge; there he accepted a horse blanket from one of his troopers and used it to buff himself dry in the pale, fog-filtered sun. "I know you and Count Trocero can defend this siege," he continued, "so I leave it to you. I will be gone from Ianthe for a time."

"But, Conan," Trocero gasped, "my king, what mean you? Do you still intend to ride north and join Prospero in his Nemedian campaign? I warn you, Sire, if we cannot contain this Kothian bandit, he could have the city circled within days." The count shook his head somberly, gazing close into Conan's eyes. "It will be more inconvenient then for you to return with a legion and break the siege. . . . Sire, are you in your senses?"

"I trust you to deal with Armiro the Koth," the king said, donning common breeches and a singlet handed him by an officer. "Also to oversee my royal guests, Delvyn and Amlunia. If the fight comes to a full siege, better that I am gone, since defense was never my best skill." After pulling the shirt down over his head, he leant nearer the count and addressed him confidentially. "Trocero, I ride to Khoraja. Alone, to see to the welfare of an old . . . ally of mine. I have heard tell she is ill-used, and even as king I cannot neglect such a trust."

"Conan . . . Your Majesty," Trocero sputtered, finding it difficult to keep his voice low. "Can you truly abandon your conquests to go galloping off after an old flame? What of our enemies? If you lust after a foreign queen, why not send an army hence to free her?"

"An army is too slow!" the king shot back in a fierce whisper. "As for my enemy—if anyone can tell me how to lay low young Armiro, Supreme Tyrant of Khoraja, why, Yasmela can!"

CHAPTER 8
The Tarnhold

Conan the Cimmerian, self-crowned King of Aquilonia, was a hard man not to recognize. He had ranged the wide world from sea-lapped Argos to fabled Khitai and back to Zingara, not once but many times. Especially along this trans-Hyborian Road of Kings had he marched, galloped, slunk, and been dragged in chains at various times, with trouble usually racing just ahead of him or close at his heels. Not a man to be forgotten, he—rather, one to be awaited with a tickle of sweat on the brow. The kind to watch carefully, and to conceal one's wealth and marriageable daughters from.

Down the years, Conan's name had been bruited abroad as that of criminal, rebel, savior, and conqueror. Under the name Conan and other names, in a score of lands, he had won more friends than enemies—at least, than surviving enemies. Men and women alike had rallied to his side and had prospered or died in his service. Most recently, they had hailed him as monarch of the greatest nation of the Hyborian world. Not the man to pass most easily was Conan, alone and anonymous, through enemy Koth.

To compound the difficulty, he was a rare sort of foreigner—a northern savage by birth, whose square features and icy blue eyes set him apart in this land of dusky, oval-faced southerners. His robust size and obvious strength, tempered with the catlike grace of movement he had ever possessed, merely posed further obstacles to a discreet passage eastward.

A remedy to all this was, firstly, the coarse, common garb and weapons Conan wore. The hooded cloak he draped over himself was soon frayed and dusted liberally by travel, enough to avoid any seeming of kingliness. For horseflesh, he resorted to a pair of sturdy common mounts, mud-colored and heavy in the shanks, one to ride upon and one to trail behind him. At a larcenous rate of exchange, before leaving Ophir, he traded his purseful of pure Aquilonian gold staters for the baser coinage of eastern realms, which would be far less noticed.

He let his beard grow out coarse and gray-grizzled, eschewing for a time the morning kiss of the steel that rode ever keen at his side. At times he feigned a limp; it was not difficult, in view of the painful effect of the long days' rides on the perfidious wound that marred a private part of his anatomy. While keeping his injuries clean, over the rest of his person he cultivated a smell shrewdly calculated to fend off the few hostlers and stablers he had contact with, to hold them at long range and avert idle conversation.

Most important and most difficult, perhaps—since Conan as both thief and king was best known for his fighting prowess and quickness of temper—he disguised himself by affecting a meek, reclusive nature. In spite of several brisk encounters on the road and in lodging places along the way, he reined back his ire and refused to heed the urgings of steel—the steel which, all his days, had saddled and ridden him across the world in much the same way he rode unreflecting horses and camels.

So King Conan traversed the scorched, conquered farmlands of southern Ophir, and the castled, meadowed vastnesses of Koth. As far as he could tell, he went unrecognized and unremembered. Even so, if some of the innkeepers and horse-tenders he dealt with looked closely at the Aquilonian silver groats among the bastard coin they handed him in change, they might have seen gleaming up at them the very face of the sullen, hurrying stranger who had spent the previous night in their hayloft, arriving at dusk and departing well before dawn.

Now, forsaking Koth's hilly plains for the narrow valleys of the mountain kingdom Khoraja, Conan had ample time to dwell on his memories of the country's former Princess-Regent Yasmela: how she had boldly chosen him, the first stranger she met on a nighted city street, to command her nation's armies in obedience to some wild vision she had of the god Mitra's will. How together they defeated the undead sorcerer Natohk, known to men as the Black Colossus, and celebrated their triumph one moonlit, passionate night amid desert ruins.

His brow furrowed as he recalled how, when subsequently he courted her, she had grown less compliant to him, weighted by concerns of family and kingdom; how she sacrificed all her time and passion to palliate the land's misrule by her brother King Khossus; and how, after Conan's departure, she ended by using her womanly charms to sway nobles of high blood—whether as a player or a pawn in the age-old game of courtly intrigue, neither she nor anyone else could say.

Since his kingship, news of Khoraja had come to Conan primarily through legates and spies. He knew that King Khossus had died some time ago—of an illness, it was publicly stated, though such a death could also result from some highly-placed person's ill-will. Princess-Regent Yasmela, instead of acceding directly to the throne, played some unclear and diminishing role in the long, slow waltz of barons, pretenders, chancellors, and princes-designate. These successions ultimately led to an obscure princeling's seizure of power as Supreme Tyrant—a title most likely invented by Armiro himself, to enhance his power. In any event, Khoraja's political tempests soon must have seemed petty to him, subsumed as they were into the grander turmoil of Koth, the new arena for the Khorajan upstart's ambitions.

Whatever the upheavals in the mountain kingdom, Conan had assumed that Yasmela, as sweetheart of Khoraja—and, through his own efforts, its savior—would retain an honored, protected place in public life. It had taken a schemer as high-handed as Armiro to shut her away from sight in the Tarnhold; whether she still lived, lying tortured and starved in one of its catacombs, was the king's gnawing concern. It preyed on him as he descended the forested slopes from the northern border passes, into the rumor-haunted valley and down to the dark, ill-regarded tarn.

He remembered hearing in earlier days of the remote castle and sometime prison known as the Tarnhold. Now it lay before him, a massive keep asprawl with layers and accretions of masonry added on over the centuries in ungainly, clashing styles. The whole was surrounded by a sheer, battlemented wall, with rank forest growing without. Both keep and curtain wall edged directly on the mountain tarn, even extending some distance out into its waters. Such was true of many of the squirely fastnesses of lake-rich Khoraja; yet most of them managed to avoid the forbidding aspect of this place.

From horseback atop a hummock in the lakeside trail, Conan tried to judge what made the Tarnhold look so menacing. Possibly it was the grayish-black hue of the massive stonework, unaccountably darker than the bleached granite of the surrounding cliffs. Or the patchiness of the vegetation—blighted, possibly, by a rising water level. Maybe it was the murky look of the pond itself; for it seemed to catch the heavens' light and deaden it to grayish-green, rather than hurling it back skyward in sun glints and daybright reflections as most mountain lakes would. It could be due to the brooding clots of cloud impaled atop the nearby mountain peaks; their sullen shadows seemed to flow down the forested slopes, pooling darkly around the Tarnhold and its prisoned shoreline.

It seemed to Conan that, in a setting so bleak, Yasmela could hardly be enjoying life and health. He knew with certainty that a pedlar he had tried to ask about the Tarnhold, at the inn in the neighboring valley, had reacted to his questions with fear and evasion. Reluctant to discuss the castle at all, the man had cut off their talk guiltily and abruptly when Princess-Regent Yasmela's name was mentioned—an open admission, as Conan saw it, of her misfortune. The anonymous king had decided not to press the matter to knuckle-edge or knifepoint, lest some hint of his own veiled intentions should reach the castle's warders.

The few guards his questing eyes now saw did not seem any too formidable: gray-liveried figures bearing their halberds to and fro along the battlements, with no look of hardness or readiness about them. Scaling the wall would pose no challenge, in view of the age and crudity of the stonework. The warders, he guessed, would keep more vigilant watch inward than outward. It would be easy to slip past, even slay them if he felt a need for it, moving stealthily by night.

Except that he had no intention of waiting so long. Night was a poor time for spying; little could be seen, and most telltale activities were halted. Furthermore, entering a strange abode in darkness required the use of a light, sure to draw attention to the bearer. He had resolved to enter by daylight, if only to learn the inner scheme of the place. He would wait in hiding within or, if necessary, return later.

He guided his horses off the trail, hobbling, the animals near plenty of water and forage where a sparse forest of scrub trees and dead-white snags screened them from the castle. He rubbed them down and replaced his saddle and traps on their backs, leaving them ready for a quick escape. Then, stripping off most of his own garments and weapons, he crept to the lakeside.

The tarn was warm, reeking faintly of sulfur. He guessed that the action of submerged hot springs or brimstone seeps accounted for its murky color. Along its rim, amid tangles of sedge and reed, floated thick clumps of algae. Conan slid into the water and laved himself well in it, using handfuls of the muddy scum as soap—since the unwashed smell that had helped conceal him could now just as easily betray him. He edged deeper then into the lake until the water rose to his eyes, and paddled forward in the direction of the fortress.

Even in the tepid water, he felt goose-prickles of dread at assaulting an enemy fort nearly naked. Yet his breechclout of thin, twisted silk would drain water swiftly and silently. So would his black mane, tied back as it was behind his ears. A sheathed dagger, looped to the thong at his waist, completed his attire. If he had need of clothing, such as a guard's uniform, it could be obtained later inside the Tarnhold.

The wound in his posterior was healed now and well nigh forgotten. His skin, he knew, was burned dark enough not to flash whitely in daylight; even so, he would have to swim deep beneath the surface for long intervals to avoid detection. Paddling smoothly, his feet brushing the rank, weedy slope of the tarn bottom, he rounded a stand of cattail reeds and confronted one massive side of the keep.

It rose dark and sheer, a brisk swim away across open water. The less lofty curtain wall joined it at one corner. No guards were visible on the angle of the battlement overlooking the tarn, and so Conan dove deep and swam a few dozen strokes out into the open before surfacing to examine the looming pile again.

The only windows on this side were small chinks high up in the gray-black face. The masonry looked old and creviced; even so, it would be a long, vulnerable climb up to the windows, or to the roof edge that beetled over them. Better to scale the wall alongside the keep, where the joints between ancient and merely antique stonework promised to provide more toeholds.

But first, Conan decided to inspect the bases of the walls beneath the water; there might be gaps or outflows there that would provide a stealthier means of entry. Filling his lungs, he dove beneath the surface with his eyes skinned open.

Below, in a gallery of skylit yellow-green, Conan marvelled at the sight that awaited him. The water level had indeed risen by two or three fathoms sometime in recent centuries—likely the result of a dam or avalanche downstream. Here on the tarn's weedy floor lay the former dock and lakeside entry of the castle.

A stone pier extended straight below him, half-buried now in silt and feathery moss; behind it was a broad terrace, half silted under and littered with sunken, waterlogged limbs and snags. At the back, centered in the shaggy green wall of the keep, yawned a high, rounded archway. It had given access to the lowest levels of the Tarnhold, which now presumably were flooded.

Such a passage, if still open, was precisely what Conan sought. Lungs straining, he angled his course upward and returned to the lake surface close beside the sheltering wall of the keep. There, judging himself unlikely to be seen, he took an extended rest. Breathing deeply, he filled himself with air in the manner of Vilayet pearl-divers; meanwhile he clung to the wall with one hand and one foot. The weathered stonework was green-slimed beneath the water, dry and crusted above. Small seasonal variations in the tarn's level were recorded on its surface in horizontal lines of chalky white. The stone crevices at the waterline were filled with dry, papery skins of spiderlike water creatures, abandoned husks which crumbled away at Conan's touch.

He took his time, resting well for the dive he intended. There was still no sound or motion from the windows high above, and the curtain wall was invisible from here. No boats or other habitations were in evidence around the tarn, which stretched away darkly to brushy shores fanged by rocks and the bleached spikes of dead trees. Conan thought of tender Yasmela subjected daily to this desolate prospect—if indeed she lived and had sight. Then he drew a last breath and vanished beneath the surface.

The submerged archway was dark and menacing, with weeds trailing across its cavern-maw, yet Conan could waste no time cutting them away. Feeling the weight of water crinkling at the back of his jaw, he propelled himself downward and inward beneath the keystone of the arch, groping through slimy, ticklish streamers.

The corridor was deep, and his eyes had little time to adjust to the gloom, but he saw something ahead. Not a door, as he had feared, but a grillwork of vertical bars radiating down from the ceiling. The metal rods looked swollen and deformed with rust, and the grill's pattern was already bent and uneven, so there seemed an excellent chance of slipping past it. With only eight or so of the vertical bars screening a passage as wide as the height of a man, there was almost room to squirm through already.

Swimming up to the grill, he braced a shoulder against one of the bars, clamped a second one with fist and levered forearm, and set his feet against a third. Then he thrust, using all the strength of his shoulders, back, and legs. He felt the metal of the nether bar give way perceptibly. He was just about to renew his effort when a sudden, giddy awareness transformed his underwater world.

He felt the rods moving in his clutch, shifting forcibly of their own accord; he saw them flex, too, loosely jointed at the swellings he had thought mere ulcerations of rust. He imagined at first that the grill was collapsing, crushed down, perhaps, by a deadfall of masonry in the tunnel.

Then, peering upward into the murky gloom, he grasped a truth that nearly made him spew out all the breath from his lungs and forfeit life at once: the bars he clutched were not metal rods, but living limbs, the armored legs of a huge underwater spider that had been nesting in the archway. If once asleep, it was now awake; he could see two huge eyes, greenly luminous, glaring down at him from the rim of a blunt, spiderlike body. He could make out mandibles, too—a pale nest of them in the creature's underside, stirring and writhing in what looked like newly roused hunger. As he watched, two jointed, medium-sized appendages extended downward. Their pointed tips flexed into hooks, making ready to rake him up toward the creature's eager mouth-parts.

Convulsively he kicked free, clawing at water to propel himself away toward the archway. But his path was blocked by more of the creature's legs, which had shifted silently around him, penning him in like the bars of a tall, narrow cage. He twisted in the water and thrust his body halfway out between two of the prisoning legs; simultaneously, nimbly, the limbs moved together to scissor his waist in a tight, jagged embrace.

Squirming helplessly, Conan fumbled for his hip-thong and wrenched free his dagger. He used the short blade to fence futilely with the hooked talons that poked and probed at his nether limbs, then to hack and stab at one of the jointed legs that held him prisoned. But the armor was hopelessly thick and tough, the joints as tightly sealed and leathery as those of a lobster or crayfish.

The truth, he knew in his anguished soul, was that the monster had no real need to eat him alive, nor even crush him. All it had to do was detain him there another dozen heartbeats, until his tortured lungs burst and life fled from him in a silvery gush of upward-racing bubbles. His strength was waning fast; he felt himself growing dizzy and weak as he struggled. Defying certain fate, he thrashed ever more desperately, kicking at the legs and feelers, clawing at streamers of weed that softly caressed him and twined in his long, swirling hair.

Yet his struggles had some effect on the water dweller: still hovering in the middle of the tunnel, the thing was buoyed slowly upward and outward toward the archway—whether by its victim's frantic strivings, or by the elemental yearning of the air hoarded in the captive's lungs to fly back to the surface. Conan, nearly blind with asphyxiation, felt himself drifting upward, and felt his head bump the vaulting of the tunnel's ceiling. With a convulsive effort he stabbed and clawed at the weedy stones overhead, dragging the water spider another few hand's-breadths after him.

That brought him to the rim of the entryway, the outermost arch. Hauling himself abreast of it by main force, he reached around the corner and wedged the blade of his dagger in a slimy crevice of stone. Planting both his hands on the hilt, he pulled against the spider-thing's grip with all his might.

Conan's effort did not break the spider's clutch around his waist. Nor was the creature drawn out of its rocky lair, where it must have seized a firm claw-hold with some of its remaining legs. Instead, the keystone of the arch was torn free. It plummeted down past Conan onto the monster, dragging them both toward the bottom. After it, with a slow, deliberate rumble, came a further avalanche of loosened stones. Conan felt himself caught up in a mighty surge of water and billowing debris. It smote him; it drove the air out of him, and with it, his life.

Chapter 9
The Realm of Illusion

Hell was a dark, cold place.

Often Conan had wondered what it would be like. He had heard Barachan pirates warn of a watery afterworld, and dying Shemites bemoan lakes of unquenchable fire. Aesir ballads, on the other hand, told of a dismal, icy waste curiously like the singers' northern home. But this particular hell—his own private one, perhaps, or mighty Crom's repository of spent souls—was a cold, sightless vacancy of hard-edged stone and dripping water. It stank of damp, musty decay.

He lay on a harsh angular surface—a stone stairway, it seemed to be. The lower half of his body trailed in water and was numbed by its chill. He stirred weakly, his limbs feeling—where they had sensation—sore and bruised, as if a dozen demons had thrashed and pummelled him already for his misdeeds. Nevertheless, he was able to drag himself forward to the first dry step and sit upright on it. A short while later, after his numb dizziness diminished, he climbed shakily to his feet and braced himself against a stone wall rising vertical beside him. It felt vertical, at least—but who could say for certain in this sightless, directionless nether realm?

There seemed, in any event, to be a direction the gods wanted him to go, and he followed it: up the stairs, groping his way step by step. The stairway ended on a level pavement, bounded by another stone wall opposite the first, parallel and just beyond continuous reach of it. It was only a corridor, logic told him, trying rationally to fill in the invisible boundaries. Nevertheless, when passing between the two walls—in the giddy moment after his reluctant hand abandoned one damp, rough surface, and before his other questing hand encountered the second—he felt tempted to fall prone and clutch the stone floor, lest he be hurled blindly off into black, limitless space.

And yet he persevered. The corridor had turnings, he soon learned. It also had doors, iron-plated, scaled with rust, and fastened or corroded firmly shut. The odor wafting through the doors' barred grills, in any event, was too sour and too anciently dead to make him want to pass within. Would he, he wondered, eventually find one door unlatched and open, yawning to receive him?

At a branching of the corridor, he found a treasure. It hung in the air high out of reach, shining and scintillating like the rarest, brightest of gems: a sloping bar of light, firm and steady, illuminating a few scattered dust-motes that drifted overhead.

The ray did not cast any light on him nor on his surroundings; so far out of reach was it, he could not even find its source and terminus. They were concealed, most likely, by the shelves or buttresses of the vault's construction. The walls were too wide apart for any mortal to span, and too smooth for even a hillman to climb, so he had to content himself with craning his stiff, sore neck and watching the sliver of light play on wandering motes.

He found that by jumping high and swiping at air, he could make dust swirl across the beam in shifting patterns. This he did repeatedly; though it was idiot's play, it reassured him of his own reality. Holding one hand high against the faint scintillation, he saw that he could almost trace its familiar shape: four thick fingers and a callused thumb. He still had shape, that meant—and the sun still shone. Somewhere beyond this inky void the heavens still turned; just possibly, there was a way for him to regain them.

The discovery caused stirrings deep in his battered awareness. He recalled a long journeying, a swim, a struggle, a clutching menace . . . perhaps he was not in hell yet, after all. With new resolve he groped onward along a branching wall of the corridor, seeking escape.

The doorway he next found had no door in its arch. Peering into vacant blackness in search of new light traces, he edged forward—and felt the stones beneath him buckle and slip away into a void. He fell back against the column of the doorway, grasping it and hauling himself up from the devouring abyss. The stones that had collapsed, meanwhile, splashed thunderously into a well that lay unseen beneath.

Panting in relief, Conan regained his feet in the archway and listened to the lapping of wavelets raised by the fall. There was something strange about the sound, something oddly heavy and viscous. The deep, plopping echoes suggested that the room was floorless and vaulted, a collapsed gallery. Yet the picture his mind formed was different somehow—the image of a pond or fountain, broad and circular, fringed by ruins silhouetted under skies of mottled black. The fluid lapping and tossing in the pool, his inner vision told him, was not water; it was thicker, inky black and oily, and it rippled not with wind but with some mysterious inner force. As he stood listening, the splashing deepened and mingled with a more forceful gushing or gurgling, as of bubbles rising from far beneath the surface. The noise sustained an eerie timbre, almost that of articulate speech.

Then, as Conan stood caught in his reverie, it became evident that something more portentous was occurring. The gushing and bubbling became a draining sound, that of broad sheets and runnels of inky fluid cascading noisily downward as some massive thing raised itself slowly and ponderously from the center of the pool. . . .

Sensing a peril not to his body but to his very soul, he turned and bolted from the doorway. He staggered, groping, along the wall, running blindly, scarcely pausing to wonder whether the floor dropped away again just ahead. The sounds did not pursue him, yet he fled on, up an incline, across the trackless vacancy of another arch or corridor. His motion carried him against a wood panel, a door, which burst rottenly open before his weight. He staggered through into the space beyond, clawed smothering fabric aside . . . and halted, dazzled.

The room ahead of him was full of the brightness of day. He had to shut his eyes—yes, and raise his hands to shield his tissue-thin eyelids against the light's intensity. But not before he had glimpsed someone—a female form, soft and graceful—starting up within the room.

"Conan? Is it you?"

The voice was familiar to him, hauntingly so.

"Is it, can it really be Conan of Cimmeria? I have dreamed of you for the last three nights!" He felt gentle hands prying his fingers aside from his face, letting in light that scorched his eyelids. "Yes, you are my Conan! You have aged but little—nay, you are comelier than ever." He felt soft kisses placed on his eyelids, his cheeks, his dry, panting lips. "And you are a king!" The face that pressed his, he realized, was wet with tears.

"Yasmela—by Ishtar, girl, I have found you!" Rather than remaining in an ungainly crouch intended for flight, he sank to one knee on the thick carpet beneath their feet. "A moment ago I thought I was in hell. Now I know I am in paradise!"

He forced his eyelids open briefly, admitting a slit of searing brightness; it conveyed a beauty that seemed every bit as searing. With eyelids clamped tight again, he dwelt long on the afterimage: berry-stained lips, deep brown eyes, finely sculptured features, and dark hair fringed with golden radiance.

"You are even more beautiful, Yasmela, if that were possible!" He pressed closer and she cradled his head in her arms. With her body shielding him from the light, he was able to blink his eyes open again, to see before him the soft olive skin of her bosom nestled in fringed, gauzy fabric and adorned with the delicate chain of a gold pendant.

The two clung together in silence for many moments; by the time they eased apart and Conan rose to his feet, his eyes were tuned to take in every detail of the place with a steady, blue-glinting gaze.

It was a lavish apartment, broad-arched between gracefully carved pillars, fitted with the richest furnishings and draperies. At its far side, a three-panelled balcony doorway opened on a view of a mountain lake, its waters bright with afternoon sun. An exit to an adjoining room stood open at one side. The portal by which he had burst in was a plain one, its planks gray with age, now hanging ajar in its splintered wooden jamb. It had been concealed by a richly embroidered arras, which trailed to the floor from a broken pole.

"That way leads to the cellars," Yasmela said. "They are flooded and unhealthy, as you probably know." She left his side and went to close the door.

"Aye, shut it well." Conan went along with her to help. "You might catch an ague . . . or something might catch you." Breaking off a piece of thick wooden splinter, he laid it against the jamb, then drove the door shut with the sole of his foot, wedging it tight. "This should be made faster yet, with spikes," he added, turning to her. "But tell me, Yasmela, what is this place? Are we still in the Tarnhold? My mind has been afuddled ever since I awoke in yon crypt."

"Why yes, we are in Tarnhold. My window overlooks Aubril Tarn. 'Tis even more beautiful at sunset, if you will but stay. . . ."

"Yes, certainly—but confound it, Yasmela, it is not the same! That lake is wholesome to look on, and the trees outside your window live and flourish." He strode toward the tall glazed doors, whose curtains were tied back in graceful knots. "This room of yours, and the balcony—the ramshackle prison I saw could never contain such wealth and ease!"

"Oh yes, Conan, I understand." She followed him across the room, detaining him with a gentle touch on his arm. "This castle, the Tarnhold, is an ancient place. Over the centuries it has housed highborn folk of Khoraja who are out of favor, and who . . . seek refuge here. Powerful warding spells have been placed on the estate to make it seem forbidding, so as to turn outsiders away. Doubtless when first you saw it, you were ensnared by the illusion."

"I see—at least, I think I do. But what of the spider-thing that nearly drowned me in the lake? Was that an illusion, too?" Stopping short at the sill of the balcony, lest it melt away beneath his feet, he cocked his head suspiciously outside. Sun played bright on the marble tile of the terrace, and flowers spilled in many-hued riot down the sides of urns set into the carved balustrade.

"Of the monster you mention, Conan, I do not know; it may have been illusion." Yasmela clung to him without apparent unease at his showing himself before the window. "Tarnhold has many secrets, and many wardings. Some are false, some may be only too real."

"Hmm." Conan turned back into the room. "Maybe all of this, then, is false." He moved to the wall and fingered the silky stuff of a tapestry, then hefted a jade urn that stood on a side-table beneath it. "Perhaps all here in Tarnhold is really squalid ruin, and we inside are the bedazzled ones."

"I only know what I see and feel, Conan—what I am." She touched the vase as he set it down, then the arm that held it, trailing her fingertips finally up to his naked chest. "Are you your same fierce, barbarous self?"

He grunted thoughtfully, glancing down at his soiled, abraded limbs, his soggy breech-wrap, and his dust-caked feet. "Aye, I reckon so. I would wash myself in the lake, if I knew the water spiders were but wraiths."

"There is a steaming spring in the yard below. I will bathe you, Conan." She clapped her hands together suddenly, sharply, and the sound was answered by the scraping of a door in the next room. Conan turned and waited warily for a servant or guard to appear. It turned out to be a woman, middle-aged and matronly, clad in a long, belted gown. She looked up once at Conan, wide-eyed, then discreetly lowered her eyes and bowed to her mistress.

"Vateesa, gather up linens for a bath," Yasmela instructed her. "And be sure that our evening meal is . . . ample enough for our guest." She turned to Conan. "Come with me, and none will gainsay us."

Following the servant, Yasmela led him through two more rooms as sumptuous as the first, and then down a broad stairway to a vestibule. Conan hesitated before stepping into the castle yard, but Yasmela exited blithely and beckoned to him, so he ventured out. The few other servants who were in evidence, gardeners and stablehands, seemed to vanish discreetly soon after their emergence. The courtyard was sunlit and pleasant, with garden plots and orchard trees cultivated along the base of the wall. Even the jumbled architecture of the keep was more appealing from this angle. Of sentries on the wall top there was no sign, and access to the lake was unobstructed via a low, stone-curbed terrace. In all, the place wore an utterly different aspect from within.

Gushing at the far corner of the court, beneath an arbor of grapevines that fruited unseasonably due to its warmth, a mineral spring flowed through a pool of lime-encrusted marble. From its surface curled a haze of steam redolent of the same sulfurous perfume Conan had noted in the tarn's water.

At the smell, and at the noise of the water welling up from deep within the earth, Conan hesitated—but here the sound was seductive. He shed his damp clout and stepped into the spring, gasping at its scalding warmth. Moments later, once her maid had helped Yasmela remove her gown, she followed. She retained as raiment only the comb in her hair and the delicate neck chain, from which the gold pendant dangled down between her firm breasts.

She met her guest in a tender embrace, which she then had some difficulty breaking free of—but together, at length, they sat down on the pool curb and began easing by slow degrees into the steaming cauldron. No sooner had they immersed themselves fully than they found it necessary to climb out again, to cool and rest themselves in the afternoon's rising shadows. The patient Vateesa helped Yasmela lave Conan's limbs and knead and pound his travel-weary, battle-sore thews as he lay stretched on the stone. Then the handmaid withdrew, leaving the two alone to minister more attentively to one another.

On Yasmela's balcony at sunset, over a table scattered with bread husks, nutshells, and razed remains of fruit and fowl, they continued their talk. Conan, belching in a thoughtful, restrained way, said to her, "From within the keep, I see no guards on the walls."

"No, the guards are few," Yasmela replied. "As I told you, the Tarnhold relies on other wardings."

"Hmm. I see." Conan nodded grudgingly. "With protectors like those, you do not need human guardians." He looked closely at her. "You are not, then, a prisoner here?"

"A prisoner?" She gave a slow shake of her head. "No, though some may put it forth that I am. I have merely retired from Khorajan political life."

"Retired, so meekly? That does not sound like you, Yasmela, to lay down arms and surrender the field."

"No, perhaps not. But, Conan," she said, taking his hand across the table, "you should know that I am not the fiery princess-regent I once was. For so many years I lived in the shadow of my brother the king, trying to right the wrongs and mend the weaknesses his rule left in the fabric of our state. Even after his death, fickle Khoraja proved beyond the power of one woman to master. I remained a player in the web of royal intrigue at the palace—whether triumphantly or not, to this day I cannot say for sure. Such things can weary one over the years—the factions, the conspiracies, the consorts and liaisons. You have had many lovers, I take it?"

Conan nodded. "Many," he assured her.

Yasmela sighed. "Well, you may not understand, but love is far less joyous when the coupling is freighted with political cares and dictated by expediencies. The courtly men I have known were glib-tongued, most of them, but even less loyal than the fickle mob of common folk. After years of such half dealings, there comes a time when one is grateful to leave the nation in the hands of someone who can guide it surely, someone strong and ruthless enough to—"

"Armiro, you mean." Conan shifted awkwardly in his seat. "Yasmela, does the prince keep you here as his concubine?"

She laughed, surprised. "Prince Armiro? Why, no!" She flushed slightly, but assumed an attitude of thoughtfulness as she recollected herself. "I do not even know if the prince has time or inclination for affairs of the flesh, so fixed is he on securing and extending his power. If he did have such a hankering, 'twould be for a woman younger than myself, I am sure."

"You seem young enough to me, Yasmela," Conan told her frankly. "But I warn you, this Armiro is my bounden enemy. No man who has played me so false as he has can be allowed to live."

Yasmela's eyes registered faint alarm. "But, Conan, I caution you, Armiro is not one to be easily undone. And he is not an ill ruler, really. In truth, some say he is the greatest Khorajan leader since our land was carved out of the mountainous backside of Shem! He has done an able job of maintaining order in Koth, as you must have seen on your journey here." Her hand earnestly pressed his across the table. "Unlike any Khorajan monarch of recent time, Armiro carries his ambitions and his wars outside our border, which in itself is a great relief. And I have not heard that his rule over the subject domains is unduly harsh."

"I know not," Conan answered impatiently. "The fellow is a quick and sly commander, I'll vouchsafe. But does that make up for treachery, I ask you? Or for cowardice?" He must have gripped Yasmela's hand with too great a fraction of his vengeful strength, for she jerked it back across the table with an injured cry.

"The wretch broke the rule of single combat," Conan grated at her, hardly noticing her unease. "He set upon me with slinking assassins under the very eyes of his troops—who cheered and hailed him for the foul deed! One of his murdering dogs pricked me in the fundament—here, where no self-respecting warrior should bear a scar!" Conan half rose from the table and slapped himself demonstratively on the injured spot, though he did not lower his borrowed britches to prove the point.

"I tell you," he went on, seating himself righteously, "there is not room in all of Hyboria for him and me! I would be a-warring at him now, except for the rumor I heard that you were ill-used at his hands—Crom, the mortal despite it aroused in me!" The monarch scowled at her across the table. "If he were but a lowly clod or swineherd, I would still want to shred his living gizzard—all the more so a prince, who arrogates himself to be my equal!" Conan shook his black mane, frowning in contempt. "Where does he hail from, anyway?"

Yasmela was evidently distressed by her lover's wrath—indeed, he now saw, almost to the point of tears. In answering, she chose her words carefully. "He is but an orphan of the cynical Khorajan court, made callous like so many others by its snubs and restraints." She shook her head in evident melancholy. "Years ago, he was just one of a handful of pretenders pressing credible claims to the throne—but he was smarter and more industrious than the rest, and so he has outlived them all." She shook her head and sighed, as at the untidiness of the table before her, and of her entire life. "But tell me, Conan, my worldly king, can you not see that the customs and manners of a foreigner might reasonably differ from your own? You too were reviled as a savage in your early days, remember! Can you not tolerate the same kind of harsh individuality in the ruler of a far-off realm?"

Conan frowned, shaking his head. "Nay, Yasmela. For such as Armiro there is no room in my heart!" Scowling, he groped for words. "One of the things I have been shown as king is that the world is but a small place, really—a tiny village of kings, vying at arms and statecraft. In such a paltry village, it does not pay to tolerate a bad neighbor."

"You intend to be king of the village, then," Yasmela concluded for him. "You have advisors who tell you this?"

"Indeed." Conan nodded frankly. "I have one friend in particular, a witty fellow named Delvyn, who has told me more about myself than I could have learned in a dozen lifetimes."

Yasmela nodded knowingly. "Many kings have such friends. But I would caution you to proceed carefully—Armiro has his advisors, too."

"At times I think you must be one of them," Conan told her. "But I know you better than to believe that you would throw in your lot with one as treacherous as Armiro."

"Nay, you are right," Yasmela conceded, "he is too deceitful for my liking." She shook her head sadly. "Even so, if you will bide here with me this night, you may hear that which will change your estimation of Armiro." She sighed wistfully, as if troubled by a related concern. "For my own part, I worry that I have been less than honest with you. For I must tell you, Conan, I am not as I seem."

At this Conan blinked. "Pray, girl, do not tell me I have bathed and bedded with some ancient, bearded sorcerer, or a deathless vampire who means to guzzle my lifeblood!" Though his remark was uttered lightly, as a jest, he could not keep a glint of real suspicion from his eyes, and a feathery-keen thrill of fear from his voice.

"Oh, but that is practically true, my love," Yasmela said in dismal seriousness. "For, in regard to what you said earlier about the deceptions of this place—whether the Tarnhold's beauty is its true reality, or whether its ugliness is—I confess that I, too, am under such a charm! This amulet''—she pressed the object on the gold chain about her neck, which nested now in the none too voluminous twist of gossamer enfolding her bosom—''is enchanted from olden times. It was ensorcelled to bestow on its wearer a false appearance of youth. I must tell you, Conan, that beneath it, I am old! Lacking its spell, I would not seem so desirable to you.'' Her speech ended with a faint catch in her voice. Clasping the pendant to her chest with one hand, she covered her eyes in shame with the other.

''Now, girl!'' Conan protested, rising from his bench and coming around the table to her. ''Your years cannot be more plenteous than mine—at least, not by many.'' He stopped and sat on the edge of the tabletop before her. ''And know you, I am not old! Any liar who says I am, I challenge to a bout of swords or ale noggins!'' Leaning forward, he ruffled Yasmela's chestnut tresses and patted her cheek, whose softness dampened his fingers with tears.

''Yes, Conan,'' she answered, her voice faint and shy. ''But everyone knows that men grow more winsome with age, while women shrivel and droop like spent weeds.''

''Nonsense,'' he told her gently. The light in the sky above the lake had faded to the purplest shadow of sunset. He reached beside him and moved the guttering oil lamp to the edge of the table, where it better illuminated Yasmela's seated form. ''You have no need of that amulet,'' he said, holding forth his cupped hand. ''Give it to me.''

Sitting disconsolate with one elbow propped on the table, her hand still covering her eyes, Yasmela sat stubbornly clutching the charm with her other hand against the ribbon of filmy stuff across her bosom. This, and loose harem pants of the same diaphanous cloth, were the only garb she wore, or needed in the mild evening air. The pendant, as he knew from earlier, closer examination, was in the shape of a stoneflower, the symbol of youth, embellished with blue-jewelled stamens.

"Come," he instructed her again, "hand it over."

Finally, at his urging, she stirred. With a brisk, careless motion that dislodged another sob from her throat, she lifted the chain over her head, held it out, and dropped it into his extended hand. He accepted it and stuffed it into a pocket at his waist. Meanwhile he kept his eyes fixed on his lover's half-averted face and sylph-like body, feeling eerie anticipation and a trace of dread.

The changes came subtly and slowly. Yasmela's taut breasts, slung in their nets of gauzy blue fabric, seemed to soften and relax; they spread to rounder, more luxuriant shapes against her chest, even as the breastbone beneath heaved with pent-up anguish. Her flat belly swelled for a moment, almost as if ripening with child; but then it stopped, arrested in soft, dimpled convexity that balanced the gentle curves of her upper body. Her thighs and hips, seen plainly through the single layer of filmy cloth, now deepened and strengthened, lending vigor and a firmer foundation to the entire woman.

Shoulders and neck filled in graciously, too; in all, her appearance changed from dollish, boyish youthfulness to vibrant queenliness. Her aspect, poised there in the backless chair, put Conan in mind of the unclothed demigoddesses carved in stone who fled, fought, and loved their way across the lofty architraves of the Temple of Mitra at Tarantia.

Yasmela's face, as she blinked up at Conan from beneath her shielding hand, was a more richly charactered portrait of her former one. Years had gone to rest there, as had sorrows, leaving their traces in the more melancholy curvature of her lips and the soft lines at the corners of her eyes. But Conan saw tracks of humor, too, at the sides of her mouth; a greater worldly wisdom, and a new capacity for lusty, fleshly abandon that seemed only to have been confirmed by its many trials.

Her cheeks glistened now with tears; despair showed off her features, perhaps, to their worst advantage. Yet her eyes bore, if anything, a surer wit. Quicker to read his stare, perhaps, they gleamed at him now with what might be hope. In answer, still seated on the table edge, he extended an arm to her.

"Up, woman, and come here to me . . . but first remove those flimsy shreds. And forget your enchanted bauble! This time I want you naked."

Chapter 10
Night Marauders

Late each afternoon, when the weary sun god retires for his rest—so the legends chanted by tribes in the remote southern part of Stygia tell it—he unleashes his hungry black panther Night to prowl forth and guard his earthly domain. Most mortals, left lying in the beast's ebon shadow, dare only cower in sleep. But others, notably thieves and lovers, undertake their greatest exertions as the shaggy black belly passes over.

Yet no matter how patiently and tirelessly one may toil—even if one's efforts are aided by others' eager hands, and slaked by however many draughts of cooling wine—'tis hard to labor the long night through. Toward dawn, most inevitably, thieves of love and of less precious goods seek out a soft place to lay themselves down. They forsake their earthly cares, resting for the return of bright day. It was from such a rest that Conan and Yasmela, lying across their bed in a tangle of slack limbs and silken coverlets, were awakened by a scream.

'Twas Vateesa's, they knew instantly, coming as it did from the adjoining room. Its shrill, frightened peal was silenced by a savage blow; whether dealt by flesh or steel, the stroke sounded mortal.

In an instant Conan slipped from the bed and snatched up a bronze statuette for his defense. Simultaneously, the door banged open and a black-clad figure darted through. Another instant, and the intruder toppled dead to the floor, his brains spattered across a priceless tapestry by the heft of the figurine. The marauder's wickedly edged shortsword did not clatter to the floor; it already shaved the air in Conan's grasp.

A rush of footsteps signalled that the fight was not over, as a half-dozen more dim figures spilled into the room. Abruptly a dark lamp was unshuttered; it played a lurid, blinding beam on Conan, and on the half-draped figure of his royal mistress behind him.

"So, Yasmela!" a hard, sharp voice proclaimed in aristocratic Kothian. "You now openly conspire with my enemies! A violation of our understanding, this, and a heinous treachery to me—"

"Fault not the queen," Conan interrupted. "She bears no blame if a foreign warrior bursts into her room uninvited! My arrival was no more heralded than yours, Armiro—for in sooth, the voice I hear sounds like Armiro's, though I know not how it comes here, by what sorcerous ploy or illusion—"

"Sorcery? Illusion?" As the brittle voice erupted in spiteful laughter, its dark-clad owner edged forward into the fringe of lamp glare. "Do you not think I have spies, O Conan of Aquilonia—in embattled Ophir, and in your royal legions as well? Do you not think I have slaves, sedans, coaches, and good swift roads, to carry me here faster than any lone man on horseback?''

''Very well then, rascal,'' Conan barked back at him, ''you are here! You have already shown that you are no duellist! Tell your dogs to have at me, and I will test their steel!''

''I would not bid them sully their blades with such a small chore,'' Armiro proclaimed, drawing his sword with a razory rasp. ''Keep back, men, this fight is mine!'' The prince sprang forward, a lean, crouching silhouette in the lamplight.

The two fighters met with a grating, scraping clash that rattled the curios in far corners of the chamber. The two blades were equally short and keen, well-chosen for battling in close quarters. Conan's near nudity gave him a disadvantage; he was wrapped only in short, flimsy breeks from Yasmela's guest closet, while Armiro appeared to be sheathed in soft leather under his cloak. But this did not keep the Aquilonian from pressing the attack, raining energetic slashes and thrusts which drove his adversary back and forced his henchmen to step aside and allow room.

Then, in a sudden turn of events, Conan's deft skein of attack began to unwind just as swiftly. Armiro, with his back to the wall, snatched his cape loose from its fastening at his throat and whipped it expertly over his free arm. Using it as a shield to deflect the Aquilonian's sword-cuts, the smaller, leaner man fought his way to the center of the room and beyond. Conan had to give ground, darting gingerly to keep his unprotected skin clear of a casual but potentially fatal brush with steel.

The prince, leading with his swathed arm, lashed out viciously from under its cover with his flashing, clanging blade. Conan, for his part, never quite gained the balance and momentum to deliver a blow that would shear through cape and arm alike. His retreat led the fight away from the bed, where Yasmela sat gasping with each stroke. Her bright eyes shone with fear as they followed the duel—on whose behalf, it was not entirely clear.

Then Conan was forced back against the wall—and with a roar and a clang, the fight turned again. The Aquilonian king snatched up not a cloak but a side-table, swinging it against Armiro's sword-arm with a force that propelled the younger man bodily into the center of the room. There the prince staggered and fell to one knee, not visibly injured but clearly overcome, his blade raised defensively in a jarred, unsteady hand. Meanwhile Conan dashed forward, throwing aside the broken table. His skin shone pale in the lamplight as his back arched for a killing thrust.

"No, Conan, spare him! He is my son!"

Yasmela's cry, ringing out in the gloom, may have stayed her lover's hand for a fateful instant. In any event it did not matter—for even before her plea could echo in the close chamber, Armiro's men had rushed forward on all sides, seizing hold of Conan and rescuing their prince. At the onslaught, the savage king's blade lashed powerfully to one side, chopping into bone and flesh; but its maimed victim must have had the unheard-of courage to grasp the weapon and bear it down with him. In moments the king was unarmed, pressed to the floor by the remaining half-dozen guards. There he lay pinioned and gasping, with a pair of Kothian blades crossed at his throat.

"Why, thank you, dear Mother," Armiro told Yasmela as he arose to his feet. "Your intercession on my behalf softens my heart toward you. I shan't entertain such drastic remedies for your . . . malfeasances . . . as I was considering before. Though this unseemly alliance of yours"—he pointed with his sword to the still-struggling man on the floor—"is hardly a small indiscretion.'

"Spare him, Armiro, please!" Yasmela cried. "Show him the same forbearance he would have shown you, for my sake." Clutching her bedclothes pathetically against her breast, she leaned forward across the mattress and raised tear-stained eyes and a supplicating hand to her son. "Conan and I are dear friends of old. In truth, he did not force himself on me!"

Armiro laughed—a brittle, supercilious note. "No great surprise, Mother," he said with chilly levity. "But tell me no more, I caution you. Remember, I have not always shown kindness or mercy to your 'dear old friends!' "

He glanced down again to the thrashing figure on the floor, hedged in by the tight-ranked knot of his bodyguards. These men did not make the mistake of laughing along with their prince at such delicate personal matters; in any event they were too busy with their captive, whom they managed to pin down ruthlessly and efficiently.

"But this one," the prince decided, "is too useful to kill, at least for now. He will make a valuable hostage or lure—perhaps even a manageable puppet king," he added tauntingly, "someday. Marius, strings for our puppet!" He issued the command with a hard snap of his fingers.

Obediently a soldier, one of the two whose swords were crossed at Conan's throat, reached to his belt and produced a coil of rawhide thongs. These he shook out into long loops. His fellow guards undertook the formidable task of forcing their captive's wrists together behind his back.

"For your part, Mother," Armiro went on, "I fear that your sojourn here is ended. You must continue your retreat from Khorajan state affairs, and your own fleshly ones, in some stronghold more remote and secure than this. I will undertake to see that your physical comfort is not greatly diminished." The prince sheathed his sword and continued speaking in cold, authoritative accents. "The Tarnhold, henceforth, will be more heavily guarded. It will serve as a prison for this captive, and a trap for any venturesome souls who essay his rescue. Marius, once he is securely bound, have the servants ready one of the cells on the lower floor for him. And tell them to pack my mother's things for a journey." Armiro laid a hand tentatively on Yasmela's tousled brow, then let it drop. "Mother, dear, you may dress yourself, but pray do so in the next room. Come." Motioning briskly to her, he turned and quitted the room himself.

"Conan, I am sorry! I did not mean for you to be caught. . . ." Yasmela's voice dissolved into sobs, which retreated from him unseen as she took her leave. A moment later he heard her give a sharp cry of anguish, presumably on seeing the fallen Vateesa in the next room. Of the maidservant's fate Conan could hear nothing. The intervening door slammed sharply, and the voices beyond were reduced to a murmur.

The king himself was trussed face-down on the floor, wrists and ankles bound together and both knots anchored to the heavy wooden bedstead. The hard, sharp thongs were knotted expertly, Conan could tell. With each loop cross-braided to the next in a sort of cuff, they restrained him securely, while only mildly numbing his hands and feet.

When the task was finished, the guard named Marius felt safe in leaving his captive untended on the floor. He departed the room with some of his fellows, telling off a pair of them to remain and keep watch. The voices of these two could shortly be heard from the balcony, commenting idly on the approach of sunrise over the lake.

Conan, lying in the chamber's interior gloom, struggled futilely, tugging and prying at his bonds. While keeping as silent as he could, he inwardly cursed Yasmela, the Tarnhold, Armiro, his guardsmen, and most vehemently of all, himself. He had been a great fool to trust the princess-regent, who had always been a slave to her highborn family and kingdom. Now, it appeared, one of her high courtly liaisons had saddled her with a scheming offspring—complete with false pedigree, no doubt, and a boundless lust for true rank and power. Out of her years of bitter experience, Yasmela must have trained him well; the princeling's resources, his energy, his cunning and cruelty in pursuit of conquest all seemed limitless.

Even his fencing, as it happened, was not bad; Conan had to yield him a grudging ounce of respect on that score. Though for a shameless whelp first to hide behind the skirts of his mother, and then publicly to scorn and revile her, was most reprehensible of all! If Conan could but escape this place and arm himself, why, nothing would keep him from maiming and flaying the wretched miscreant, be he Yasmela's son or her pampered fancy-boy!

But that was mere bluster, he told himself, lying weaponless and hog-tied as he was. The wine of revenge against a foe as cunning as Armiro might have to be aged far longer, and savored chill. For the moment he knew, more realistically, that if he could break free of these bonds, no earthly force could keep him from the balcony and the lake beyond. Now was the best time for it; in darkness he could certainly get clear of the Tarnhold.

But what stratagem could avail him? He had no weapon, and none was in reach. Teeth and toes were his only free-ranging digits, and neither could grasp the hard, tight knots which held him. The bed itself could scarcely be made to inch across the floor, at least not without noise. He had no wish to amuse and edify his captors with clumsy, futile efforts.

The one object he had on his person, he remembered now, was the neck-charm he had taken from Yasmela. It nestled in a pouch at the front of his waist. Unthinkingly, he began straining his lashed wrists sideways around his hips, trying to reach it with a hooked forefinger. But what might he do with it, even so? Offer it as a bribe to his guards? Call on its magical powers, perhaps, to disguise himself, by making his bluff, battle-scarred features look as comely and persuasive as those of the effete prince? He snorted in disdain at the thought of such a wizardly ploy.

Nevertheless, the charm might be of use. By arching and twisting his shoulders as far as he could, he brought his finger to the lip of the narrow pouch. Its end probed inside and hooked the slender gold chain, which, by careful inches, he withdrew. The jewelled pendant stuck in the seam, then came free; in a moment it trailed loosely from his hand.

By inexorable logic the thought came to him. He arched his elbows away from his body and flipped the chain up over the bonds that held his wrist. Then he waited. The wait was a tense, uncertain thing—can mortal flesh sense magic at work, by some tingle or warmth? Could he feel it acting behind his back, even close up against his bare skin?

In moments he felt the change: the thongs about his wrists began to stretch and soften under the charm. As the hard cowhide slackened and became more supple and youthful, he worked tirelessly at it, methodically flexing and twisting his powerful arms. Over long moments the hide gave way; his hands pulled free, and he set to work on the bonds at his ankles.

CHAPTER 11
The Thing from the Pit

"Immortal Kthantos, I am here—" In a far, twilit place the dwarf Delvyn stood at the edge of a softly lapping black fountain. "As well you know, O Godling! What do you wish of me this time?"

The pond's dark substance stirred, not in any discernible wind. Yet it shivered perceptibly from rim to rim as if in mild distaste.

"Not wish, but require." The deep, bodiless voice bubbled up from the pond's center. "I require, first, that you use a more worshipful term of address for me than 'Godling'—something commensurate with my divinity and limitless power."

"Very well, Demigod! But I hope that is not all you have summoned me here for." With an air of impatience, the jester shifted his weight from one foot to the other at the pond's stone curb. "I gather that your power continues to grow. In fact, I see that you have made repairs hereabouts—most tasteful ones, too.'' His gaze surveyed the monumental stonework surrounding the pool. The fluted columns and stately entablatures were no longer ragged and crumbing; their dark silhouettes jutted up knife-edged, in stark perspective against the starless, paling sky. ''Even so,'' Delvyn ventured, ''I would hardly call your powers limitless.''

''Limits are but a fleeting thing,'' the bubbling voice replied. ''Although from your low vantage they may seem insurmountable, to a god's lofty perspective they are slight.''

''Low as my perspective may be, O godly Kthantos, 'tis loftier than yours.'' The dwarf stood calmly regarding the pond at his feet. ''If you seek respect from your worshipers, you might consider clothing your divinity in some shape more prepossessing than an oily puddle.''

''Something more tangible, you mean,'' Kthantos answered warningly. ''Some emblem or eidolon, perhaps, such as can easily fit into the puny minds and imaginations of earthbound mortals.'' As the demigod spoke, a localized stirring occurred beneath the pond's surface. Delvyn, feeling a sudden chill of unease, watched dark eddies moving and swirling closer to his place on the pond's rim.

''Some symbol they can whittle copies of,'' the god rumbled on, ''to carry about in their grimy shirtwaists, or house in humble shrines by the roadside. Would such a shape as this serve?''

Against the deep, sardonic bubbling of the voice, a dripping, trickling object raised itself up abruptly from the mire: a manlike form, yet skeletally thin, it glistened all over with the black, oily substance of the pond—or at least of its thicker bottom-muck. Rising up directly before the dwarf, it towered menacingly over him at a height several times his own.

"Is this incarnation lofty enough for you, little man?" While the godly voice blurted forth the question, the tarry skeleton's lower jaw wagged along with it in a crude parody of speech.

Delvyn backed judiciously away from the looming shape; at this, the creature's gaunt arms lifted from its sides. They unfolded, extended, then continued impossibly to unfold and extend far beyond the reach of any naturally formed being. At a point well behind the dwarf's faltering steps, the hands drew together and almost met, effectively blocking his path of retreat with their bony, encircling clutch.

Each skeletal arm, the jester saw on uncomfortably close examination, was composed of a dozen or more ordinary human arm-bones jointed rudely together. Each long-taloned finger and thumb was a similar unlikely amalgam of human-looking joints. The limbs, though ungainly, did not seem to be impaired in leverage or dexterity by their unnatural structure; they flexed and twitched, as if eager to close on soft, mortal substance.

"Well, what think you?" Kthantos asked, bubbling forth copious amusement. "Is this a fitting emblem of my godhood?"

"Most impressive, Immortal One," Delvyn responded carefully, "especially if it is intended as a threat to our enemies or a scourge of sinners. 'Twere better, perhaps, if such a frighting face were shown to unbelievers, rather than to our faithful adherents."

"No matter, 'tis but a toy! I keep these mortal remains and other oddments here for my amusement." Noiselessly, swiftly, the freakish skeleton folded in its extremities and settled back beneath the surface. "There has been precious little else to occupy me," Kthantos said, "during the weary millennia my power has been confined to this pool." At the godling's whim, skeletal parts reassembled themselves at the surface of the pool and danced in random patterns there. Bony, disembodied hands slapped together in rhythm, and legs splashed to the clacking of oily black skeletal jaws. Meanwhile, spines and rib-cages swam and dove like schools of frolicking dolphins.

"Truly," Kthantos continued, "this is but idle exercise. When in time I bestir myself to command the world from this puddle, there will be no question of my godliness. Speaking of that, acolyte, how goes our campaign?"

Delvyn, called thus suddenly to account, nodded with a careful appearance of satisfaction. "It goest well, Immortal One. The king whom I have chosen is a swift and furious fighter, a commander able to hold his own against any rival on earth. Thus far he has overrun half of one kingdom and unleashed war on a second, posing a formidable challenge to his enemy's flank."

"Which king, then, are you referring to?" the godly voice asked. "The barbarous brute Conan or the sly Armiro?"

"Why, King Conan of Aquilonia, O Immortal One!" In replying to his master, the jester sounded somewhat startled and unsure. "Though 'tis true, if the Aquilonian were bested in this world-spanning conflict, our hopes would then ride on the one named Armiro. I would swiftly gain his ear and use my persuasions on him, but I doubt that he would prove as tractable as the northern monarch." The supplicant stood thoughtfully silent a moment before he spoke again. "Since you have so much knowledge, Immortal One, regarding a matter I have not heretofore troubled you with, 'tis evident that you have other, varied sources of information."

"Varied enough to know that your champion's glorious quest for world conquest has been halted this past fortnight, with your king vanished from his subjects' sight. Abdicated, captured, or, as the ever-spreading whisper has it, dead—such a state bodes not well for his hope of empire."

"Nay, Immortal Kthantos," the dwarf protested, "King Conan is not dead! I would know if he were! Remember, he is a great leader, a man of truly royal whims. He is entering upon a time of turbulent passions—standing as he does, at my urging, on the threshold of world dominion." The dwarf shrugged as if to minimize the king's absence. "So he betakes himself where he will without warning, delegating his great projects to his followers, who are unfailingly capable, unquestioningly loyal. All this has been foreseen, and is merely a part of my great strategy." Delvyn gestured theatrically, building an eloquent defense. " 'Tis consistent with our plans that he seize every chance, and for the best—after all, the last time he did so, a great city fell into his outstretched hand like an overripe plum."

"You are a glib mortal!" Kthantos said. "And yet, can you honestly claim that his long absence from the battlefront and from your control does not endanger our purpose?" From the dark surface of the pond, a crowd of skeletal arms now raised stubs of frail, rotted swords and fenced with one another in mock combat. "If he is off spying or adventuring, why are you not with him? What if he is slain or captured? How can you possibly hope to protect him—or else betray him timely, and fall in with his vanquisher?"

"Aye, great Kthantos, I must admit"—the dwarf allowed his shoulders to slump with an air of confession—"my control is less than complete. True, he is a slave of his own pride and lust, as befits a king; and he seems fully enamored of the goals I have set for him. His sudden whims and excesses, as a rule, only serve to strengthen my hand. But down the course of his life, if I gather correctly, his path has oft been unduly swayed by women. There is his queen, Zenobia, always a threat—her I plan to counterbalance with the wanton Amlunia, who is a safe, predictable force, a player of our own sort. But now emerges another female, a queen in the enemy camp, named Yasmela. How great her role may be, I cannot say; but I do not like it. It is to her rescue that Conan has flown—"

"Would it help your scheming," Kthantos' bubbling voice insinuated, "if I told you that the woman Yasmela is Prince Armiro's mother?"

"So! Then 'tis far worse than I thought." Delvyn fell to one knee and stared into the mirrorlike stillness of the pool a long moment. "Forgive me, Immortal Lord! I did not sufficiently credit your wisdom." The dwarf bowed in obeisance, then shook his head. "Pray, Kthantos, if your powers extend far enough to gather this earthly knowledge—is it then possible that you could reach out and affect the fall of events in the mortal world? For, assuming indeed that our champion still lives—"

"Conan lives, you spoke true in that." The god's voice dribbled forth without discernible wrath or reproach from the pond's surface, which had grown smooth and unbroken. "For although Queen Yasmela is a doting mother, she harbors a most unmotherly, astonishing attachment to her son's sworn, blooded enemy. In answer to your question—yes, I can affect the earthly world. I told you before that I have the power to kill."

"Pray use it, then, Lord! This woman, Yasmela—the damage she might do is unthinkable, a menace to your plans and to your renewed godhead—"

"Enough! 'Twill be done even as you pray! Not this moment—'tis hard to reach so far and pluck a life. But as you see, my power increases daily. It need not wait long."

"The woman Zenobia, too, Lord Kthantos—I had not thought to ask it. But the one death may rebound, and necessitate another. . . ."

"My, what a greedy little man you are—greedy for death. Although I am a bountiful god, you must not ask so many favors at once! The first boon I have granted. As to the other—we must wait and see."

Chapter 12
Roads of Conquest

In the days and weeks that followed, the courts of Hyboria resounded with the fall of kings and trembled with the uneasy shifting of alliances. From inn to farmstead to lordly manor, a grim word was murmured; it spread northward and inland faster than the burgeoning of new green buds in spring. The word was "war."

Well might the alarm be spread, since Aquilonia and Koth stood snarling at one another across the prone, gutted body of Ophir, like lion and hyena tearing at a slain antelope. Then, of a sudden, the ill-tempered Aquilonian cat swept forth its thorny paw to tear a living, bleeding chunk from the side of kingless Nemedia as well. And meanwhile, the stirrings and skirmishings of armies in western Ophir came near enough to the border of Argos to cause mutterings of concern in the nation's seaport capital, Messantia.

In Ophir itself the opposing forces lay stalemated,

perhaps because both commands had been abandoned by their kings to less aggressive subordinates. Swift marches culminating in a fierce attack on the bridgehead by Captain Egilrude's lancers, and subtle feints by Count Trocero, had driven the Kothians back across the Red River—but without the final, crushing victory the Aquilonian commander sought. Armiro's forces, by dint of stubborn obedience and patient drill, withdrew intact across their timber bridge.

The very next morning, as if in retaliation, a Kothian attack spearheaded by siege towers and wall-smashing rams penetrated the eastern half of the capital. Kothian troops, flushed with victory, pressed inward all the way to the river. Only after days of fighting was the city wall retaken by Trocero and Lionnard. The transpontine half of Ianthe lay in ruins, burned—as was Armiro's bridge, part of its length still standing out from the east bank of the Red River as a charred monument to the vain ambitions of war.

The King of Aquilonia returned ragged and travel-weary to the Ophirean capital. His long absence was attributed variously by his observers and detractors to pagan religious devotions, a galloping brain-fever, or the secret negotiation of foreign alliances. Though his officers half expected another enemy capital to have fallen to their king during his travels, he was grimly silent about the nature and success of his expedition. When asked privately by Trocero whether he had made progress toward unseating Armiro, he answered with a snarled curse, saying:

"I only learned that which will make it harder to undo him."

The count's reaction was noncommittal. As he had learned from sore experience, it would take consummate generalship to defeat the legions of Armiro the Koth.

The king's sojourn in Ianthe was brief. After a single day and a night, and these spent first in festive eating, then locked in a bedchamber with the courtesan Amlunia, Conan left the Ophirean campaign in the patient hands of Trocero and Ottobrand. Departing northward with Amlunia, the jester Delvyn, and a sizeable corps of Black Dragon guards under the newly promoted Egilrude, the king rode to join Prospero in Nemedia. His parting words to Trocero were:

"Remember, old friend, keep Armiro's legions occupied on this front. I'll roll up his northern flank until Ophir falls of its own weight. We shall go on conquering, if need be, until Koth and Khoraja are but islands amid a vast Aquilonian sea!"

The ride to Nemedia was longer than it had been, because Aquilonia had annexed extensive territory in the fertile valley known as the Tybor Gap. The farmers and herders who dwelt there were not much in evidence; their wealth and numbers had been too much depleted by conscripting and foraging armies. Their farms and fields looked abandoned but little harmed; it was further northward and eastward, approaching the Nemedian capital Belverus, that the ravages of war were fully seen—in broken castles, looted towns, and scorched farmsteads. In some roadside hamlets, widows and black-clad mothers knelt and keened over newly filled graves. In others, where no living humans remained to bury the dead, harsh-voiced crows did the keening.

The king had recently completed an epic journey and was mindful of many tedious battles to come. So he passed the trip as restfully as possible. Part of each day he lounged in the high saddle of his great black destrier Shalmaneser. Alternately, he rode with his companions Delvyn and Amlunia in his heavy brazen war chariot, pulled by a team of four Zamboulan bay geldings. The chariot provided a chance for banter, wine-toping, and even merrymaking, insofar as the often grim aspect of their surroundings would allow.

King Conan, oddly enough, seemed more touched by the scenes of desolation and despair than did his fresh-faced concubine or his comic dwarf. Perhaps the cause lay in the knowledge of his own sovereign responsibility for them. As kings will, he sought the rare opportunity to do good, dispensing a word where it might allay suffering, a coin or a loaf in the hope of redeeming a life. Yet most of the sufferers, rather than awaiting his boon, fled or cowered away from his sight, regarding him as their ruthless conqueror. The resulting ridicule and witticisms from Delvyn and Amlunia the king bore stoically, as a bitter dose that was somehow his due.

The capital Belverus rose into sight still intact, its roofs and spires sharp against blue sky. Its massive outer wall loomed imperially, although smoke-blackened in places, notched and trailing rubble in others. The fighting that had finally ruptured the gate had come from within, from forces loyal to the Aquilonian nominee Baron Halk. The baron, an avowed ally of the western conquerors, now ruled the city under Aquilonia's flag. At first sight of the black and gold lion banner flying above the gate, Conan's column of troops halted in the road and raised a lusty cheer.

The king kept his troops in tight order within the city. He had to spur his horse ahead to stop Amlunia from driving the chariot recklessly through the market district, at cost of innocent life and limb; otherwise the procession passed safely to the royal palace. The domed, minaretted pile was battle-scarred, with broken portals under hasty repair, but scarcely looted and still sumptuous.

Baron Halk was not in Belverus; he had ridden eastward with Prospero, to subdue fractious outer provinces and lay siege to Numalia. The baron's troops held the capital well in hand; Conan noticed that the citizens quailed even more from the gray-cloaked provincial guards than from the aloof, well-disciplined Aquilonian invaders.

Halk and his supporters hailed from the northwestern provinces of Nemedia, close up against Aquilonia. The northerly barons were harsh men, battle-hard from strife against raiding Cimmerians and the adventuring warlords of the Border Kingdoms. No love was lost between Halk's faction and the southern Nemedians, who had long held imperial sway over the country from the remote and, to a northerner's eye, decadent splendor of Belverus.

Hence, in the turmoil following close on the death of a king, Halk and his neighboring barons sided with the Aquilonians. Rightly or not, they expected greater license and hegemony as clients of invaders than they had yet enjoyed under native Nemedian monarchs.

With matters so firmly in control, Conan did not linger long in Belverus. One afternoon's rest for his troops, and one night's carouse with local authorities and officers—during which he made a point of drinking the hardiest of them under the feast table—was more than enough. Late the next morning, when the last of his troopers had been rounded up from stews and brothels in the teeming joy-district, he set forth again on the Road of Kings.

Scenes of devastation greeted them—more recent

ones here, with some vanquished castles still smoking on their hilltops, and some corpses still bloating unscavenged in the grass. Captured spies and turncoats tossed and moaned, too, on crosstrees raised at road junctions. They were placed there by time-honored Nemedian custom, probably at Baron Halk's order.

Amlunia, seated beside her king, had a constructive suggestion to offer as the war chariot drew near the first of these unfortunates. "Arrow practice, Conan!" she blithely cried. "Or javelins, if you prefer. Each strike to the heart wins a tot of ale . . . or shall we shoot for the crosspiece instead? That would be harder, a throat or eye shot—"

"Quiet, wench," the king warned her, speaking with gruff restraint. "I once had my own taste of crucifixion, and I can tell you, 'twas no idle sport."

"But oh, Master," Amlunia cried, clinging to the Aquilonian's shoulder in the teasing, coaxing fashion that was her wont. "Please, Conan, to lighten the boredom of this march! It would serve the wretches well, by granting them a merciful death!"

"Aye, true, Milord Throat-piercer! You should not mind that!" Delvyn spoke up from his place on a packing chest at the front chariot rail, where, in full armor, he stood holding the reins. "Know you, Amlunia, royal Conan is a great mercy killer. I first laid eyes on him easing the pangs of his dying battle foes. He would have done the same for me, in his kingly zeal, had I not pointed out to him that I was not injured. . . ."

"Enough!" Conan spoke in a voice whose restraint was cracking, with as much real ire as he had yet shown his sycophants. "Egilrude!" he called out resoundingly. "Captain, over here!" Having compelled his chariot mates' silence with grim looks, he rapped out orders that a party of troopers take pincers and extract the spikes holding the crucified men in place. Those who survived the ordeal of their liberation were to be left with stocks of bread and water by the roadside, to live as they might. "If they be real traitors," Conan declared, "then their countrymen will slay them after we are gone."

So passed the march, winding on for days, until the royal party overtook Prospero's Aquilonian legions and the host of Nemedian troops loyal to Baron Halk. They lay encamped before the gates of Numalia, the great walled city of the eastern realm.

From afar across the plain could be seen upward-angling campfire smoke in an arc about the city. A line of tents and rough fortifications stretched in a circle just outside bowshot of the wall. As the marchers drew nearer, the snap and thud of catapults became audible, counting off a steady, monotonous barrage. At length the arching projectiles were visible, glinting in a thin haze of dust their impacts raised over the town's west gate and the massive square towers that flanked it. Aside from raising dust, the bombardment had done no apparent damage.

At last, to the heralding blare of trumpets, the Black Dragons rode into the main camp. On the arrival of the king, a well-drilled cheer rang up heavenward from the besieging troopers:

"Hail, Conan the Great!"

The cry echoed faintly away northward and southward as it spread along the siege perimeter. The king, flanked by his guards, spurred his mount straight up to the command pavilion, bright with gold-embroidered flaps and pennons. There a handful of officers stood assembled.

"Conan! Hail, O King!" Prospero exclaimed. Foremost in the delegation, he knelt in a low, elegant bow before stepping forward to the monarch's horse. "Happy we are to have you here, milord. And how timely your arrival!" He turned to the nobleman beside him, who was still recovering from his bow. "This is Baron Halk, our Nemedian ally, a fierce and unyielding fighter," he announced, helping the man to his feet.

The Baron, though middle-aged and hale-looking, was stout and heavily armored, which may have accounted for his difficulty in rising. He seemed slightly flushed, unused to making obeisances. Or perhaps, the king thought, his ungainliness and reddish color were the result of excessive drink. Conan felt the baron's purplish gaze on him as he swung down from the saddle, and when he turned to the delegation, Halk's hand was extended. The baron fumblingly grasped the king's arm, palm to wrist, in the legionary fashion, half in greeting and half to steady himself on his feet.

"Greetings, Sir King," he declared, giving Conan's forearm a middling squeeze. "You are indeed Cimmerian bred, 'tis plain from the cast of your face. There is Cimmerian blood in my royal line as well, the legacy of fierce northern invaders." He relinquished Conan's arm and laid his own on the shoulder nearest him, for better support. "Glad I am that you sent the silver-tongued Prospero to drink and dicker with me, for it has proven a profitable alliance." The taint of wine was evident in his words, as on his wafting breath. "It befits well that we of northern blood should clap these womanish southerners under our yoke."

"I differ not between northern and southern blood—nor does my sword. In fact it may be that I have more enemies north of the Gunder Marches than south."

Conan returned the other's gaze coldly, knowing that in any case the baron would remember little of this meeting. "But I trust Prospero's rede that you will be my loyal confederate and an able guardian of this realm, once it is subdued and given over into your keeping." He turned to the Poitanian. "Both of you have done well so far. I commend you. But, Prospero," he declared to the count, "as I look about the camp today, your force seems to be standing idle."

"Aye, Your Majesty," the Poitanian answered, his lips pursing noncommittally between mustache and goatee. "So it would seem."

"You have offered the city magisters fair terms of surrender?"

"Yes, milord. Our envoy was sent dragging back to us hog-tied, his hair glued to his horse's tail with pitch and pine resin."

"I see. A flagrant insult." Conan scowled grimly around him, then pointed. "Those catapults, now—do you truly think they will have any effect on the bronze gate, or its granite bastions and butments? Their missiles only peck at it, man, like pigeons at a stone granary!"

"Yes, Sire, you are right." Prospero nodded in frank concurrence with his king. "The catapults seem to be doing no damage whatever."

"Well, good Count," Conan said, rounding again on his subordinate, "I never thought I would have to spur you to greater effort in reducing a city! Know you, a lengthy siege never helped an army's fighting spirit." He drew Prospero a little aside to keep from upbraiding him too publicly. "Plague and starvation will tell as sorely on us as on the defenders—they drain a trooper's will. And I, for one, lack the time to wait. A long siege here, followed by another and yet another, though each were victorious, would lose us this campaign!" Abruptly the king ceased his tirade. Reluctant to abuse his long-time friend and counsellor further, he left the final word to Prospero. "Well, man, what have you to say for yourself?"

For a moment there was no sound except a distant artillery officer's shout, the snap of the catapult, and the crack of a projectile against unyielding stone. Then the count raised his arm innocently and pointed. "When yonder candle burns out, the gates of Numalia will fall."

"What?" The king's gaze followed Prospero's pointing finger. On a camp table under the tent's broad canopy sat a crystal chimney mounted on an ornate bronze base; within it, the remains of a white tallow candle burned. The taper which remained was less than a stub, its wax all but consumed, its wick doubling over and near to sputtering out. Conan, registering these facts, sized up the figure who stood over the lamp, intent upon its glow—a scrawny, elderly man with a balding gray pate, clad in a silk jerkin and pantaloons that looked dusty black in the shade of the awning.

"What, Prospero," Conan asked in a gruff, restrained voice, "you have resorted to wizardy? You know my opinion of such things. Although, to shorten a siege—"

"Nay, my king, 'tis not sorcery!" Evidently the Poitanian, having finished with some private joke, was now anxious to reassure Conan lest the king betray unseemly ignorance to the others present. "The venerable Minias there is a sapper, captain of a whole company of miners brought to us by Baron Halk. The dirt in those breastworks"—he pointed to a line of field defenses, apparently raised to fend off sallies out of the city—"has been dug from beneath the north gate tower, and carried here through tunnels engineered by Minias." At the further mention of his name, the elderly captain looked around long enough to give a respectful nod to Conan, then turned back to his candle. Prospero continued, "This pelting by catapults is meant only to cover the noise of the sappers' digging, so the Numalians will not sink shafts of their own and send miners to attack ours."

"I see," Conan said with an air of sagacity he did not truly feel. "It sounds like the methods used by certain thieves of my youthful acquaintance, when I dwelt in Zamora." He glanced back to the camp table with a slightly puzzled look. "But tell me, how will the snuffing of yon candle make the gate fall? Is it a signal?"

Prospero concealed any amusement he may have felt, but was still groping for words as Minias turned to answer the king. "Your Majesty," the engineer said in Nemedian, "I sent an identical candle, lit at the same instant, down into the mines to pace my men's labor. It will burn out too, at the same time. By now timber props are set in place, the supporting earthen walls cut away, and ropes connected to the last braces to trigger a cave-in." The engineer gave a guarded look around the expanse of tents, troopers, and makeshift defenses. "Your troops stand ready, O King, by Lord Prospero's order. We have taken pains to look at ease, so as not to alert the watchers on the city wall. But believe me, all is in readiness."

To a questioning look from Conan, Prospero responded with a nod. "In truth, Your Majesty . . . the horses have been saddled behind cover, the assault equipment laid out, and the men ordered to await our signal.'' The count's neat mustache semaphored upward as he smiled confidently over the camp and the looming wall. ''Inside the city, most of the enemy will be taking their afternoon rest. The arrival of the royal party has doubtless heightened their watchfulness—and so, Sire, I think it especially important that no alarm be given now.''

All the lesser nobles and officers, including Delvyn and the strutting Amlunia, had dismounted and come forward to hear the exchange between Conan and Prospero. The dwarf in his battle regalia drew astonished looks from the troops and officers, as did the leman in her tight suit of leather and bronze. For caution's sake, the king now ordered his entourage to disperse to nearby tents and stand at ease. He likewise passed orders for the rest of the Black Dragons to dismount and lead their horses away without fanfare.

Then he waited with the others in false, watchful idleness. The wisp of candle left inside the bronze lamp burned with stubborn tenacity, consuming the last droplets of wax in its socket. The wick curled in its final throes, filling the flask with gray vapor, and died.

An uneasy silence ensued. The wall and gate towers stood unaffected, bright in the westering sun.

Then, in the middle of the broken field between the siege camp and the wall, a narrow hole in the ground appeared. Half-naked men, short and earth-smeared, began scrambling out of the cavity like nether devils. Their sudden appearance caused the battery officer to hold back his order, and for the first time since Conan's arrival, the catapult barrage fell silent. These changes brought a shout from one of the sentries on the wall. Behind the lofty battlement, a new stirring of helmeted heads could be seen.

Then, eerily, the earth shuddered underfoot. A billowing fountain of dust vented from the hole in the apron before the wall, blowing with it the last of the scurrying dirt-streaked troglodytes. The thick masonry of the nearest square tower began visibly to shift; it flashed in sunlight, then twisted and settled outward and downward. From its edge, tiny human figures toppled forward into vacant air.

Then came the sound: a vast, shuddering rumble accompanied by the shriek of tearing timbers and by thinner human screams. The din continued for long moments, as did the agitation of the earth, subsiding only when the tower lay in a sloping heap of rubble beneath clouds of sun-shafted dust.

"Curse of Gehenna, the gate still stands!" Conan's oath rang out in the tremulous silence.

"Aye, Your Majesty!" Prospero cried, turning to his engineer. "What say you to this, Minias?"

"Held up by its crossbar, no doubt." Shading his eyes, the sapper peered thoughtfully up into the dust cloud. The metal-clad edge of the gate could be seen jutting outward at an awkward angle. He stroked his gray-grizzled jaw, but offered no further suggestion.

"Macha and Nemain, it matters not!" Conan wheeled to find his horse. "Launch the attack, we'll have the wall in a trice! Ladders and bill-hooks are ready at hand, are they not? Cavalry, mount up!"

"Aye." Prospero hesitated as others around them started to move. "But there is no breach for cavalry to pass through—horses cannot cross that pile of rubble!"

"Shalmaneser can," the king said, swinging up into his warhorse's saddle. "Follow me!"

Egilrude and Baron Halk had passed Conan's attack order down the ranks; now trumpets blared, making a din greater than that of the tower's collapse. As their shrieking faded, it was taken up by trumpets farther down the line. The note diminished in the distance, drowned by the cheers of an army surging forward to its fate.

"Onward, dogs, for loot and empire!" Conan led the charge, a lone mounted warrior at the head of a foot-borne horde raising spears, bows, and siege ladders toward the wall. Man and horse outdistanced the running troops swiftly; then they thundered through the crowd of sappers, who parted for them, cheering. Coming to the fringe of the rubble hill where the gate tower had once stood, the king reined his horse aside in search of the surest way forward. The stallion, unwilling to be restrained, reared momentarily and pawed the air, whinnying fiercely. Then the beast lunged onto the smoking granite pile.

"By Bel and Asura!" The ride at once became rough and jarring, as wild as a turn astride a raw Hyrkanian mustang. The footing was loose and uneven beneath the stallion's massive hooves, and Conan seized Shalmaneser's mane to stay in the saddle, clamping his knees against the heaving, laboring rib cage. The mighty horse plunged and sideslipped, staggered over obstacles, trod half-buried bodies under, and leaped to clear the jagged gaps between man-sized stones. He scrabbled and faltered, starting small avalanches of shifting wreckage. Yet horse and man mounted gradually toward the ruin's jagged crest.

"Smokes of Belia! Faugh!" The air was yellow with rock dust and the fumes of abraded flints; yet the acrid cloud did not screen the horseman from marksmen atop the wall. Arrows and slung stones pattered onto the rocks around him, sent by a handful of city defenders who had ventured out onto the jagged edge of parapet above the fallen tower. Conan had naught but sword and ax strapped to his waist. Even if he had possessed spear or bow, he could not have loosed his grip on Shalmaneser long enough to ply them against the enemy. The siege catapults might have cleared the broken rampart, but their barrage had not resumed—understandably, in view of his own royal presence close under the wall.

"Come, dogs, here to me!" By now the first of the following horsemen—officers, mainly, and Black Dragon guards—had reached the stone pile. Conan's swift backward look told him they were making uncertain progress. A few spurred their steeds up the apron of rubble; others dismounted to drag their horses forward, or else abandoned them and climbed on foot. The first wave of footsoldiers jogged not far behind, their projectiles already striking high on the wall. But the returning rain of stones and shafts was heavy, and helmeted heads milled thickly atop the long, V-notched parapet. It appeared that, apart from the immediate devastation of the tower, the defense of the city would be vigorous.

"By Crom's ravening hounds!" Conan, clinging to the steeply canted back of his lunging, surging mount, suddenly faced a greater obstacle. As he reached the lowest point of the breach in the wall, he saw that the wreckage did not trail smoothly down into the city. The tower, undermined from without, had slumped outward, leaving a vertical drop of four or five man-lengths inside, above the paved courts of the town. There was no ramp nor stair remaining, and no chance for a safe descent. Instead, as the king gaped over the precipice into the town, his regal silhouette drew more arrow flights from below. Shafts whistled past him and clanked on his armor, augmenting those which continued to rain down from above.

Luckily man and horse were fully armored, and their plunging motion made both difficult targets. They never paused; Conan flicked the reins to command his fearless steed, and the stallion knew what to do. With a whickering scream he hurled his ebon bulk up onto the broad, crumbling fringe of the city wall, driving upward toward the jagged edge of the topmost parapet.

"Crom Cruaich! By the bent, bloody Lord of the Mound!" Conan roared forth a savage war-cry, dragging his great sword out of its sheath.

The archers had taken their most skillful shots as the horse labored below them, and had missed. Now they loosed hastily, anxious to turn back the red-nostriled steed and its bellowing rider. But their shafts, failing to find chinks in the polished armor of horse or king, glanced harmlessly aside. A pair of them dropped their bows and turned to snatch up halberds, but they were too late.

"Manannan's fiery blood!" With a pantherish leap, the black destrier launched himself and his rider onto the broken rim of the wall top, bowling over one of the archers and knocking him senseless with flailing, sledgelike hooves. For a desperate moment the stallion struggled at the crumbling masonry edge. He scrabbled wildly on fetlocks and steel-shod hooves, sending loose stones showering down on the heads of the infantry below. Then, triumphantly, the horse gained the parapet with all four limbs and catapulted forward. One of the rallying pikemen was knocked from the wall by his lunge. The other died under Conan's sword; the great blade fell, rose, and fell again as the man turned to flee, splitting first his halberd, then his steel-helmeted skull. The last remaining archer, already in full flight, went a half-dozen strides before he was battered to a bloody shred beneath flying, steel-shod hooves. Like the others, he had had no choice but to fight or flee along the wall. On one side ran the battlement, on the other a bone-crushing drop to the alley below, with no possible escape.

Thus was unleashed, so legends tell, Crom's holy vengeance on the city of Numalia. The parapet lay open ahead; the runway atop it was broad—and so was Shalmaneser, massive in black-draped armor and savagely afire with battle lust. The smooth, level course freed Conan's hands to wield both sword and ax from the saddle; the king, wise with the horse lore of Turan, rode as one with his mount, leaning agilely left and right to let his blades reap a rich red harvest. Limbs, heads, and entire bodies fell sundered in their hurtling wake, while the mad-eyed demon steed lashed out with hooves and gnashing, red-stained teeth.

The Numalians on the parapet stood little chance before Conan's onslaught. Summoned hastily to meet the challenge from below, they had no time or means to defend against a marauding horseman. Conan galloped the length of the wall, riding men down, scathing them with steel, or driving them from the edge. Those few who found shelter on ladders and stairways cringed helpless at his passing. Man and horse thundered by so rapidly, clearing the way as they went, that none could hope to pursue them; even an arrow flight seemed a forlorn chance.

The Aquilonian king's ride was well-timed for his host. In his wake, those defenders who mounted to the battlement found themselves face to face with besiegers swarming from knotted ropes and siege ladders. Their fight was joined late, on terms fatally advantageous to the city's foes.

Conan, his vision bathed in a pulsating red mist, watched each enemy loom before him, receive his blow, and crumple aside in a welter of red. Slash with sword, strike with ax; some died facing him, some plunging madly away. The king's mailed body moved with the supple swiftness of a rattlesnake, arching, leaning, and striking from the saddle. His knees clung to his mount's heaving sides, giving subtle guidance to the horse; the surging, clamoring rhythm of the charge was altered only when Shalmaneser veered aside to ride down an occasional shrinking coward. Conan had no care for what lay ahead; he might circle the whole city wall and then, for all he knew, turn and circle it again. He was Crom's holy warrior, lost in the moment, only vaguely aware of the cheers and battle cries roaring up at him from one side of the wall and the screams, moans, and imprecations rising from the other.

A halberdier raised his blade high, but then faltered. He turned to flee and died beneath Conan's pitiless ax. An archer dropped his bow, sought to lower himself down the edge of the wall, and slipped out of sight with a forlorn cry. Another threw himself flat on the parapet, in evident hope that the horse would avoid him—a mistaken hope, as Shalmaneser's only momentarily broken, muffled gait told.

Ahead a group of striving bodies signalled a fight. A ladder was set against the battlement, and black-helmeted men atop it fenced and sparred with Numalians who tried to dislodge them. Most of the nearby defenders had rushed to the spot, their swords and hook-headed pikes flashing in the sunlight. Shalmaneser, momentarily unopposed, broke into a faster pace, eager to rend and crush the mass of puny mortals ahead.

Then the hindmost of the defenders turned—the captain of a spear company, judging by his gray tunic, unarmored but metal-capped. The long steel blade of his spear swung down through the air toward the fast-closing horseman. He grounded the butt of his weapon in a pavement-crack and crouched in place over the base of the shaft, holding the blade up at a low, vicious angle.

There was no time to slow the frenzied horse, and no place to veer; the stallion continued his charge straight onto the unmoving warrior. With a dragging, sickening impact, Conan felt the spearpoint lodge in Shalmaneser's vitals. Yet the enraged horse lunged and staggered onward. Though impaled, he strained his massive neck forward as the spearman arose from his crouch. With a shrill, whinnying scream, he sank his teeth into the man's throat.

The hellish paroxysms of rage and pain that followed bore horse, rider, and horse's victim over the back edge of the parapet. Conan felt himself plummeting through empty air; he clutched the mane and saddle before him, clawing at horseflesh for purchase. Then he was dashed face-first into the rough horsehair, striking, as luck would have it, atop his mount rather than beneath.

The breath battered out of his lungs was slow in returning. His armor had protected him in places and crimped his flesh painfully in others. Beyond that, he felt no grave injury.

Expecting to be set upon at any moment by the vengeful inhabitants, he hauled himself up. He retrieved his sword, which had clashed to earth nearby. But the alleyway he found himself in was empty of watchers. Except for a distant clamor from the wall above, it lay silent. The great stallion was dead, as was his heroic slayer, who lay in a spatter of blood mere paces away.

Sheathing the sword and turning from the carnage, he strode back along the alley toward the embattled gate. The narrow lane was one of a series that ran in the shadow of the wall. Where clusters of ramshackle buildings leaned up against the massive structure for support, the way angled into the town. The few defenders and city folk he saw did not pause to challenge him. Most Numalians had evidently left the neighborhood of the wall, or taken refuge indoors, forsaking the streets.

The only active fighters Conan saw were those who looked down from the wall top—and who occasionally plunged to the pavement near him with a bone-breaking crash, or rolled and slithered down the adjoining roofs. All of those were dcfenders, some already dead, some merely wounded as their side was driven from the wall. Drawing near an open casement of stairs leading up to the parapet, Conan saw it hastily abandoned by a last few Numalian soldiers. They ran into the slums and disappeared, leaving the upper flights of the stairway crowded with descending Aquilonians and Nemedian allies. Cheering as they spied Conan, they rallied at the bottom to his lusty cry:

"Follow me, troopers, to the city gate!"

Some, but not all, fell in after him, and their ranks swelled with fresh arrivals as they went.

But the west gate, when at length they found it, had already been forced. Infantry or sappers had managed to deepen the breach in the wall; in so doing they had created a new, inward-sloping pile of rubble, its jagged surface interspersed with dusty, arrow-pierced bodies.

Down this grisly ramp the attackers must have swarmed, to seize the remaining gate tower and open the unblocked valve of the gate from within. Windrows of gray-clad Numalian corpses, mingled with a few in black and brown uniforms, attested to the savagery of the fight. Now boisterous invaders moved through the plaza with a stream of black-mailed horsemen clattering in through the gate, probably following Prospero to the assault on the municipal palace.

Conan scanned the crowd for a horse to commandeer. The first he saw was too small and light for him, though it already bore two riders: the leather-clad Amlunia, waving a flask of Numalian wine, and, riding pillion behind her, the dwarf Delvyn in his brass armor.

Conan glanced back and found his troop disintegrating in the frenzied atmosphere of the gateyard. He told their ranking officer to lead them against the citadel, pointing him the way. Then he strode forward and hailed his companions.

"Hail, Conan the Invulnerable," Delvyn cried as the horse wheeled to a stop. "Lone conqueror of the great wall of Numalia—can you be slain by any mortal hand?" He raised his dagger Hearts-pang and flourished it overhead. The gesture summoned cheers and salutes from passing soldiers, to whom Conan waved magnanimously.

"If I am invulnerable," the king confided to his boon friends, "I wish the last foeman had aimed his spear at me, and not at my horse! Alas, brave Shalmaneser's like will not be found soon."

"Not likely," Amlunia agreed, leaning down from her saddle to tip her wine flask to Conan's lips. "But what matters a horse, O Master of the World? You can mount any horse—or any other creature you want, any time!'' She laughed boldly and straightened up in the saddle. ''Numalia is yours, Lord! You told me you once lived as a thief in these streets—now you have stolen the whole city!''

''Aye,'' Conan said, casting about restlessly. ''But I would trade the whole miserable place for a strong horse. I need one to carry me to the fight at the palace.''

''Another fight?'' Amlunia cried petulantly. ''Have you not had enough of fighting this day? The wall is breached, the city is ours! Now it is time for pillage and massacre, for rapine and frenzy in the true barbaric spirit!''

''Indeed, Master,'' Delvyn added solemnly from behind the leman, ''the cry of havoc is already loosed. The troops have begun the sack, and by tomorrow this once proud town will be on her knees.''

''A great mistake, that, if it makes them forget their duty to me!'' Conan growled. ''But ho, Baron Halk! And Egilrude, what tidings?''

The two riders trotted up and reined in their steeds. ''Hail, O King! How happy to find you well! I saw you unhorsed—'' Egilrude swung down from his saddle even as he spoke. ''Here, milord, take my steed! The west and north walls are cleared, thanks to your noble charge, and the south garrison has accepted our terms—''

''Aye, good fighting, King Cimmerian!' the baron chimed in. ''A fine show of horsemanship you gave us, an example to both our armies! But dry work, I'll wager.'' Halk unslung a wineskin from his plump armored chest, swigged from it, and held it forth to Conan as the king eased into Egilrude's saddle. ''Now this southern fleshpot is ours, and the pickings will be rich! My men and I have waited long for this day."

"Restrain your men, Baron, till the central district falls and the outer garrisons are subdued." Conan did not reach out for the wineskin. "I do not want our troops diverted from the palace fight."

"I see no problem in that, Your Majesty," Egilrude said. "Men of both armies are flocking to the palace—more men than can possibly take part."

"Aye, of course," Baron Halk cried, "for the loot will be richest there! But, O King, do not imagine we can prevent them from despoiling the town. Not my troops, nor yours either. The egg is broken and cannot soon be put back together."

"So say you, Baron? And you, Egilrude?" Conan frowned. "Well enough, then, I suppose! I never had any love for Numalia." The king shrugged and accepted Halk's wine flask, raising its spout thirstily to his lips. "So long as our victory is complete, let them do what they want!"

CHAPTER 13
Cradle of Empire

Bright lights and swirling shadows played against the high lancet windows of the royal palace at Tarantia. From its stately archways, dim in summer night, echoes of music and festivity drifted. Courtiers and privileged citizens gathered, as they had done so often in recent months, to celebrate the departure of fresh Aquilonian recruits to the foreign campaigns. On the morrow the young officers would ride off to follow the lure of wealth and glamorous peril abroad; but tonight was set aside for revelry, for lavish food and drink, and for fond goodbyes murmured to sweethearts in the palace gardens.

On the broad inner veranda at the garden's edge, Queen Zenobia reclined on a cushioned seat, clad in jewels and a gown of intricate, gathered lace. Beneath the soft-hued glow of paper-covered lanterns she sat, keeping apart from the festive throng. Through crystalpaned doors at the rear of the terrace could be seen the heads and shoulders of officers and ladies, moving rhythmically to measured phrases of reed, timbrel, and horn. Guarding the doors and the outer corners of the balcony stood mute, helmeted Black Dragon guards; in a chair drawn intimately near sat her current visitor. It was balding, grandfatherly Publius, Chancellor of Aquilonia and the queen's most senior advisor.

"The ball proceeds smoothly, Your Majesty," he assured her with a swift, nodding bow of his head. "The palace staff seems well-used to these affairs, not bored or overburdened."

" 'Tis well," the queen said with a wan smile. "It gives us a chance to show and spend some of the wealth my husband sends back from his conquerings. I want these young men to have something fine to remember their home by, before they ride off to hardships from which they may never return." As she spoke, her smile faded, possibly out of concern for her own absent campaigner.

Publius said in his unctuous manner, "Your gatherings, milady, are certainly more tranquil and civilized than our king would have had them. So far we have had no duels nor mock combats, no bouts of drinking and storytelling, and no troupes of naked foreign dancers." The chancellor met Zenobia's raised eyes with a prim, unctuous smirk. "I confess, Your Majesty, these festivities of yours are more in keeping with my own taste."

The queen frowned slightly. "Indeed, Publius? I make it my place to promote the gentler arts and traditions of Aquilonia, lest we be proclaimed a savage nation with an uncouth king. But do not dismiss too lightly the virtue of a primitive soul, or the strength of an unbridled spirit. Sometimes a foreign eye can pierce the veils of obsolete assumptions." She waved a shapely hand in air, as if brushing aside cobwebs, and turned in her seat away from Publius. "Sometimes," she continued, "a rough-accented voice can make itself heard over self-righteous mumblings of pious dogma. It may even, at times, rally a nation."

Falling silent, Queen Zenobia looked out over the garden's dark expanse, softly lit by constellations of paper lamps dangling from trees. A young uniformed officer and his maiden, half embracing, moved slowly past the splashing fountain toward the invisible paths and arbors of the lower garden. The girl was no aristocrat, but one of the palace servants, draped from neck to knees in a modest gown belted with a silken cord for the occasion. Even so, she clung to the lad's neck and paused frequently to lavish on him kisses and breathless whispers; she seemed generally eager to aid the war effort by sending him off happy the next morn. As the two disappeared beneath the elms, Zenobia heaved a faint sigh and turned back to Publius.

"It was Conan's savagery, not his kingliness, that made me love him the first moment I saw him."

The impact of the queen's earlier reproach to Publius was dissipated by her obvious melancholy, and so he was able to shrug off his discomfiture and offer further flattery. " 'Tis an appropriate turn of history, milady: our king's recent conquest of Nemedia gives Your Majesty sway over Belverus, your native city."

"Aye, 'tis an irony indeed—I, who once was a slave girl there! And yet I am queen in fact only, since Conan has given nominal power to the local barons. I wonder, Publius . . . I wonder if he will someday try to conquer his native land of Cimmeria? I doubt that even he could subdue such a savage, untamed place!" The queen shook her head wistfully. "Publius, do you really think he intends to conquer the entire world?"

The chancellor shrugged. "Who can say? In my latest dispatches I have cautioned him not to declare such a goal openly, since it would turn every Hyborian sovereign against him. But in light of his recent conquests, some of them are bound to assume so anyway."

Interested, Zenobia leaned a little closer. "Can you not dissuade him?"

Publius shook his head. "The king is not one to abandon a plan lightly, as you know. I am told the idea burns strongly in his breast. 'Tis hard to see what could turn him from it, short of his own . . ." Seeing the queen's anxious look, he subtly altered the word which had formed on his tongue: ". . . defeat. And yet, if I am told aright," he elaborated more hopefully, "King Conan's great desire just now is to destroy the schemer Armiro. If he were to achieve that goal, with a suitable expenditure of blood and Cimmerian sweat, it might sate his lust for conquest. At least temporarily, I should think. . . ." Publius, remembering himself and wondering if he had spoken too freely, let his voice trail off.

But Zenobia seized immediately on the substance of his words. "Yes, I understand, he might be content with victory over Koth. So far, after all, he has only seized the holdings of the two kings who warred against him. Armiro opposed him in that. . . ."

"And now, if he snatches territory from his new-made enemy, who can fault him for it?" Publius spoke enthusiastically, feeling suddenly at home in his special fiefdom of diplomacy. "The onslaught of our puppet barons against eastern Nemedia is clearly an internal matter. Aquilonian presence there can be seen as a move to threaten Armiro's northern flank in Ophir and in Koth.'' The stuffy look on the chancellor's face was the same affectation he would have used on a foreign legate. ''Tomorrow, on the king's order brought by today's courier, I am to open negotiations with the Corinthian embassy, to allow passage of our army southward through their territory to strike at Koth. Such a compact will be of use to Conan, whether he intends to respect Corinthia's neutrality or not.''

''I see.'' At the prospect of a broader war, the queen grew somber again. ''I suppose Conan must settle his dispute with Armiro,'' she sighed. ''It surprises me that the two have remained in a standoff so long.''

''Both men are astute commanders,'' Publius declared. ''In all of Hyboria, the Kothian army is the only one that can stand against Aquilonia's. Nevertheless, if our two countries should fall to open war and weaken one another, the neighboring lands would be quick to crowd in and divide up the spoils, as Armiro sought to do in Ophir. Both your husband and his adversary perceive this only too well. So they bide their time, each awaiting the chance for a deft, decisive stroke that will leave the victor relatively strong.''

''I see it well,'' Zenobia said. ''Like angry lions they circle, surrounded by a horde of slavering jackals. A nasty business, war is—a foul one!'' She sighed again, glancing this time toward the banquet hall, where the strains of a bright new galliard were just starting up.

''And yet,'' she continued, ''to us here in Tarantia, war brings only wealth and gaiety. To our idle young it promises fame, plunder, and military rank. War does not slay our sons, it turns them into immortal heroes. For every few farm lads who fall in battle, one is newly created the thane or earl of an estate in the Tybor Gap, and so their rural families are happy. My husband is called the greatest Aquilonian hero of all time—if only I knew that it would always be so! The cost to our nation has been slight so far. At length I fear that we will pay the butcher's bill in full, with sore complaint."

"In other lands," Publius said, "our king is not now seen as hero or liberator. Spies tell me the lords of Brythunia and Corinthia are warning their peoples to fortify against the coming of Conan the Ravager and Conan the Locust. Those nations will not be as divided and ill-prepared as we found the Nemedians. But hold, here comes another mighty chieftain!"

Publius turned in his seat to welcome young Conn, who had marched onto the terrace. The lad wore a porridge-bowl helmet and waved a wooden sword as he strutted proudly forward, leading an army consisting of one youthful but harried-looking nursemaid.

"Your Majesty," the woman said to Zenobia with a deep bow, "I have been trying to conduct Prince Conn to bed, so that he may conquer the world of dream. But first he wants milady's blessing."

"Oh, my sweet darling!" Zenobia reached forth and gathered up the young warrior in lace-covered arms. "You have my blessing, dear one—my boon and my shriving as well! Go forth and conquer great dreams for me!"

"A stirring sendoff, Your Majesty!" A firm, deep voice spoke up as the child was swept out of the queen's arms and bundled off by his nurse. "I can see why the lad's father conquers foreign lands so efficiently."

"Why, Trocero!" Publius said in surprise.

"Ah, Count, good evening!" Zenobia sat upright on her lounge and regarded the caped, breastplated noble, who bent down to tweak Conn's ear as the nursemaid hurried him through the doorway. "We did not expect you to arrive so soon! How went your journey? I have been eager to hear first-hand news of affairs in Ophir."

"Conditions there are—stable, Your Majesty." The count bent to kiss the queen's extended hand; he exchanged handclasps of greeting with Publius before seating himself on a chair beside the chancellor. "Now that the Red River is guarded by a chain of forts, there is less threat of Kothian attack. With King Conan's approval, I judged it urgent to return home and see to matters in the south."

"The south?" Publius asked in evident puzzlement. "You mean, in southern Aquilonia?"

"Yes, Chancellor," Trocero replied, his sun-darkened features almost imperceptibly coloring. "I did not know if informants had brought word to you yet, but apparently not—so I assume Her Majesty, too, has not heard . . . ?" At Zenobia's impatient headshake, the count proceeded.

"Prince Armiro has extended the western end of our battleline in Ophir, by striking out into Argos. Five days ago his troops seized the Arond district and passed from there across the border. The Argosseans have not been able to bring their main force to bear as yet, but we can depend on them to send their fleet up the Khorotas River. There would not be much danger to our southern flank—were it not for the rumors that Koth has formed a secret alliance with Zingara. As it stands, I had best alert the southern lords personally, and bid them build their forces to readiness."

"A threat to our southern border!" Zenobia shook her head. "Armiro playing the same game with us that we play with him in the north! Truly, events outrun my fears." She shook her head in wonderment, then looked at Publius. "But Zingara has been Aquilonia's ally, at least since Conan took the throne! And Argos is a mighty kingdom, a deadly enemy for Koth."

"Perhaps, Your Majesty." Publius nodded uncertainly. "Yet Argos is principally a maritime nation, not nearly so powerful on land. As such, they often find themselves in conflict with Zingara over ports and coastal trade." The chancellor massaged his high, gray-wisped forehead with his fingertips as he spoke. "The Zingaran court might not find it amiss to enter an alliance against their southern neighbor, even at risk of war with us, their longtime ally." Visibly swallowing further musings, he regarded his queen. "But rest assured, milady, I will mobilize all my forces on the diplomatic front to avert any such misjudgment."

A threatened silence ensued among them, mocked in counterpoint by the gay dance music that lilted from the crowded ballroom; all three were aware, perhaps, that they relaxed in the serene eye of a war storm which boded soon to sweep the whole world.

It was Zenobia who spoke up at last. "And so, Count Trocero, how fares my husband in his foreign adventurings? I know he has faced risks I scarcely dare to think of—and won vast triumphs, as is his way. He brings glory to us all. But does he miss his home and family, I wonder?"

Trocero shifted his booted feet on the marble terrace so as to half-bow graciously in his seat. "Your Majesty, I can assure you that King Conan's every march and conquest, his every step and sword-thrust, are made in devoutest, most loving tribute to yourself and little Conn."

"I see." The queen digested this information a moment, to the drifting strains of music. "And what of his little ragamuffin, the dwarfish Delvyn? Does the jester still accompany him on his travels?''

''Aye, milady,'' Trocero said. ''The fool even dons armor and rides into battle. He postures and shakes his puny weapons at the enemy, when the king permits it.''

''And he sings and japes during victory feasts, I do not doubt. I have heard tales of wild revels held in conquered foreign cities by our lord and liege—have you not, Count? Though I realize, of course, that your role in the war is largely defensive.''

''Ah, yes, indeed.'' Trocero seemed uneasy at the direction the conversation was taking. He shifted briskly in his seat and muttered something about the stress of battle and the importance of troopers' morale.

''And yet he leaves you to your own devices, does he not? I hear tell that he rides away on long quests, such as a visit to his former lover Yasmela in the East.''

Seeing the warrior's voiceless discomfiture at this, Zenobia pressed him mercilessly. ''Come, do not deny it! If he goes to visit an old flame or rescue a captive queen, why should I not hear of it? I know of the slut Amlunia, too—I have my spies and astrologers to inform me of these things—''

''Your Majesty!'' interrupted Publius, sounding deeply shocked. ''You know that if you require a seer, or need a horoscope cast, I am at Your Highness's service! It does not do for one so highly placed to heed rumor-mongers and charlatans—I have warned milady of the danger, and it is greatest in these troubled times. Pray, do not give ear to invidious gossip—''

''Quiet, Publius!'' Zenobia hissed, sitting bolt upright on her divan. ''I already know your game! You fear that if I learn too much, I will turn on Conan and do harm to the empire. But I . . . I am greater than that! Yes, I know of his lights-o'-love! I would tear their throats out, send assassins to kill them if I could!" Her eyes flashed like steel in the soft light. "But I love Conan and shall remain faithful to him. He is not only my husband . . . he is my king!"

"There now, Vateesa, dear! Does that make you feel better? Here, I'll lower your head for you."

Princess-Regent Yasmela, kneeling beside the cot on which her servant lay, set down the goblet of water on the bedside table. Cradling the invalid's gray head in one gentle hand, she smoothed out the satin pillow beneath it with the other and let her patient lie back undisturbed. She judged from the level of liquid in the cup that Vateesa had swallowed a few sips; but the woman made no answer to her questions. Her eyes continued to gaze straight ahead, gleaming dull brown in the candlelight.

"Are you comfortable, Vateesa? Rest now, you will be up and about soon."

Arising from her knees with the aid of the bedframe, Yasmela turned and moved the candle to the far corner of the table. There it glared less brightly into the unblinking eyes, and played less luridly on the disfigured side of the woman's face. Though her visible wound was healed, Vateesa had lain thus stuporous since leaving the Tarnhold, where she had been struck with a club wielded by one of Armiro's bodyguards. She was Yasmela's only maidservant; now the roles of servant and lady were reversed. But the noblewoman knew she might care for Vateesa the rest of her days without repaying a tenth part of the woman's faithful service to her.

The princess-regent turned restlessly away. She

moved to the tall window, lifted aside the curtain, and peered out through one of the lozenge-shaped panes. There was no moon, and therefore no view—only a scattering of stars obscured at the bottom by the outlines of peaks, whose jagged shapes she had not yet learned. No great disappointment, that; even the midday view of bleak, stony mountains and dark forest slopes would have provided little comfort to her. The night draught falling from the windowpanes was chill, so she closed the curtains and turned away again.

This remote, nameless tower was her punishment, she knew: a further remove from the care and devotion of her son, sparse enough as those formerly had been. Armiro's attitude toward Vateesa, too, had been frighteningly cold-blooded—discounting her injury as that of a mere maidservant, even though she had been as a second mother to him, helping to raise him from boyhood. At times Yasmela wondered what she herself had wrought on the world, by making her son so precocious, schooling him so well in the ways of power, yet foolishly denying him a legitimate parentage.

And yet, Armiro was her only son! She could do nothing but love him and protect him, after all, since some secrets were too dangerous to tell. . . .

His antipathy to any lover of hers was understandable, given his early and ill-starred relations with the shallow, scheming men of the Khorajan court. And Conan, upon learning of her tie to Armiro, likely thought it fitting to abandon her to a sorrow that was, quite literally, of her own making. Now the two were implacable enemies, and would remain so until one of them finally slew or imprisoned the other . . . these, the last two males she cared about in all the world!

Her barren eyes had no tears left to shed over it all.

Here, penned up in this remote part of Khoraja, guarded by surly, unfeeling troopers loyal only to Armiro, she was helpless to save king or prince, nation or world. Life had brought all her grand, courtly schemes to a standstill. There was nothing left but to try and comfort a poor injured serving-maid, and in so doing possibly save her own soul.

Her brooding thoughts had carried her to her bed cabinet; there she stood wondering whether to shut herself away and pursue sleep in the musky dark, or whether to continue her wraithlike wakeful state, sporting queenly finery for Vateesa's sightless eyes in the gray candlelight. Her attention was caught by a sound outside her chamber door, on the stair that spiralled up from the common hall and the guardrooms below.

A night sentry, perhaps, going up to stand his vigil on the tower's topmost bastion. Or so she thought—until she heard a fumbling at the oaken door. It was locked, she knew, with a swivel catch that kept the outside latch from being depressed. Nevertheless, with a feeling of unreality that changed swiftly to alarm, she saw the hinged bar lift slowly in its brackets. She saw it disengage, and saw the door swing inward with a deep, muted creak of iron hinges.

The figure that stood outside on the narrow landing was dark and inscrutable—a tall, lean form in a hooded gray cloak, whose hem brushed the ground and whose voluminous sleeves depended from the ends of unseen arms. Only the garment was visible—she might have thought it empty, suspended there in the hall, had it not glided toward her across the threshold with a measured, deliberate step.

"Who is it?" She addressed herself to the obscurity shaded deep within the hanging folds of the intruder's cowl. "Begone. I have retired for the night, and desire no visitors." Suddenly, the thought occurred to her that it might be Conan. The eager, rising light of her glance then belied her previous statement.

No, she saw, it could not be he, for the figure was willow-thin. Nor was it Armiro, her cherished son, who would have been little taller than herself. This visitor was much taller, his cowl having brushed the lintel as he glided in. But another thought occurred to her.

"Are you a messenger sent by Armiro?" she asked. "Or by some other, perhaps, to tell me of his injury or—death?" Her voice quickened with anxiety before stumbling over the dreaded word. "Come, speak you and allay my fears, before I summon the guard! If this is a prank of the garrison, you will face harsh punishment!"

"No . . . not death." The voice of the stranger as he loomed in the doorway was full and timbrous, as deep almost as the creaking of the hinges had been, but with a certain supple fluidity the rusting metal lacked. "I bring you tidings not of death, but of a joyous birth."

"What do you mean?" At the eerie sound of the intruder's voice, Yasmela edged toward her dressing table beyond the window, for it included amidst its freight of combs, mirrors, and cosmetic ointments, a long, straight dagger. "You are not of the garrison," she challenged the stranger, "and you are no courier! If you do not leave at once—I warn you, I will scream!"

"So, scream away," the liquescent voice gloated. "What more fitting sound than a woman's screams to accompany a grand and glorious birth?" Having found his eerie voice at last, the cloaked stranger now waxed eloquent. "I speak of your own birth, Noble Lady, into the favor and protection of an all-knowing god who has decided to resume his seat of power here on earth. . . ."

The breath for a full-bodied shriek gathered in Yasmela's lungs—and caught there, prisoned in by the fear-taut cords of her throat, as she watched what now unfolded in the doorway. Quite literally, unfolded—for, instead of striding forward, the weird visitor reached effortlessly across the room toward her. There was a shapeless stirring within the long, loose sleeves of the hooded robe, and from it protruded black-glistening, bony talons of impossible grasp and rapidly growing length.

It was not human, she knew, nor anything earthly; more than the threat of the skeletal touch, she sensed a dark, chilling peril to her mortal soul. By an instantaneous motion she avoided the death clutch; she lunged backward, feeling the window curtain and leaded glass give way behind her—first jagged resistance, then only rushing wind. The dark menace passed over her, the talons clutching empty night. Her scream came at last, and she felt her soul soaring joyously free. Her body, meanwhile, plunged to the hard stones of the mountainside to lie broken and still.

Chapter 14
Hail the Mighty!

"Delvyn, strike up a song!" King Conan roared from his stolen throne. "Night draws nigh and our guest is travel-weary. We must get our roistering done early this day!"

The chair he sprawled on was not a true throne, but it was tall and stately nevertheless, the official seat of the recently departed First Magister of Numalia. Conan, leaning awry in it, with a booted leg cocked over its gold-leafed arm and a twelve-pointed crown resting askew on his brow, looked every bit the brawling barbarian conqueror.

The council hall before him lay in disarray, with long tables disordered and benches overturned. The ashes of a bonfire marred the center of the bright mosaic floor. Scattered all around were crusts, bones, wine jar fragments, and other debris of two nights' pillage and feasting. Most noticeable of all was the Magistry Chamber's once mighty bronze door, battered free of its mountings and lying flat across the floor. Much of the high stone archway had tumbled inward with it and now lay strewn nearby, but the ceiling above had held. A broad, jagged opening looked out over the courtyard and the broken crest of the breached curtain wall.

Beyond, sunset reddened the western sky. Against its deepening glory, smoke plumes from fires in the town could still be seen, as well as wheeling specks that were black carrion birds.

The dwarf Delvyn sat cross-legged on the broad mantle of the cavernous, unlit fireplace. Now he commenced strumming and plucking, as ordered by the king. The score or so of Aquilonian and Nemedian officers who lounged about the room showed scant enthusiasm for his chords. And the visitor Conan had referred to, after casting his gaze disapprovingly about the ravaged palace, stepped forward and raised a protest. It was Publius, the gray-haired Chancellor of Aquilonia, newly arrived from Tarantia.

"My liege," the brittle elder voice objected, "it would seem to me the time is riper for discussing matters of state than for revel and orgy—"

"Publius, Publius," Conan interrupted him, waving a flagon imperiously overhead, " 'twould seem to me but this: that I must conquer the world faster if I am to outrun your helpful advice!" Over the laughter which followed his quip, the king added, "But what I crave now is a song. Jester!"

Delvyn's strumming, which had receded during the exchange, swelled again to the fore and was joined by the minstrel's high, firm voice. The stately tune was evidently unfamiliar to the company, who fell silent and listened attentively.

Bold hero's blood and fertile northern soil,
The red and black of Aquilonia's crest;
From these two shall be born in battle toil,
A boundless land with mystic vision blest.

The first verse led to an instrumental interlude paced by Delvyn's skilled fingers. During its elaborate twinings and chimings, the warrior Amlunia seemed suddenly inspired: lithely, from her footstool before Conan's throne, she sprang up in a spontaneous dance for the company.

Drawing both sword and dagger, she discarded her weapon-belt; then she plied the tapering steel blades in an agile, graceful parody of combat. Before long she cast aside her fur-trimmed cloak, letting her scanty vest, breeks, and boots of black leather show off her creamy pale skin to striking advantage. The watching officers were awed to silence as she stalked and thrust to the soul-felt music, and Delvyn's next stanzas were heard as clearly as the first.

Barbaric souls and hotly tempered steel,
Strike forth and toll the glory of our days!
Grind foemen's flags beneath the chariot wheel
And scourge away the sin of foreign ways.

Hyboria! Thy will proclaims the right!
With iron rigor reigns your godlike king.
Hyboria, thy god grant us the might!
For thee we conquer, and to thee we sing.

Delvyn's lyric rang to a halt, to be saluted with lusty cheers and raised tankards from the company. The king himself sloshed his drink overhead and called out,

"Well sung, little bard! And well danced, sword girl!" But meanwhile the tempo of the jester's strumming continued, and gradually quickened. The attention of all remained focused on Amlunia, who still strode and turned in the center of the hall.

Darting and gliding, she alternated swift, leaping motions with slow, intent ones. She scuffed through the bonfire's cold ashes to dance in front of Publius, who sat primly at the end of a long bench. His unwillingness to react, and the leman's teasing efforts to make him flinch with near passes of her weapons, raised hoots and guffaws from the watchers.

Of a sudden, a burly Nemedian knight arose from Baron Halk's side at one of the long tables and came from behind it. Drawing a short thrusting-sword and propping it obscenely between his legs, he pranced toward Amlunia with a loutish, suggestive gait. Laughter dinned on him from all sides, drowning out the music—all the more so as the girl dancer spun and rushed at him. Her weapons flashed in a graceful, darting pass; her motion bowled him over and made him yelp with pain. As she whirled triumphantly away, the knight scuttled back behind the table, cursing and clutching a blood-streaming arm. The cheers of the watchers shook the chamber, threatening to make more of the broken archway collapse.

Conan, whose laughter was most uproarious of all, bellowed at last over the din, "Enough music! Enough dancing, while I still have officers left! Amlunia, you little trollop, come up here and share my throne! Ho, servants, fetch our dinner, and light more torches against the evening's dark! Be not stingy, the spoils of a city are ours to burn!"

While the conquered servants scurried to obey, Publius came forward and stubbornly begged to speak with his king ". . . before Your Majesty sinks any deeper into his cups," as the chancellor put it.

"There are matters which press most urgently for milord's attention," Publius began. "To wit: the devastation of newly conquered areas, and their imminent fate." The chancellor ruffled his fur shoulder-cape expressively. "Upon arriving here I was appalled, Sire, to see troops running riot in town—drinking, procuring women, and stripping the place of its wealth. Wanton destruction, too, with fire and steel—if this is by Your Majesty's leave, I would point out that it is milord's own newly won property and subjects that are being plundered and abused."

"By the horns of Erlik!" Conan exclaimed. "What, Publius, would you expect to see in a conquered city? You will find no strings of enchained slaves plodding the streets, and no piles of lopped heads in the marketplace! Who can accuse me of misrule? Would you, Amlunia?" He turned up the shapely chin of the girl, whose limber weight rested against him. "Likely so, wench, since you are more bloodthirsty and hard-handed than I! You need not answer. But say, Delvyn, what think you of these charges?"

From his seat on the mantlepiece, the dwarf spoke up readily. "As courtly wag, King Nose-cruncher, I like misrule! It provides meat for my jests." He followed the sally with a strum on his mandolin.

"Fit words for an accomplished fool!" Publius retorted, ignoring the scatter of laughter. "But I, as the king's loyal counsellor, must speak in earnest." His glance swept aside to include Delvyn and Amlunia. "Milord, methinks the chaos in the city but mirrors the disorder of your own kingly, ah, affairs. At the very least, Your Majesty should give thought to appearances. Count Prospero is establishing good order in Belverus, and your court in Tarantia may yet weather the strain. But here in Numalia—''

''Enough!'' Conan growled. ''In some matters, Publius, I will not accept your counsel. I am no gray-bearded sage, to mince every step with caution—and I am no miser, to deny the rewards of conquest to my troops. I have told my men to treat the vanquished folk of Numalia fairly, as I myself would.'' He paused to sip from a flagon thrust up to his lips by Amlunia, who reclined easily across his knees. ''If there is cruelty, blame it on Baron Halk's troops and their freight of ancient grudges.''

His remark was made without a glance for his ally, and may have gone unnoticed by Halk. The baron was drinking and jesting just then at the expense of his wounded knight, whose arm was being poulticed by a serving-maid.

''Aye, milord, perhaps,'' Publius answered the king patiently. ''And yet it remains for us to curb them, if we do not want the whole city laid waste. I fear that our conquests bring us into partnership with ruthless, self-interested sorts, while our true allies only learn to mistrust us.''

''Allies?'' Conan demanded, his brow knitting imperiously. ''What allies have we, except puppets like Halk and Lionnard?'' His tone was unrestrained and once again careless of who might overhear. ''Has any Hyborian king offered to aid me against the threat of Armiro the Koth? Argos would not, until the varlet attacked them! And now Zingara makes ready to turn colors. Corinthia's highborn nobles will not join me against the villain, nor even grant my army safe passage across their territory to get at him! They threaten to league against me with their neighbors if I try!''

Impatiently the king pushed Amlunia's proffered cup aside from his lips. In so doing, he splashed part of its foam down her feather bodice, which caused him to be distracted a moment with her squeals and squirms. ''The lords of Hyboria,'' he finished at length, ''are rogues and traitors all, and will one day kneel to me!''

''Doubtless so, if you wish it, Your Majesty.'' Publius shifted his feet doggedly before the throne. ''And yet, Sire, until it comes to pass, may we not keep them as friends? Forgive me, Sire, but when milord bluffs and postures so, and lets his minstrels sing anthems of world conquest,'' he added with a glance to the watching Delvyn, ''it gains Aquilonia no friends.''

''Nonsense!'' the king said. ''I am no mealy-mouthed diplomat, to hide my true intentions!'' Obdurate against his advisor's questioning, he drew Amlunia further on his lap, where she lounged like a Stygian cat. ''Know you, Publius, once I strike out for my goal, no man or nation will stand against me.''

''You would undertake, then, to attack your neighbors openly and at once, without first dividing them amongst themselves?'' So offended was Publius by this idea that he omitted any respectful form of address; yet the monarch did not seem to notice.

''When I am ready to reap foreign kingdoms, they will fall to my sword like ripe grain!'' From the ire that flashed hot in Conan's eyes as he glanced around the hall, he lapsed into somber speculation. ''Think on it, Publius—it has been in my head much of late. How can I have survived thus far, braved so many perils and endured so many hardships, if I am not marked by the gods for some special purpose? I offer myself to enemies in combat, scorn their blades, dance on their battlements, and receive for it but a scratch and a thump! Know you, Crom and Mitra have favored me in the past—surely they are the source of all this bounty and luck!" He thumbed his chin slowly, meditatively. "Or mayhap, as Delvyn has it, there is godly stuffing in my own self. Belike I have slain enough godlets and demogorgons in my time to soak up a touch of divinity." He paused again, his pensiveness deepening into a frown, before resuming. "Since none can gainsay me this great power—and with it the fame and repute of a god—'twould be foolish not to use it and make myself truly and eternally great. After all, why should a man have to die to achieve godhood?"

"Remember, Old Gray-grizzle," Delvyn chimed in suddenly from his chimneypiece, "you deal here with a great king! When did the advice of a tame old mouse ever bind a lion? Men like Conan the Neck-twister are not shackled by the laws of common men! Great men do great crimes! They are honored for breaking and remaking mortal laws!"

The jester spoke with an uncharacteristic vehemence and lack of ribaldry. But his tirade held the ears of all those present as he went on:

"A king's one duty is the exercise of power—for if powers are not used and extended, they fade to dust and withered parchment! A king's true task is to invent new powers, and test them to their limits—especially those powers that command the lives and deaths of his subjects. In fact, I would say, the use of power is a goal in itself, the one true aim of existence. If the power seized is grand enough, its wielder becomes a god!"

"Hear, hear!" Conan thundered at the conclusion of

the speech. "Publius, list ye well, for yon fool speaks with the voice of true wisdom."

To all this, Publius for once seemed at a loss to reply. Whether he stood silenced by the merits of the argument, or by despair of his king's sobriety, his wizened countenance was too subtle to reveal.

In any event, the feast had been readied, and so the attention of all was diverted. A high table was placed near the throne, with specially tasted meat and drink for Conan and his consort, and a special high stool for Delvyn. Meanwhile, the comeliest and most pliant Numalian castle maidens dispensed viands. Publius retreated to the tables and took a seat on Baron Halk's right hand, where he set about smoothing any rumpled seams of diplomacy. The meal wore on with obligatory toast and tune, sport and sally, many of them at the chancellor's expense, as the sky grew dark outside and the twinkling stars peered in.

It was after a half-dozen courses of food that a messenger entered, flanked by two Black Dragon guards. Plastered with mud and dust from the road, he reeled slightly with saddle-stiffness. Yet he strode up and addressed the king directly.

"Sir, I bring news of Khoraja via Ophir and Belverus, relayed to you by Count Prospero's order."

"Excellent," Conan said, waving to a servant. "Pour the man a cup of ale, that he may regale us less hoarsely. What news?"

"Then, Sire, you have had no word of it before now?" Accepting his flagon, the man looked up across its foaming brim at Conan, seeming oddly hesitant to drink. "No news from Khoraja?"

"Nay, courier, I think not. But how am I to know unless you tell me?" Impatiently the king leaned forward across his preening lap-kitten Amlunia. "Come, dog, spit it out!"

"My liege . . . word has it that Yasmela, the princess-regent of Khoraja, is dead."

The silence that followed the pronouncement was momentous. To the watchers, it was clear that mighty emotions stirred and battled in Conan's breast. Yet his stern kingly dignity scarcely permitted him to wail in anguish or sob forth his grief—if such he felt for this woman whom, after all, none of them knew. The bearer of the ill tidings stood stock-straight, unsure whether or not to fear for his own neck. Even Amlunia, twined in the monarch's lap, grew quiet and watched him with alert, suspicious eyes. It was as if she tried to gauge how much power a woman could have over this man—the depth of his injury, and the expression it would find.

It was Publius who, sensing the danger of the moment and anxious to cover his king's public discomfiture, edged up from behind the messenger to continue the questioning. "Queen Yasmela, dead? Tell me, has it been put forth what caused her death?"

The messenger turned aside and nodded, eager to discharge his duty. " 'Tis said she died of a fall, milord Chancellor. Not at Castle Tarnhold where she had lived, but at some unknown rural retreat."

"Are there rumors of foul play, then?" At the man's awkward but expressive silence, Publius continued, "Of course, such is always a likelihood in noble deaths. How does her passing affect the rulership of Khoraja and Koth?"

" 'Tis thought that Prince Armiro's rule of Khoraja is strengthened," the man said, "and with it, his sway over Koth." Reporting this last, he evidently felt safer—

long-lived enough, at least, to take a swallow of ale from his cup.

"A fall," the sullen king muttered. These, his first words in some moments, were spoken from beneath a brooding, thunder-clouded brow. "And yet, methinks a greater fall will follow."

"Your Majesty sees a . . . baneful influence in this?" Publius regarded his king carefully.

"Baneful, yes . . . to the unnatural whelp Armiro, in Crom's own time!" The king sat unmoving, his hands gripping the chair arms. "There is no doubt he ordered her killed . . . Yasmela, his own mother! I myself heard him threaten her before me." Conan's voice gradually intensified, grinding like a stone mill that remorselessly grated anguish into rage. "Does that leave you any doubt as to what kind of viperous enemy we face? . . . what stamp of low, perfidious skulkard?"

About the hall knights arose angrily from their seats, answering the king's exhortation with a chorus of rough, angry shouts.

"That is why I vow to throttle him with this good hand!" Conan, too, bolted upright, dumping Amlunia unceremoniously from his lap. She was kept from falling to the floor only by a sure grip on her wrist from his free hand—the one that was not raised above his head, clutching and crushing air for the benefit of the watchers. "By Crom and Mitra, Manannan and Kubal, Macha and Set, and by any other fell god who will accept my oath, I swear it!"

That night and the ensuing days brought more discussion of war, more preparation for war, and more war. The last few fractious Nemedian loyals withdrew to the country's eastern borderlands—there to be joined, it was rumored, by foreign mercenaries sent to keep Conan's conquest of Nemedia from being too swift and easy. Numalia was placed under a military governor nominated by Baron Halk, and the city's stocks were plundered more deeply for the army's refit.

Meanwhile, through the near provinces, word of Nemedia's subjugation spread. Peasant and squire alike murmured the wildfire reputation of Conan the Great. But more often, among inhabitants of settled districts fearful of invasion, the whispers were of Conan the Ravager, Conan the Despoiler, Conan the Terrible. However cruel the existing rulership, its downfall in war could be seen only as a great calamity. To provide against it, farmers dug shelters in the forest, buried their winter stores of seed and provender, and hid away their oxen and women.

Then in eastern Nemedia a trap was sprung. Die-hard loyalists were lured in strength out of their border forest, pursuing what they thought was a small force of Baron Halk's knights. Once in brushy meadowland, they found themselves encircled by a full Aquilonian legion that had marched up and deployed secretly the night before. The cavalry battle was wide-ranging, with lightning strike and counterstrike; the clash of infantry was short and brutal. Conan's regiments won the day, writing an end to the Nemedian Resistance as a fighting force.

It was a small battle, the harsh conclusion of a whirlwind campaign. But it was remembered for a rumor which arose there, to be repeated with wonder and dread by King Conan's foes and friends alike. Whether true or false, it was woven into the many-hued cloak of legendry that adorned his name in later years.

The tale, or rather the vision, attended the thickest

part of the fight. Survivors told of seeing the emperor's chariot sweep across the battlefield, its horses red-eyed and foaming at their bits, guided negligently or not at all by a dwarf who rode postilion, straddling the left-most horse. With his legs locked tightly in the brute's harness, the mannikin strummed on a lute as he rode, letting the team's reins trail through mud and blood and over the bodies of the slain.

On the chariot's platform—so the tale went—mindless of its giddy course and of the swords and spears raised all around, Conan and his battle-mistress Amlunia stood locked in a wild, passionate embrace. Bereft of much of their armor and clothing, they stripped away more as they strove together in frenzy, baring one another's flesh like immortals scornful of earthly barb or edge. Mouth to greedy mouth they clung as their vehicle plummeted through crowds of footmen and horsemen. Their mad transports of lust were the last terrible vision of many a dying man, so it was whispered, and a sight to haunt the battle's survivors for the remainder of their days.

Chapter 15
Dark Communion

Armiro, Supreme Tyrant of Khoraja and High Prince Designate of Koth, awoke from a troubled sleep into gusty alien darkness.

At least, he dreamt that he awoke. He came to himself standing upright out-of-doors, clad in the black silk shirt and pantaloons he usually slept in for the sake of ready concealment from night assassins. His feet, he sensed, were shod in the same soft boots he remembered placing beside his cot that evening; but of the familiar dagger he kept hidden beneath his pillow, there was no trace on his person.

His surroundings were not totally obscure. As he peered about him, a feathery crescent moon edged from behind a vaporous cloud overhead and lit the scene eerily. He stood in a plaza of monumental stonework—walls, pillars and entablatures, all quaint and ancient-seeming in design. Yet they stood here untouched by time, looming straight and square against a moon-pale firmament masked by racing cloudlets.

Something about those pale stars bothered him. He stepped forward to view them better, and found the surface of this dream world as hard and smooth under his feet as polished stone ought to be. But after a pace or two he stopped, dazzled. Light sprang up suddenly ahead—basins of low, reddish flame blossoming upward from carved sconces and braziers set around the courtyard.

No hand had lit them, as far as he could see. No human servants stood by to tend and refill them. Except for the prince himself, the place was deserted.

The flames, he noted, glinted on the wavelets of a circular, oily-dark pool at the center of the court. Its surface rippled, possibly with the same faint, chill stirrings of air that tugged and fretted the hems of his garments; unless, as it almost seemed, the pond harbored a restless life of its own. It was the central feature of the place, and the only other moving object; somehow the dream-jaded prince was hardly surprised when a deep liquid voice bubbled up from its center in sensible, intelligible accents.

"Welcome, Prince Armiro, Lord of Koth, and seeker of an even broader empire. It gratifies me to allow such noble feet to tread the ancient stones of my temple."

"Who are you,' Armiro challenged directly, "to waft me here at this ungracious hour and vex my rightful slumbers?"

"Come now, my dear prince," the voice bubbled forth humorously, "are you claiming that a peaceful rest was interrupted? I know better! But then, who would expect one of your precarious station—and your, shall we say, firm manner of dealing with others—to be blessed with easy dreams?"

Armiro barked a cynical laugh. "You know me well, phantom! In truth, my dreams were of hard blows being struck, and harridans' coarse, cruel laughter, and of murderers creeping upon me in the dark. Such is the usual content of my dreams. Never, till lately, have they contained phantasms and disembodied voices!"

"Good; then you are attuned to my growing and returning power. Mere days ago I would have lacked the ability to reach into your dreams, much less bring a rank nonbeliever such as yourself here to my side."

"Who are you, I ask again, and what is this eldritch place?" Staying a half-dozen paces back from the low curb of the pool, Armiro nevertheless drew himself up straighter and looked around in a confident, commanding manner. "Is this our familiar world? If so, your power includes that of moving the stars in the celestial spheres, for the constellations overhead are oddly disfigured to my eye. But hold! —this cannot be the earth I know, for yonder hangs another moon." His air of lordly unconcern was shaken slightly as he raised an arm to point. There, in the wake of a drifting bank of cloud low down near the horizon, skulked a second, coarser crescent.

"Now, now, my prince," the bubbling voice chided him, "do not assume that this is other than your home. Know you, the stars swirl across the sky in their own infinitely slow evolutions like dust motes in a breeze. If these heavens seem strange, perhaps it is because I prefer to recall a time when this earth of yours had two moons!

"As for myself," the liquid voice simmered on, "I am Kthantos, a god. I was, in times long past, the greatest god . . . the only one, to all purposes. My power declined, due in part to the predictable folly of my priests, who let themselves be violently hated. More foolishly, they let themselves be wiped out." The bubblings slowed a moment, then plopped heavily, emitting what could be construed as a yawn. "My grasp declined too, I admit, through my own diminished interest in my worshipers and a weariness with their petty affairs."

Armiro asked guardedly, "Your worshipers were men?"

"Men? Yes, of course—or nearly so, it matters not. Down the ages your race has changed less markedly than the face of the heavens." A riffle of unarticulated bubbles gave the impression of something shifting restlessly beneath the pool's surface. "In any case, I have decided to resume my seat as ruler of this world—as divine ruler, that is, with a place beneath me for a mortal monarch of virtually limitless power. Accordingly, I now find it appropriate to gather followers, to shade the course of history with dreams, visions, and summonings, and even to reach forth in small excursions into your world. Though time troubles a god less than a mortal, I have spent enough eons in this pond to grow weary of its dank emptiness."

"You remain here always?" Armiro asked with an air of casualness.

"Unless I choose to emerge—but I seldom do. This was once my sacrificial pool, and I remember it fondly as the sanguine, rippling heart of a world-spanning empire. What I miss most is a warm soul to keep me company. I have these few relics, of course"—from the surface of the pond there abruptly broke skeletal arms, some brandishing swords and rusted shields, others flailing aimlessly; then, just as unceremoniously, they sank and disappeared beneath the surface—"but they are mere residue. Their mortal essences, which can stir and tickle so pleasantly, are long since consumed and dissipated. I did encounter a fine soul recently—a warm, vibrant, sensitive spirit. I touched it and almost seized it for my own—but alas, it slipped away from me, likely into the care of some lesser, meeker god. A sore pity!"

"I warn you, Kthantos," Armiro said, his voice echoing out across the pond, "you would not find my soul so warm or tickling in nature. Do not think to snatch it from me."

"Nay, Prince! For you, I have another proposal. I know of your overweening ambition—also of your competence and your freedom from the nagging traditionalism that shackles so many able rulers. You do not care too deeply, I gather, for your fellow beings."

"Care?" Armiro asked negligently. "Why should I care? None has yet cared for me—nobody, that is, who had the power to give me what I craved."

"Ah, Prince, I see more clearly the hard, bristly shape of your soul. In truth, it is not one that I would choose to comfort me. Still, your independence and resourcefulness are your best strengths."

"And why not?" Armiro asked bitterly. "I always had to do for myself."

"Of late you have shown even less compunction—as on your army's march into neutral Argos, whose lands you are now laying waste. Do you not find yourself progressively freer of the petty constraints of humanity and mercy?"

"Yes . . . of late I have suffered a loss," the prince replied. "Not a loss that, in itself, would unhinge or weaken me, or warrant a show of unprincely grief—but by confirming my long-held belief in human frailty and deceit, and the ultimate futility of human life, the affair has sobered me." Armiro stood tall and straight, scanning the pond and the pillars beyond it with composed features. "Sobered me, yes, and made me firmer in my purpose."

"Firmness is called for, it would seem, considering the strength and ferocity of those who oppose you."

"Strength? Ferocity?" This time Armiro's laugh was scornful. "Say rather, luck and bombast!" Suddenly restless, he turned aside, strode a pace or two, and wheeled back to face the pond. "My chief enemy just now is a boob so uncultured, a lout so rough and rude, that I can summon no respect or kinship for him as a monarch! In truth, I scarcely regard him as a man, but as some spouting, posturing relic of a mythical past age. He knows scant little of diplomacy, even less of the science of modern war, and is borne up in his conquests on the shoulders of his generals and advisors, serving as a sort of archaic figurehead—with all his twaddle of noble savagery and the unconquerable will! A beef-slabbed idol with a crowned, gilded brow, and feet of dung!

"And yet," the prince continued, "he has intruded upon me in an unpardonable way. Not just lately, in regard to my troublesome loss; I find that once before he made the mistake so many others have, of playing a dubious part in my despised past." Armiro frowned with a deep inner vexation. "So it becomes my duty and my special pleasure to silence his noxious blatting. In time I shall settle on a punishment for him that is condign."

"Truly a diverting struggle, even to one of my world-weariness—between two mortal kings who are, whatever you may say, formidable. Your maneuvers in this burgeoning war strike one as being careful and measured, neither impetuous nor hurried."

"What needs hurry, when my aim is to draw him inevitably into conflict with other foes, whom I can in turn cajole—but stay!'' Armiro brought himself up short. ''I never was one to disclose my plans, and I do not feel inclined to do so now. Not even in a dream, within the dark, cavernous reaches of my own benighted skull.''

''If you think this shrine lies within your skull, then you have a somber image of your own spirit, my prince.'' The bubbles in the flame-lit pond roiled and tossed luridly a moment, then subsided. ''Here, in any case, is my proposal: every earthly conqueror needs a god to conquer righteously for. Given your fealty to me, I will guide your war to a clear and imminent confrontation between you and your principal foe. If you prove yourself the better king, I will ensure the completeness of your triumph.''

''Hmm, you may just be capable of it.'' Armiro's parleying face was rigid and unexpressive, his arms folded across his chest, his attitude of intense thought signalled by only a slight forward inclination of his head. ''And yet, your guarantee to me is no guarantee at all. You double-deal with that brigand Conan as well, methinks. But I gather that you find my view of the world more congenial to your own.''

The submerged voice riffled forth a cluster of bubbles. ''The question is this: can you accept me, Kthantos, as the One True God? And can you accept and honor my high priest, in whatever odd shape he may come to you?'' The dark surface stilled for a moment. ''Think on these things, Prince Armiro. You need not render me an answer now. . . .''

Of a sudden, the nests of flame in the braziers began to sink and gutter low. The unearthly prospect was gradually obscured; even the stars and the tissue moons faded. Then was darkness, turbid and restless—followed by blazing light, as Armiro blinked open his eyes on the misty sun-glare of a bright Argossean morning.

"Mmm. Uhh. Guards. . . ." Screening his eyes one-handed against the seam of fiery light that edged the tent flaps, the prince hauled himself up to a sitting position in his field cot.

The day-glare intensified briefly as a trooper let himself into the tent, and then was mercifully blocked by his armored bulk. "Ready at your order, O Prince!"

"Guard, why have I been allowed to sleep so late? 'Tis past sunrise."

"Sire, your seneschal was unable to rouse you. You muttered in your sleep, and so we all retired outside lest we overhear portentous state secrets."

"I see. All of you? That was wise." Armiro finished tugging his boots on unassisted, arose, and unhooked his gold-embroidered tunic of rank from the nearby wardrobe. "Assemble my officers."

Moments later, the high command of the Kothian Army stood in a neat, attentive circle on the finely woven Aghrapur carpet laid outside the tent. As they waited, the prince himself parted the draperies in the entryway. As he stepped forth, warm morning sun bathed his square, youthful face and gold-berobed figure.

"Vassals, attend my words," Armiro told the assembled ministers and generals. "I have had a holy vision."

Queen Zenobia, wife of the world's mightiest conqueror, sat alone in her chamber savoring grief's bitter dregs. She who controlled more wealth than any other woman in the world, whose empire was enlarged daily by the swiftest marches of armies at its remotest ends, distilled the bitter wine of sorrow from her own salt tears. Gentle Zenobia, mother of a loving son, governess of a land prosperous and unscathed by recent wars, sat alone knotting her patient skeins of anger, interweaving strands of spite, renunciation, and murder.

The brightness of her lodging belied the gloom of her spirit. The broad, vaulted chamber was rich with furniture, tapestries, and bedclothes bartered, or wrested at swordpoint, from exotic corners of the world. The room shone brilliant with a brave expense of tallow candles blazing in candelabra set all around. Zenobia's beauty, even in grief, had no cause to hide from the light. The tears that fell from her eyes twinkled like precious, fleeting gems in the candleglow.

Her wrath and sorrow were not primarily against Conan, her husband. Him she could not hope to know or control. Men were puzzling elemental forces, like water or molten red stone flowing down to their own level: transparently simple at times, and laughably predictable. But their boyish immaturity had a way of linking with the boyishness of other males to cause remarkable upheavals that could transform the world—like the great explosions said to occur when the sea flowed into volcanoes along the Zingaran coast.

No, Conan was both above and beneath blame for his actions. He would never hesitate an instant to place his life, and his kingdom, at stake in defense of the curious code he equated with manhood. Though a king, he was moved by inner turbulent forces he himself understood least of all. Zenobia could more easily blame others—power-seekers who sought to divert Conan's relentless energy and, like herself, share in the result. Such others, women mostly, she could identify as threats; these she could hate.

This Amlunia, for instance—a cheap baggage, eager to

vend her body and play up to a warrior's fantasies of what a woman's nature and cravings should be. The rumors and spy reports, lurid as they sounded, could not conceal her true nature from Zenobia—the little slut knew exactly what she was doing! Her infamous cruelty and wantonness made it hard even to imagine an adequate punishment for her perfidy: powdered glass in her kohl and rouge, perhaps, or a handsome, seductive young assassin with a blade where his love-hilt ought to be.

Indeed, if Zenobia had her truest wish, she would go confront the bitch and pluck out her hair with bare hands, and her eyes as well. Yet the queen entertained no serious thought of riding forth from the capital, abandoning her duties of governance, and dashing to the frontier to rescue her husband from his indiscretions. She would never dare such an extreme—would she?

As to the other snares in her path, and in Conan's—the woman Yasmela was a mystery, even though Zenobia had heard Conan speak of her in his frank, tactless way. A queen, she held unknown power from her place in Conan's past; likely she sought to use it all now, to make him help her recover her lost or faltering throne. And yet, she did not seem to have sought Conan out; rather, the opposite. Characteristically, Zenobia's husband had thrown aside everything, and jeopardized his wife's standing and safety, to aid another woman in distress.

In all, the Khorajan queen's influence was less vexing than that of Conan's closest companion, the insidious dwarf. Though not female, he had a scheming woman's indirectness of purpose—the eunuch-like skill of wielding his power from a position of seeming weakness. Here, Zenobia felt, lay the real source of the threat to her husband. And Delvyn was male, at least nominally. So Conan's ministers might be willing to move against him, rather than showing him the same blind loyalty and protection they gave the king in his amorous strayings.

Yet how could she reveal her hurt—the painful rift in her heart that threatened to widen and deepen until it tore apart a whole empire? So far she had almost managed to keep it inside her, for the sake of her son and his future, for the welfare of the kingdom, and for Conan's safety. After all, the harsh perils he faced in his daily campaigning were perhaps the sorest point of her fear; though hurt and humiliated, she would not wish to endanger him further with marital discord or political intrigue. At least not yet. Consequently, she had borne it all—the fears, the rumors, the tears and the dark, puzzling dreams—proudly and silently, except in the lonely refuge of her sleeping chamber. She had prayed to Mitra and other gods, so far in vain. She might know better how to proceed, if only she could confide in someone; the burden was hardest to bear when one lacked guidance, even a word.

And yet, past experience told her it might all end at any moment. Conan could return unannounced, to regale and romance her grandly and put to rest her fears of abandonment. He thought of her still, from time to time, as proven by the loot and gifts he sent back from abroad in his impulsive generosity—most notably, the rich feather bed that now bulked enormous against the broad wall of the chamber. Its satin bolsters and blankets made a show in the candlelight that was far too garish to be considered an invitation to sleep; its fine ebony frame and posts, with erotic human forms carved flowingly into the polished wood, served only as a pang and a reproach to the lonely queen. She hesitated to brave such a bed alone.

Arising, dabbing at her eyes with a damp lace handkerchief, for what she knew would not be the last time that evening, she reached across her writing-table. From it she took up a long, spoon-shaped gold snuffer, and began making the rounds of the room. She preferred not to summon a servant for such chores; stopping at each candelabrum, she snuffed out all but the tallest central candle, leaving the room at last with a dim, diffuse light spreading from its corners.

She had just begun removing her clothing, beginning with her long white shawl, when a knock sounded. Not at the room's main door, but at the rear one that communicated with the other bedchambers, the privy, and the postern gate. It was not unknown for her to have visitors at this hour—a spy, most likely, sent through by the guard captain in obedience to her standing order. Draping her shawl across a chair, she walked to the door and unlatched it.

The figure loomed gaunt and thin. It was concealed entirely in the folds of a long black cloak, which hung loosely at the sleeves and trailed along the ground. Its cowl opened narrowly on a dark void, within which no face was clearly visible. Even so, the visitor seemed strangely familiar to Zenobia—perhaps from her dreams. She blinked, mindful of her prayers to the gods of Hyboria.

"You come, then," she found herself asking, "to bring me some wisdom or solace, amid all the turmoil that frets the world?" Stepping back, she opened the door wider. "Very well, stranger, enter!"

Chapter 16
Hero of the Realm

Corps Marshall Egilrude guided his horse along the forested ridge. The high parts of the ridge were rocky and treeless, the tallest and most exposed trees having been burnt or splintered by lightning storms that evidently struck this wild land with devastating frequency. In consequence of this, the marshall soon came to a place where a view opened out on more forested ridges—rank upon rank of them, extending to the jagged wall of the Karpash Mountains in the blue southerly haze.

With a further clattering of loose stones beneath rough-shod hooves, Egilrude's two adjutants reined up beside him. Neither said a word, but one of them pointed. The marshall followed the thrust of his callused, coarse-nailed finger. On one of the ridges rising close under the mountains' piny flank stood the outline of a stone tower. The square battlement looked worn and dinted, whether by combat or by the force of hurled lightnings, it was hard to say. But the movement of sentries, metal-glinting in the sun, could be seen on its top.

"Not a strong keep," was Egilrude's comment. "But why garrison a watchtower in this wild region?" He turned and gazed at the visored, sun-dark face of one of his subordinates. "Is there a village nearby?"

"We do not know yet, Sire. Scouts have been dispatched to give us an appreciation of the defenses, but their return is doubtful. Even if our host has not already been sighted, it will be hard to approach such an outpost unseen."

"Exactly," the marshall said, "so we must advance in strength and press what surprise we may yet enjoy. Having pushed so far into Corinthia, and bloodied a good many noses doing it, 'twould be unsoldierly to turn back without gaining this bit of intelligence." Reining his steed around, Egilrude led the others diagonally back down the ridge toward the valley trail.

Even without sentry posts, the ruggedness of the craggy hill country made it risky ground for invaders. But the marshall was counting on the remoteness and sparse population of the district to render it helpless against the considerable force he commanded.

He had sworn to distinguish himself in leading this mission, his first truly independent one. His rank, after all, had been specially decreed by the conqueror himself, King Conan of Aquilonia, and soon to be Lord of All the World. It was the king's way of singling him out—a gesture of special favor, and a test. Such a chance was too precious to let pass lightly. All his days he had looked on Conan as a hero; and ever since seeing him enter a banquet hall teeming with his enemies, single-handed, to emerge unscathed and ruler of a vast new kingdom, Egilrude had viewed the doughty Cimmerian with an awe that bordered upon worship. The power and enlightenment such a godlike warrior might bestow on him were impossible to imagine; perhaps someday, with a touch of his hand or of his gleaming sword, he might bestow on Egilrude, too, the gift of godhood.

Such thoughts were visionary, perhaps, foolishly at odds with the sweaty, dusty realities of soldierhood that daily filled his nostrils and smudged his face. But the strange, spectral dreams he had had in his tent of late, though somber and foreboding, seemed somehow to convey this kernel of mystic promise. It felt right to him, just a part of the reckless euphoria that drove this campaign of world conquest onward, and he sensed that the others he rode with shared the same dream.

In any event, his lot was cast; years ago, when faced with a choice of whether to march with the legions or stay and toil in the flat grainlands of Bossonia under the stern hand of his father, he had chosen his life path. He had resolved to do his best, and it was not like an Aquilonian officer to turn aside from his goal.

Egilrude rejoined the center of the legion which had, by his order, continued its southeastward march. The trail was narrow but the valley bottom was flat; so, by galloping through reaches of meadow and stream bank, it was not hard to bypass most of the column. Once back at the head of the force, he and his adjutants exchanged their winded steeds for unburdened spares.

So the morning progressed, without any return or mirror signal by the far-ranging scouts. The midday stop was made; mess carts stoked with charcoal fires fed the companies hot stew by shifts in a streamside camp, dispatching companies as fast as new ones marched up. At every crest in the trail, Egilrude scanned the hills ahead for the square outline of the watchtower, knowing it would not be long before the column came in view of it.

What he did encounter, he did not expect: a long line of foreign troops, Corinthian and Brythunian by their banners, threading down a mountainous cross-trail to cut the route of his march.

The force had not had time, the marshall judged, to deploy in ambush or defense; but they were armed and ready, with light cavalry lancers well-suited to the mountainous terrain riding in the fore. Egilrude drew up his lead phalanx of mounted archers at the stream ford just below the trail junction. He directed the following infantry to continue forward and fill in on either side of the flat, steep-walled valley. Better, he reasoned, to keep the rearmost, slowest elements of the army moving, and make ready to fight in a solid, compact front. At the same time, he issued orders to be relayed by semaphore to his outriders along the nearby ridges.

Before many minutes had passed, the lead contingent of Corinthian cavalry and officers faced Egilrude's command party on the opposite bank of the stream. Grounding their bannered lances in a circle to signify a parley, the leaders left them behind and rode to the water's edge. Egilrude gestured his two adjutants and a pair of cavalry officers forward; they sat in their saddles on the near bank, awaiting the foreigners' words.

The Corinthian leader chose the language of once proud Nemedia as a common tongue. "Interlopers, we renounce your presence on Corinthian soil! We order you to depart our sovereign territory at once. I bring with me a decree of our governing council." The gold-crested horseman appeared to be of a rank equivalent to legion captain. He now waved high a scroll, red-tasselled, of regal-looking authority. "It states that all Aquilonian and tributary forces are to withdraw behind western borders in a space of two days, on pain of battle."

"So you say." Egilrude, sitting unruffled in his saddle, used the same gruff Nemedian dialect to reply. He spoke loudly to be heard over the gurgling of the stream. "No one in our party can read High Corinthian, so the text of your scroll must remain a matter of speculation." He tossed off the implied insult without sarcasm or undue emotion. "But I would remind you that Aquilonians first entered your land in pursuit of stateless rebels and brigands, to subdue them as a favor both to Nemedia and Corinthia. Our high command now seeks permission to pass through your country on the way to more southerly engagements, not to make war on your masters."

"Of late you passed through Nemedia, and the country now lies in ruins. We would be fools to tolerate such unmannerly guests." The gold-crested officer laughed bitterly, making low comments in Corinthian to his fellows. "If we truly sought your ruin," he continued, "we would let your army proceed southward to face the storms and vampires of the Karpash Mountains. But our orders will not permit it. Therefore you must turn back."

Egilrude sat immovable in his saddle. "Your orders, such as they are, have no sway over us. Therefore I suggest that you withdraw from the path of our march."

The Corinthian officer reddened. "I warn you, sir, you risk open war between our lands!" He raised the scroll over his head once again. "This decree is also signed by a special emissary of the King of Brythunia, whose military forces have been committed to Corinthia's aid in clearing our western border." He gestured to one of his confederates, who wore Brythunian-style fur trappings and a northern spiked helm; the outlander nodded sternly. "Failure to obey will be taken as a hostile act against both countries."

"Nonsense, we have no quarrel with Brythunia!" Egilrude shook his helmeted head with an air of dismissal. Then he shot a frank, shrewd look at the other commander. "But I warn you, since your force seems to be of no great size: my battalions are spread throughout these valleys, advancing by several parallel routes. If you would oppose me, look to your flanks."

The Corinthian shot an uneasy glance to his second officer and began muttering rapidly in his native tongue. As he did so, Egilrude tipped down the visor of his helmet, letting it fall with a sharp clang. This was a signal to his companions; as one, the horsemen spurred into the stream, drawing broadswords and maces to set upon their enemies.

Water sprayed and curtained silver in the tree-dappled light as the Aquilonians crossed the ford. Then arose a furious clanging as the two groups crossed arms. The Corinthian party knew better than to try and wheel away from their attackers; yet they lacked forward motion, and so found it hard to control their steeds. One of them, the Brythunian, slipped from his saddle into the stream, there to stain the water with a red plume issuing from a rent in his fur tunic. Egilrude hacked at the gilded Corinthian leader's offhand arm with stunning force. The marshall watched the tasselled scroll go flying from his grip into the stream, where he decided it was well lost.

The enemy officers crowded back and were soon enveloped by protecting lancers. Meanwhile, mounted forces charged from the Aquilonian side to join the fight. Arrows clipped the foliage overhead, and troopers joined battle all up and down the stream, for its summer level was low enough to wade or gallop across in most places. The two armies pressed together, and the din of weapons filled the narrow valley.

Within the hour Egilrude's side had carved out a victory—a local one, at least. The Corinthian force had not been given time to deploy fully in the valley bottom; the Aquilonian thrust pushed their lead party back, and cut them off from the trail by which the balance of their force was approaching. Having divided his foe, Egilrude pursued them relentlessly; he had not lied when he said that his own force was spread among three valleys. Now he relayed signals to his outriders to ensure that the Corinthian reinforcements were harried from two sides at least.

His central detachment hounded the heels of the Corinthian officers and cavalry tirelessly, advancing in a series of swift, concerted charges. These always succeeded in breaking up the resistance and forcing the enemy back to the next stand of forest or rocky scrub. Egilrude lost men to arrow flights and lance skirmishes; but as he advanced, it was plain that more Corinthians than Aquilonians were left moaning and bleeding among the clumps of meadow grass and the knotted roots of balsams.

Egilrude, following the famous example of his emperor, led the cavalry charges himself and took an active part in the fighting. Within the span of a hard-won quarter league his breath came in gasps, his arm and shoulder felt achingly sore and strengthless, and foamy sweat oozed from beneath the saddle blanket of his winded steed. Even so, he found in himself the will to fight on. And when finally he trapped the enemy commander in a tangled windfall of splintered trees, he felt exultation fiercer than he had ever known.

With clanging fury his mace struck the sword from the Corinthian's fist; a second blow smote the gilded helmet from his brow. Moments later the foeman lay twisted on the ground, his gaping mouth filling with a rivulet of blood from the mortal gash in his skull.

Thenceforth the surviving enemies retreated even faster, leading the harriers up the narrowing neck of the valley and over a low, meadowed pass. Beyond it, in the next, narrower valley, the square watchtower was finally visible again, though dwarfed by the broad black curtain of the Karpash peaks.

Egilrude continued to press the initiative, naggingly aware that his cavalry was drawing far ahead of his infantry and supply column. The tower keep was his immediate goal, so he would have to trust to his officers to keep his trailing forces safe and intact. To complicate matters, the afternoon grew late, and one of the local summer storms swiftly gathered. Dark-mottled clouds flowed together atop the tree-girt ridges ahead, shrouding the jagged summits of the Karpash range in billowing white and iron gray.

It was during a swift, galloping skirmish at a stream crossing that the flinty clouds finally struck forth lightning, and the first blood-warm raindrops fell.

None of the riders troubled to seek shelter, even though the onslaught of thunder terrified their plunging steeds. They fought and chased onward, with each lightning stroke illuminating the animals' staring, bloodshot eyes and bared yellow teeth. In the panic that followed, some riders were thrown or dragged from their saddles, others overtaken and slain by ravaging Aquilonian steel. The fight turned to a wild pursuit; it clattered along a stony stream-bed, whose waters flashed milky fire, and up the lane of a rude mountain village. The chase ended in a desperate fight above the town, at the gate of the looming tower keep.

The defenders, confused perhaps by the fury of the storm, had ill-advisedly lowered the drawbridge to admit their fleeing countrymen. So close on their heels were the Aquilonians, the garrison had time to raise the span no more than a hand's-breadth before it was weighted down with pelting Aquilonian destriers and their armored riders. Egilrude and the best-mounted of his companions set upon the gate guards and kept them from closing the ironbound doors or winding down the portcullis. Moments later, with more invaders arriving in the blinding downpour, the corps-marshall dismounted and led the hunt for the enemy through the dim, narrow corridors of the keep.

At the end of it, the Corinthian knights lay slain to the last man, along with the fiercest of the tower's defenders. A dozen or so bruised, sullen prisoners waited in the sodden courtyard under the command of the two score surviving Aquilonians. More numerous than both parties combined were the horses, who stood steaming and whickering in the persistent rain.

Egilrude, making an effort to shrug off his exhaustion and look fearsome, strode out of the entryway into the downpour. "Now," he barked, "I need a captive who speaks Aquilonian or Nemedian! Who of the prisoners is ready to deal with me?"

Most of the Corinthians, leathery-skinned veterans,

remained stone-faced with eyes downcast as their conqueror strode along their line. One of them, however, an elderly civilian with the look of a farmer or shepherd, could not help flashing a frightened glance up at the marshall. Egilrude stopped alongside him and, seizing his shoulder in an iron grip, jerked the man forward out of line. He fell to all fours on the muddy cobblestones.

"How many Corinthian fighters are present in these hills?" the marshall bellowed at him. "What are their orders?" He gave the man a kick in the side, sending him sprawling in the mud. "And what is the purpose of this watchtower, raised up here in the middle of nowhere?"

"Please, Captain," the man gasped in broken Nemedian, "I am but a poor shepherd, come here to sell my stock to the garrison." He looked from the prisoners to his captor with imploring eyes. "I know nothing of the wars of great empires. Please, Sire, let me go home."

Egilrude regarded the man angrily. He thought of his own kinsmen, simple folk like this. Then he thought of the mission, and of his duty to the crown.

"So, you refuse to cooperate!" he rasped. "These men are soldiers, their solemn vows prevent them from giving me information. But you . . . you are nothing, a mere peasant! By Erlik, answer me! I will have out of you your truth or your tongue!" At the shepherd's anguished silence, he turned and snapped his fingers at a group of his men standing in streaming rain. "You two, take him inside! These others can be put in the lockup below the keep. Secure the gate and drawbridge, post lookouts on the tower, and dispatch riders to guide the legion."

* * *

At dusk the rain still fell, with periodic drummings of thunder and fulminations of lightning. The body of the shepherd, his life expended in torture, had been thrown from the wall into the flooded ditch beyond. Corps Marshall Egilrude paced the tower top with his one surviving adjutant.

"So there is a western pass through the Karpash Range." Egilrude peered around at the dimming landscape, whose black ridges were now near invisible, hinted at by gray convolutions of rain and mist. Where the cloud ceiling cut across the base of the mountains, it flickered occasionally with the play of unseen lightnings high above. "An unused pass, and this tower built to guard the descent against southern invaders."

"Aye, sir. The shepherd gave us the route in considerable detail, but he had a real fear of the place." The adjutant sheltered from the rain under a shabby hide watch-cloak he had brought up from below. "Even in his last sufferings the wretch warned us against its haunts and curses. His peasant superstition was strong."

"Superstition!" Egilrude laughed bitterly. "Little needs superstition, if the place is haunted by weather like this!" He turned and paced away restlessly. "Even so, it is a valuable discovery. The emperor will be pleased and we will receive great honor." His eyes searched the dismal cloudscape in vain. It was impossible to tell in what quarter the sun was setting, much less to find any lights or movement in the nearer distance. "What did the peasant say of the armies roving hereabouts?"

"He swore the Corinthians we met were a full legion, some two thousand strong, with Brythunian auxiliaries among them. They were sent here to fall on the flank of any Aquilonian force that advanced eastward through the plain."

"So we surprised them . . . and they us." Egilrude knit his brow and pondered deeply. "Even so, we enjoy superior numbers, and they are now leaderless and bereft of cavalry. If we can reunite our host, there will be little they can do against us."

"That should not be hard," the adjutant observed. "We did not leave the main cohorts far behind."

"Aye. But in the night, with enemy harriers in the hills . . . and this devilish rain!" Egilrude snugged his travel cloak tighter, and stood outlined for a moment in a glimmer of lightning that flickered along the face of the mountains. "Those streams we galloped across in pursuit of the Corinthians are now torrents, remember. And it was hours agone that the cursed thunderclouds cut off our semaphores. If it does not clear, days could pass before we can regroup."

"Aye . . . 'tis true, Sire. . . ." The adjutant could find nothing to say against this dismal appraisal.

"Very well," Egilrude said. "Since we can see nothing anyway, have a beacon fire built and kept alight all through the night. Display my shield beside it, as a signal to our scouts in the hills. Post an officer to relieve you at midnight, and have him awaken me at dawn." Turning to the tented trap door, he ducked beneath and retired down the tower stair.

The rain continued all the next day, but some time during the following night it ceased. Dawn broke ragged through a jumble of retreating clouds, glinting brightly on new, unseasonable snow along the crest of the Karpash peaks. As the sun came to bear on sodden forest slopes, it raised up curtains of steamy mist that caught and veiled its light in unearthly beauty.

The watchers in the tower had little time to admire this spectacle, however. That same dawn revealed an enemy battalion newly arrived in the village outside their wall, mounting an attack. They dared not lower the gate and launch a cavalry charge. Instead they sped arrows and hurled stones from the parapet. Meanwhile they flashed semaphores into the hills for reinforcements, all in vain.

Given the wetness of the forest, fire was useless to the attackers. By midmorning, however, the moat was drained by means of a ditch gouged deep into the hillside. Prybars and shed-covered battering rams soon began pecking at the stones beneath the drawbridge, to good effect. By noon the gate had buckled and fallen in, allowing armored Corinthians to find their way into the keep.

King Conan and Count Prospero, having taken time to plan and refit before moving their main army southward into Corinthia, encountered scattered resistance in the Karpash foothills. Along the way, they gathered up remnants of the reconnaissance led southward by Marshall Egilrude some days before. The expedition had apparently encountered bad weather in the hills and become scattered; nevertheless, it had engaged a sizeable enemy force and kept the defenders skirmishing for days, thereby helping to clear the way for the king's advance.

Most valuable of all was the arrival of one of Egilrude's couriers, diligent and well-briefed. He told them of conditions ahead, and bore a detailed map purporting to show the king's best route through the Karpash

Mountains. The pass was said to be low, direct, and virtually undefended from either direction. It had traditionally been shunned and ill regarded, the man said, due to local supernatural beliefs. These, however, could scarcely pose a threat to a military host armed and provisioned for a major campaign. So King Conan's army pressed on toward the mountains at its best speed.

Deep in the hills, as foretold by the courier, the army arrived at a watchtower marking the approach to the pass. This was said to be the farthest point of Egilrude's march; but if the marshall had proceeded no further, there seemed little likelihood that he would be found alive. The tower with its adjacent court and keep were broken and gutted. The villagers and foreign soldiers had fled at word of Conan's approach, leaving the place abandoned.

Conan and Prospero led a company of men inside. Even before entering, the stench of death told them at some distance that the bodies had not been cleared away. The undermined gate had not been repaired, and the drained moat was but a trickling brook underfoot. Bodies of men and horses clogged the courtyard, and a trail of fallen Aquilonian and Corinthian knights led the way up a spiral staircase that was sticky with drying blood.

At its very top, on the tower parapet, Egilrude's corpse lay stiff against a rampart. He was decapitated, his head having evidently been kicked into the ashes of a fire at the parapet's center. Conan and Prospero gazed briefly down at the remains. Then they turned, inhaled the fresh mountain breeze, and gazed out at the serpentlike column of their army as it marched up the forested valley.

"A sorry death for a brave soldier," Conan remarked, scanning the view of serried ridges and the gleaming mountains ahead.

"Aye, Egilrude was brave," Prospero concurred, "and impetuous. His zeal in this expedition may well have drawn us into war with Corinthia and Brythunia."

"I hope not," Conan said. "I am not ready to fight them just yet. But I have sent Publius to meet with their emissaries. I trust him to smooth things out in that quarter."

"His greatest feat of diplomacy lies ahead of him," Prospero said, uncorking the wineskin at his side. "Meanwhile, war or no, safe passage or no, we strike southward." He raised the wineskin to his lips. "Down with Koth!"

"Aye, and death to Armiro!" Conan heartily agreed, reaching out and accepting the flask from Prospero. "And thanks once again to Egilrude, for finding us a path through the mountains." He poured a small libation of wine from the flask, choosing the officer's body rather than his disembodied head to receive the compliment.

"In finding it, he may have made some enemies hereabouts," Prospero said, glancing dubiously at the gory head rolled in ashes. "Egilrude was not the most compassionate of men. This empire-building can make them over-eager at times." With a polite, cautious gesture the count managed to retrieve his flask from Conan. It still had some wine left in it.

"Even so, he was every inch a soldier." The king turned from the rampart and strode toward the stair. "I will have him posthumously declared a Hero of the Realm."

CHAPTER 17
The Ancient Shrine

Conan treated the march into the Karpash Mountains as a welcome escape from the trials and temptations of government, conquest, and diplomacy. Skirmishing by local Corinthian forces had ceased—understandably, since the defenders would have been foolish to hinder a massive armed force now bent on leaving their territory. The king felt secure in the empire he had carved thus far; Baron Halk, after all, would defend his Nemedian satrapy to the last, and the rest of Conan's domain was in able enough hands—at least until he could strike his decisive blow against Armiro's heartland of Koth. And so he regarded his foray into the wilderness as a vacation from royal cares.

Not that he rested. Rather, he occupied himself daily at the head of the marching column, overseeing and joining in the breaking of trail. Through countless years, brush, windfalls, and avalanche debris had accumulated on the little-used route; now the progress of a well-provisioned army required the cutting of a road up the mountainside. In such tasks Conan's skill at wood-craft, gained on the rugged Pictish frontier of Aquilonia, equalled that of his most hard-bitten master sergeant.

At other times he rode beside Amlunia and Delvyn, or with Prospero, who generally stayed apart from the former two. As king he enjoyed free run of the marching column and lacked any leather-voiced superior to hound him relentlessly onward. Yet aside from that, his round did not much differ from that of a common soldier immersed in the relentless, exacting toil of man-handling stock, equipment, and supplies up the steep slopes and rocky canyons of the Karpash Range.

While Conan labored, his mind could not avoid matters which had long lain unexamined in neglected by-ways. Thinking of Zenobia and Conn, his faithful queen and adoring son, he reproached himself that their loving companionship should not be enough to satisfy him. He was prey, he knew, to a primal restlessness, a sense of incompletion and exclusion that sent him off time and again on remote, perilous adventures. Was it only boredom—his lifelong fear of rest, repletion, and the spiritual death that came along with them?

Gods knew, he despised a fat, easy life! All the worse he dreaded the thought of declining into age, growing weak and complacent—and of letting his throne and his manhood slip away or be snatched away, as he had seen so many other self-crowned kings do. Of late, he reminded himself, the telltale warnings had been there for any who had the keenness to note them—the jibes and japes at his authority, the insidious questioning of his strength, and the sniffing and pawing of hungry wolflings like Armiro, eager to unseat a regal lion such as himself.

Crom knew it was hard enough to snatch a crown, harder yet to cling to it! It had required all his wit and strength, and that of his friends, in all their loyalty, just to keep his place. Now long labors, short sleep, and the sweaty frustration of the mountain trek led him to question: why was such a challenge not enough? —kingship, and the endless work of improving his domain—strengthening Aquilonia and making it a place where art and knowledge could grow, a realm to be hailed in legend as the finest, happiest homeland a folk ever knew? Such was Zenobia's dream; why could it, and the simple joys of family life, never possess him totally, as they did her?

And yet he was also aware of his own unsatisfiable, illimitable nature. He wanted every ell of it—yes, and more. He had already tasted rewards, conquests, mortal perils and ecstacies . . . but were some souls not fated to quest even farther and mount even higher? Since his earliest years, had he not smelled the faint reek of destiny on every wind that buffeted him, however cruelly? Things had ever been . . . not easy, but *possible* for him, things that defied other men's skills and fortunes even to the point of their death.

Was not he himself, so long bathed in the glow of the gods' favor, at last ripening into a new sort of god? Already he had a god's power over men, a godlike force and clarity of will, and a virtual divine warrant of success at any task he set his hand to. He was ready now to move from the notion of declaring himself a god for kingly expediency, to that of actually *becoming* one. At times he could feel the power surging in his inmost soul—not always a bright, benign power; often grim and destructive, like the dark dreams that troubled his sleep of late, and the waking visions that ofttimes colored his sight even on the sunniest day. But power it was, to be sure: a seething fountain of dark, primal power.

"After all, King Head-chopper," Delvyn said to him on the trail one day, "men have been made gods before, but no mortal king has yet ruled all the earth. Would not the second achievement automatically entail the first?"

"Meseems it would." Conan, having dismounted from his horse to negotiate a narrow shoulder of ravine with a sharply overhanging rock wall, found it necessary to look up at Delvyn to answer. The dwarf, whose weight and height scarcely added to that of his pony and traps, had remained in the saddle ahead of the others.

"You speak wisely, Delvyn. Does he not, Amlunia?" The king glanced back to his consort, who led her steed close behind his. She was always a congenial sight with her leather laces undone, as on a sunny morning like this. "Have I the makings of a god, do you think, girl? And must I thrash the whole weary world to prove it?"

"A god, Master? To be sure! Why else do you think I cry out the names of a dozen strange gods when we lie together?" Fair as Amlunia's skin was, it scarcely colored when her pert, innocent mouth issued wanton remarks. "But truly, my king," she went on, "would you really wish to be a boring old god? My tastes run more to an imp, a djinn, or a fire demon! Or possibly a lizard-skinned incubus!"

"In truth," Conan said with a pensive frown, "the

line between gods and demons is a thin, hazy one at best.''

"What you will find, I would guess, King Skullbreaker," Delvyn opined at length, "is that gods, like kings, comprise only a small village. One would seek to become the best and most powerful god one could." The jester spoke slowly and deliberately. "To do that, one would choose one's friends carefully, and make alliance with only the greatest and most adept of the reigning gods. . . ."

So their conversations went, ranging from the outrageous and blasphemous to the merely profound. The dwarf had a clever, penetrating mind. Himself, Conan wondered how he had ever gotten so far without the jester's subtle advice. There indeed was proof of his having had divine guidance all his years. And Amlunia—in spite of her bloodlusting ways and her wanton's wont, which after all befitted a warrior's whim—she seemed devoted to him and astonishingly eager to show it. In all, he could not remember ever having had such boon marching companions.

With Prospero the king was less inclined to air his deepest ponderings. The nobleman, though courtly and sophisticated, was more linked to Conan's old life of castle and court, and more burdened down with mundane concerns of statecraft. His evident dislike of Conan's new friends—seldom stated, and masked as it was by his habit of respectful deference to his king—made Conan doubt his frankness. The monarch would have been more comfortable if Prospero had savagely denounced Delvyn and Amlunia, and gotten the matter out in the open. But he guessed that the Poitanian feared to take on the dwarf's scathing tongue and Amlunia's low-cutting sarcasm.

So open dissension did not complicate the journey. Leaders and troopers alike fell into the routine of waking, striking camp, marching, fortifying a new camp, and slumbering the night through, except for their watch duty. As they went, the way grew harder; new summits and chasms unfolded before them, each surpassing the previous one in steepness. To the fatigue of climbing was added the jarring rigor of descent, often over tangled roots and broken, sliding rock, into crevasses that would later require an even sheerer climb to escape. The roughest, narrowest parts of the trail inevitably caused the marching line to lengthen, with tiresome delays at the rear amid dusty, shadeless stones. At other times a whole long, weary day was spent hauling animals and stores up a single ragged incline by means of ropes. Those nights when the army was forced to camp divided, Conan ordered the bulk of the fighting forces into the forward camp, on the theory that the greatest threat lay in the unknown terrain ahead.

Then, when their bodies and equipment had been honed to feral leanness, the terrain all but levelled out to a high plateau of brush expanses and sparse, rocky meadows. The jagged summits of the Karpash peaks diminished to mere snags against a horizon of deep, transparent blue through which stars peered at eventide. Curiously for this higher elevation, the weather seemed to abate, with gusts less chilling and a milder, brighter sun. Even the lightning storms, which had come to be an expected relief and a tolerated threat each afternoon—since their bolts only occasionally obliterated an armored man or a pack horse—ceased to boil in from the lower valleys. Evening came now with a stillness that gradually settled over the land, and a furnacelike glow that painted the westward-facing crags a blood-drenched gold.

One such afternoon, when the forward camp had been established well before sunset on a natural defensive site, Conan went for a solitary walk. Betimes he grew weary of Delvyn's forced gaiety, Amlunia's bawdy attentions, and Prospero's unfailing politeness. Most of the soldiers had rolled into their blankets for an early sleep, in anticipation of rising before dawn on the morrow; so on the pretext of retiring for the night, the king was able to slip away from his guardians, sneak through camp, and scramble down one of the stone scarps that formed its perimeter. From there he made his way to a shallow ravine leading off into wilderness. He counted on the long mountain dusk to give him time for a brisk jog or climb.

The granite skeleton of the mountain was exposed underfoot—smooth, weathered stone with sparse grass and stunted trees rooted in its seams and fissures. Conan was aware that, if he should fail to return, it would be nigh impossible for others to trace his steps across the barren rock. He wondered if any human had ever trod here before—any lone wanderer or hunter, down the uncounted aeons of man's existence.

Then, coming over a stone hummock, he found his question indisputably answered; there before him, nestled between the rock slope and a stand of scrawny trees, was a small, squat building. It was made of stone; thick granite boulders and slabs had been cut roughly to shape, hoisted or trundled into position—and then, it appeared, carved and adorned with runes, patterns, and human figures sculpted in shallow relief. The result hulked before him in the purpling twilight, oddly uneven in shape but ornately and skillfully decorated.

Conan, deeming the place long deserted, eased down nearer to it. He squinted at the sculptures, which predominantly featured a noble, square-bearded patriarch. He decided the place must be an ancient, forgotten shrine to the god Mitra.

So this glen, rather than being primal wilderness, had known human habitation. Or perhaps it was but a way station, a shrine for devout travellers on an older, once frequented route over the pass. Conan's instinct would ordinarily be to shun hoary temples and tombs; but this edifice, suggesting as it did a benign, prosperous past, interested him. He moved near the doorway, cautiously in case the yawning hole was the lair of some wild beast. The stone posts and lintel were indeed ancient—lichen-crusted, and crumbling away at their corners. The interior gloom was difficult for his eyes to pierce with the light outside rapidly dimming.

"Look'st thou for treasure? There still may be aught inside. It is many a year since pilgrims came this way."

The voice came from behind Conan; it jarred him to action as it spoke, making him dive and roll aside over bruising rocks to land on one knee, dagger pointed ready in his hand.

But the speaker who now emerged from the thicket posed no evident threat. It was an elderly, gray-bearded man with a stoop to his walk and a quizzical smile on his seamed, sun-darkened face. With his crooked gait he advanced gingerly over the rocks and branches that littered the ground, pausing a respectful distance from the battle-ready king.

Conan returned his dagger to its sheath—a gesture hinting at contempt more than trust—and took in the stranger. He was clad in a deeply soiled, robelike garment hanging under a fur cap and fur-lined vest. He carried no weapons except a skinning knife sheathed at his waist, and a slender pole with a wire loop wagging from its end. From a strap slung over his shoulder depended a deep, roundish cage of bronze mesh—an animal trap of some kind, already seemingly weighted with the day's catch. The skirts of the old man's robe were bound up around his thighs, exposing skinny, wiry-looking shanks terminating in dusty sandalled feet. The fellow, though bent and filthy, looked capable enough of survival in this remote place or any other.

"What, then, Grandfather," Conan asked skeptically, "why do you challenge me? Are you priest or hermit of this crumbling shrine?"

"Me, a priest of Mitra?" The old one grinned crookedly, exposing a partial set of yellow-stained teeth. "Nay, stranger, I have never been a follower of haughty southern gods! I am but a wanderer like yourself, a hunter ranging these hills for my livelihood."

Conan examined the cage at the elder's side, thinking he detected the glint of beady red eyes and the probing of pointed snouts at the interstices. "You look to be naught but a rat-catcher, old fellow. Is that the noblest game to be hunted among these cliffs?"

The old one responded with a twinkle in his eye. "Not the noblest, to be sure." He shrugged crookedly. "But the most populous, certainly, and the readiest to hand. The little devils are hellish prolific—someone must hunt them, else they would overrun the world and devour all there is."

"I see." The king nodded slowly, pondering the unlikelihood of this chance meeting in the midst of nowhere. "You subsist on rats, then?"

"Rats, yes, and assorted other vermin." The old

hunter nodded judiciously. "Whatever is in season. I have been known to trap serpents as well."

"Hmm." The king took his time answering, searching for some direction in the odd conversation. The other had not asked who he was, causing Conan to feel his royal reputation slighted. Even so, he resolved not to volunteer anything, lest the fellow grow greedy for ransom; he might decide to try out one of his traps on royal game. "What of the treasure you mentioned?" Conan finally asked. "Are you here in search of that?"

"Treasure? Why, what would I want with treasure?" The old one knitted his brows in genuine-seeming astonishment. "What could it be to me, I ask you, except something too heavy to carry—till it were wrested away from me by a young tough like yourself? —and me likely killed, or further maimed in the taking! Nonsense, I need no treasure! My wants are provided for."

"I see." Conan decided not to dispute this remarkable claim. "But if I hear you aright, you think there may be treasure"—he gestured toward the yawning archway of the shrine—"and you expect me to go and seek it out."

"Treasure, yes, there must certainly be! Most indisputably!" The old one's nods seemed earnest and guileless. "But you will have to go deep, I wager. The greatest treasure always lies deepest within."

"Into that stone hut?" Conan asked, now perplexed. "How deep can one go, I ask you?"

The old man reached over his shoulder and dragged a tattered rucksack halfway forward around his side. He fished in it with a manner too abstracted to be threatening. "I will help you, if you like. Here," he said, producing a lantern and a leather pouch clearly fashioned to contain flint, steel, and tinder.

Moving forward, the old man leaned his loop-ended stave against the front of the shrine. He knelt and plied steel deftly against flint, then set his tinder flame to the wick of the mesh-chimneyed lamp. As it flared up, a brightening spark in the swiftly darkening evening, he flicked down the windscreen and stood up beside the watching king. "Here, take the lamp and follow! I will go first."

Taking up his staff, the old one stepped into the night-black archway. Conan could see no conceivable reason not to follow him. He entered, holding the lamp to one side, away from his eyes. By its beams, the shrine looked narrow and cloistered as expected; but its floor angled sharply downward into a cave or tunnel.

Ahead of him the old one made a sudden move. Conan tensed; he watched a pair of red eyes glowing from an angle of carving inside the shrine. The wire loop flicked at the end of its pole; the rustling became frantic, and the vermin was skillfully whisked to the cage at the elder's side, where a mesh lid opened and closed over it.

"Congratulations, old man! You have found your treasure already!" Conan inched the lamp forward behind his guide.

"In sooth: temples, tombs, and castles are full of rats. They like to undermine the foundations. But you must know where to look." The wire loop lashed forth again, snaring a less visible quarry from behind the noble foot of a rough-carved statue. "If you want to be a rat-catcher, you must be sly." The metal trap clashed shut again. "Sly and light-footed."

They had descended beneath ground level, and now it was apparent that the place was a cavern. Protrusions of natural stone, variously spindling and bulbous, hung from the walls and ceiling; the only path through them was the one from the shrine above, presumably cut by human hands. Lamplight played weirdly on the festoons and spires of flowstone, bringing out lurid colors in their molded, glistening surfaces. The shadows fled from the lampbearer's approach, as did the bent shadow and shape of the old man. Rats and rat spoor ceased to be in evidence; the air cooled, and the scent of mountain balsams was replaced by the dank smell of earth's innards.

"So it ever was," the old rat-catcher remarked. "Every temple of man is raised on an older sanctuary of the earth itself—even shrines of great and lofty Mitra."

"What makes you so sure this is a temple of Mitra?" Conan argued back, talking primarily to ward off the looming shadows.

"If not Mitra, then who?" The elder one twisted crookedly about to regard Conan. The lamp's glow played sharply on his wizened, impish face, highlighting its quizzical wrinkles.

"Why, old man, for all you know, it could be a temple to me!" His voice did not really quaver like a child's with the boast; only the echoes in the cave made it seem so.

"You regard yourself as one of the immortal gods?" The rat-catcher turned from him and proceeded into the cave, so that Conan was obliged to follow with the lamp just to keep him in sight. "Do you have the patience for it? I would think that the gods, forced to haunt musty sanctums such as this down the centuries, grow immortally weary of them."

"Patience was never a vice of mine," Conan said

gruffly. "If I become a god, it will be through my lack of patience."

"Hmm. 'Tis not so much patience that is required," the spirited old voice muttered back, "as an unswerving sense of your own worth. Are you struggling with imaginary wraiths and hobgoblins just to disprove or excuse your secret doubts of yourself? Or can you see a worthy goal and hold to it?"

"At the moment, old man, I can see no goal—nor anything worthwhile, including yourself! But enough of this—how much further must we go down this rathole?"

"Far, indeed." The old one glanced back to Conan with an admonishing frown. "I told you, the greatest treasures lie deep within." He walked on briskly with his crooked gait, then abruptly slowed. "But here, just ahead, may be a challenge that will keep your fickle mind distracted. Come forward—but walk lightly."

As Conan overtook the old man, he could see him stooping at the brink of a dark pit. The rim of lamplight ebbed down its farther wall as Conan approached but it did not strike any visible bottom. When the king took his place beside the rat-catcher on the edge of the abyss, he could peer down into its depths and see nothing at all—beyond a few faint contours of its stone walls a dozen man-lengths below. That it had a bottom was only suggested by echoes of faint liquid sounds from beneath.

The pit was all the more formidable, because it appeared to stretch from wall to wall of the cavern, which narrowed here to a roughly circular shape. The level part of the cave continued beyond it some way at least; this could be seen by raising the lamp high and projecting crazed shadows against crazier stone surfaces.

But the only way across to the far side of the chasm was an antique arched bridge made of roughly shaped stones.

The span was railless and unsafe; its outer edges had crumbled away, so that the level space for walking was but a single stone wide, the width of a grain sack. If there had ever been mortar in the joints between the rocks, it had long since fallen away into the void. All that remained was an improbable pile of rough stones leaning precariously together over nothingness.

"A challenge, indeed." The old rat-catcher, pulling a filthy rag out of his knapsack, stooped toward Conan and busied himself with the lamp. He unstoppered the hole in its side, and from it tipped some lamp oil onto the cloth, dousing it well. Then he raised it to the flaming chimney and, with a swift, simultaneous motion of his hand, flicked the scrap aside. The rag exploded into flame and flew out into the void, to plummet down and down.

Leaning out over the pit, both men saw it fall, flaring brightly with the rush of air past it. A long way it flew until finally its light reflected on the chasm's floor, an ebon pool.

The thin fluid of the pool looked somehow too dark to be water; it bubbled at its center, making liquescent sounds and spreading circular ripples across its surface. When the rag struck, poison vapors must have been ignited; for there came a ghostly blue flash and a *whoosh!* which caused the king and rat-catcher to step back from the rim of the pit, shading their faces.

That same instant, a rush of hot air and a tremor overtook them; the shock caused debris to sift down from the rotten bridge, while the rats fought and chittered with excitement inside the old man's cage. Conan too was momentarily abstracted; the sight of the black pond put him in mind of certain dreams he had been having of late. It brought an oily quease of fear to his stomach, and the sweat that broke out on his forehead was not wholly related to the blast of heat.

"So, onward!" the old man urged him. "Let us pass this obstacle and continue our quest. You were the one who was bored, so you may take the lead."

Conan, his brow still aprickle with sweat, protested vehemently. "Old man, I am an adventurer, not a fool! I would never trust my life to that ramshackle pile! What kind of simpleton must you think me, that you could so easily bring me to my death?"

"You fear to go." The rat-catcher pursed his pert old mouth in a way that did not necessarily imply scorn. "Very well then, you hold the lamp and I will go first. If I succeed, you must follow."

"Old fellow, do not test the bridge! I would not, even if I had your paltry few years left." Seeing that the other paid him no heed, he said, "Very well! But if you try and fail, your death be not on my head."

Conan watched as the old one walked to the end of the span, set first a foot on it, then his full weight. With careful, measured steps that were remarkably agile for one so old and crooked, he made his way forward. At the center of the bridge he stopped and looked back at Conan; then he proceeded to the far side and hopped off.

"Well?" he asked, turning back again to look across the chasm. "Are you coming?"

Conan, though admittedly relieved that the old gadfly had made the crossing, experienced a deep flush of shame that he himself had not gone first. It was almost new to him, this feeling of being bested; it smote the king in him more cruelly than the man. "What, old vermin-eater," he demanded, "you call me coward? And will you swear by the god you hold sacred that you will not poke and prod at the stones with your rat stick to send me to my death? If you try and fail, no god or demon will save you from my ire!"

"On my honor," he thought he heard the old man reply. It did not matter, for Conan was already on the bridge. Holding the lamp out for balance, he stepped gingerly in the places he had seen the other step. The bridge held, though he felt stones shift and scrape beneath his feet. He reached the center of the span, watching shadows sway with the swaying of his lamp.

Evidently the pond in the pit had remained aflame, for blue ghost-fires still eddied and shimmered across its surface far below. The bubbling at its center had also been provoked to greater activity, perhaps by the heat; now gurgling echoes drifted up that almost had the timbre of distant, angry shouts. Conan had not intended to look down, and the giddiness that followed caused him to shift his weight too abruptly. He felt the stones beneath him grate and slip dangerously.

"Old man, what—?" He should have known, his weight was far greater than the rat-catcher's, too much so to risk crossing. He did not essay a leap, for he knew the stones would never withstand the force. He felt them starting to twist and separate beneath him anyway, and saw the old scoundrel watching him with that cursed blank, interested look of his "—What should I do?"

"You must decide for yourself." The voice boomed all around him as the bridge disintegrated and hurled him into the abyss. Falling toward the flames, he gazed up at the crooked shape of the old man and gave one last, despairing shout.

"Crom!"

An instant later he awoke. His narrow camp cot had toppled over and pitched him to the floor, driving the breath out of him; but the croaking cry he issued must have been real. Now guards rushed in through the entry flap and stood about him, lanterns raised high, their eyes searching the recesses of the tent for intruders.

"To your ease!" Conan ordered, sitting up from the floor. " 'Twas nothing of consequence."

The flap fluttered again, admitting Delvyn and Amlunia and a breath of evening chill. "Alas," the dwarf said with a look of perplexity, "bad dreams are more catching lately than saddle ticks!"

Amlunia hurried forward to succor the king. But he shook her off, arising by himself and setting his bunk aright as he did so. Then Prospero burst into the tent, causing Conan to bark out impatiently, "Enough, I say! It was nothing but an evil dream. And in truth, not so much evil as . . . unsettling. I do not need anyone's help."

"I know nothing of your dreams, my liege," Prospero declared. "In sooth, I wish that what I had just heard was a mere dream. But one of our forward scouts has just returned to camp pell-mell." The count looked gravely round the circle of watchers before delivering his news. "A large host of Kothian troops has been spied ahead of us, approaching the pass."

Chapter 18
Pass Sinister

Moon dawned at the hour of deepest night. By then, additional parties had been sent from the Aquilonian camp to reconnoiter the pass. They were ordered to proceed with utmost stealth in hope of readying an ambush, or of detecting one laid by the hostile force. King Conan insisted on faring forth too, so important was the choice of terrain on which battle would be joined.

Progress was difficult by the light of cold, careless stars. But when the coarse horn of a half moon jutted over the stony flank of the nearest Karpash crag, the view began to pale. The problem became one of evading discovery by enemy scouts and pickets.

So far the Karpash Mountains had not lived up to their evil repute. No vampires had swooped out of the sky, and no ghost fogs had settled on the invaders to wilt and sicken them as they slept. But the highest reach of the pass would have seemed an eerie place even by day. The rising moon gleamed on shards of granite as white as splintered bones, and the vegetation between them was stunted at best, limited to man-sized, brittle-leaved trees, rough gorse, and rank grass.

Some concealment for troops was offered by clumps of boulders that littered the landscape here and there, feathered with crooked fern. By night it was hard to decide whether these stones had lain here since the gods forged the mountains or whether, as in places it seemed, they were the fallen, primeval ruins of some earthly race. At the fringes of the plateau, the stones turned to fields of scree that trailed off into boulder-choked stream beds. Ranging from fist-sized to oxen-sized stones, this rubble appeared impassable to horses and treacherous to infantry.

In spite of the desolation the climate remained curiously warm. No harsh winds blew; only mild, fragrant breezes wafted up from the canyons. Looking ahead, Conan could see the land beginning to fall away to southward. There was no doubt that this was the very top of the pass: an odd, fateful place for armies to meet, a potential triumph or disaster for his hopes of conquest.

From hour to hour his scouts reported the size and disposition of the the enemy force. Conan was led up the side of a rocky outcrop, to be given an intimidating view of tents and watchfires stretching down the further valley. By all accounts it was a host at least equal of his own, ten thousand and more men afoot and mounted.

A fine prize, Conan thought while riding back, if they could be caught in disarray on this harsh, broken terrain—but there was little hope of springing such an ambush. His scouts had already glimpsed enemy outriders; quite likely some were watching him and his patrol right now, making similar appraisals of his force. He shifted in his saddle, suddenly wary at the keening of a night bird startled up from the gorse at one side; one of his Black Dragons tugged his reins and cantered over to investigate.

No, Conan told himself, the main task would be avoiding any traps the enemy set for his troops. The Kothian generals were shrewd tacticians; if the cunning Armiro himself were here . . . dared Conan hope? . . . then victory might be hardest of all to seize.

Gone, at any rate, were his plans of striking freely at his enemy's vulnerable heartland; gone his schemes of snatching throne and country out from under the young tyrant. There would be no swift maneuver, no free-wheeling raids, no chance of catching the Kothians divided and whittling them down in a series of unequal battles, to seize their empire by elegant indirection. All would now be settled by a clash of roughly equal forces on field harsh and alien to both.

Timing, tenacity, and ferocity would be the deciding factors. Losses would be heavy, and the loser, even if only loser by the narrowness of a hair, would be driven to retreat down a steep, treacherous path. He would be hunted to death by the victor almost certainly. Destruction would be total, victory slim or illusory.

Here, then, lay destiny. This was the sort of epochal battle that dream and legend had prepared Conan for all his days. He was chosen to lead the army of earth's greatest empire against that of its second greatest, so to decide the fate of the world. Such would be his name and his fame—win or lose, live or perish. A splendid fate for a warrior, this, the stuff of his deepest, grimmest cravings. Why then did he balk at the prospect?

Why did the thought bring a furrow to his brow and a taut, bitter flare to his nostrils?

First came the uneasy question, what was Armiro's force doing here? If the Koth meant to strike at Conan where he was vulnerable, why would he march to the empire's eastern edge, where he was sure to find Aquilonian force in full strength and readiness? Did he mean to add his forces to those of Corinthia and Brythunia? A poor investment, that; and Conan could not imagine Corinthia any more willing to admit Kothian troops into its lands than Aquilonian ones. The assault on Aquilonia's underbelly through Argos sounded like the princeling's insidious way, but this . . . ? It made no sense, unless it concealed some devious intent or advantage on Armiro's part.

Second, after this battle, what would become of Aquilonia? The loser's empire would certainly be forfeit, more probably to greedy neighbors and rebellious factions than to this battle's victor. The winner, with his army sorely weakened and dispersed throughout the Karpash, might easily find himself bereft of his own empire by similar perils. And when Conan thought of gentle Zenobia and Conn, and of his glittering kingdom, undespoiled as yet, the stakes of battle began to seem uncomfortably high.

Interwoven through his thoughts were memories of the dream that had startled him awake that very evening. There was much truth in dreams, he guessed, whether they were sendings of the gods or only wellsprings of one's own deepest wisdom. In consequence, he felt less arrogant than he had the day before, and a good deal more inclined to walk lightly.

The mounted guardsman returned from the flank; behind him trotted a Bossonian scout on a lighter horse.

"Sire," the Black Dragon told Conan, "this man returns from a skirmish with enemy scouts. He says his partner was slain and the Kothians fled." The outrider reined his horse around in confirmation, revealing a dark bloodstain at one side of his head.

"By Bel," Conan swore, "let him return to camp with me! There is much to be done. I will have the troops deployed by sunup."

The fireless, sleepless Aquilonian camp stirred wearily in the light of false dawn. Weapons clanked, hooves rattled stones, and officers passed down orders in voices sharp with tension. All thought of rest was forgotten in the imminence of battle. Around a heap of doused ashes, the leaders of the campaign paced and discoursed. They paused to hear reports and rap out fresh orders to the subordinates who brought them before continuing their debate.

"The enemy is maneuvering up to a line, as we are," Prospero insisted. "We may expect an attack at any moment; but more certainly we can expect an immovable defense." With hands braced on his weapon belt, he looked across the cold fire with a frown near-invisible in the gloom. "On this broken, constricted ground, to attack with cavalry would be suicide."

"But remember," Conan rumbled back, "they are defending Ophir and Koth. We are the invaders! If there is no fight, they win." The king, though plainly out of sorts due to early hours and battlefield surprises, kept his voice in check, preserving a spirit of tactical debate rather than argument. "As I see it, if we strike at dawn before their force is in place, we can start them on a retreat that will soon become a rout."

"But, Sire," Prospero said doggedly, "their army is

no more scattered along the trail than ours is. Besides, it does not take an army to defend this pass! A handful of their force will serve to hold it, and the full weight of our legions cannot be brought to bear in such a narrow, broken space.'' The Poitanian shook his head in exasperation. ''There is no advantage in speed or numbers and no flank of weakness to exploit. The ones who attack will be the fools; better they be Kothian.''

Conan's rejoinder was slow in coming, and the strum of a lute from atop a flat stone nearby heralded a pronouncement of the jester Delvyn. ''Might I say, King Castle-breaker,'' the voice observed mellowly, '' 'tis not like you to argue. That you deign to do so tells me you do not think attack a wise course either.''

''True, true, mayhap,'' the king muttered vaguely. Eager for any distraction, he turned to hear the report of a cavalry captain who had dismounted and who knelt by his side.

''Sire,'' the captain said, arising, ''a returning scout reports the presence of a royal pavilion and of imperial household troops in the Kothian camp. He thinks these things signal the presence of Prince Armiro himself.''

''Good, excellent!'' Conan said. ''What of the enemy deployments?''

''Sire, their front line now crosses the pass, lying as near as a hundred paces to our own in some places. They have seized cover and high ground where possible, but they refuse the open tracts and the temple at the center.''

''Temple?'' Conan demanded. ''What temple? You mean the declivity?''

''Aye, Your Majesty. I thought you had been told of it.'' The captain spoke hurriedly, covering his nervousness with military brevity. ''There are remnants of an ancient building in the low spot. Our men can see them in the dawning light—columns and paves only, Sire, nothing defensible. Apparently the Kothians regarded the place as a dangerous salient, as we did."

"Aye, well enough," the king said. "Send forward a sentry or two, otherwise hold our troops shy of the place for now." He clapped a hand on the man's brass epauliere firmly enough to be felt through the armor. "And stand ready for orders, Euralus! Dismissed."

When the man had remounted and waved farewell, Conan turned back to his associates with a muttered curse. "Crom, must there now be a heathen temple in the midst of my battlefield? I dreamt of one last eve! Such things make the troops uneasy—and give their commander a chill, too!"

Delvyn drew his fingers musically across the dry, taut entrails of his lute. "Perhaps due to the creeping plague of dreams lately," he observed.

"Aye, that," Conan agreed, "and a long and dire experience of haunted temples before it. Anyway, Prospero," he said with a nod to his friend, "you speak rightly. We shall not attack at dawn, but wait and see if Armiro does. Meanwhile the rest of our column can move up to the fore."

"Excellent, Your Majesty," Prospero concurred. "Patience may triumph where impetuousness cannot."

"Indeed," Conan said. "In a long faceoff, I may be able to goad the stripling Armiro into something rash. But for now we have only to wait—and perhaps to dine. Where is Amlunia?"

Prospero shrugged, showing no great concern. "Is she dozing in your tent, milord?"

"Nay." To make certain of it, Conan strode to the

open entry of his own pavilion, and then to one other. "She is not here."

The dwarf shifted in his cross-legged seat on the rock. "Did she not find you earlier, King Jabber?" he piped up ingenuously. "She rode to join you on your scouting mission forward. I assumed you had left her off to rest somewhere."

"Crom's hounds!" Conan exclaimed. "You mean she has not been seen since moonrise? A woman alone in this nest of roughnecks and ravishers . . . !"

"She is not exactly defenseless," Prospero pointed out. "You might set a page to find her."

"Nay," Conan growled irritably. "Come, Delvyn, you be my page and we'll seek her out ourselves. Breakfast can wait."

The jester sprang upright and strode to his mount, which stood saddled near Conan's, dwarfed by the larger horse. "A wise thought, my king! Face-saving, in case we find her ravishing some poor, defenseless lancer or engineer."

"Your Majesty, you will not be gone long. . . ?" Prospero solicited. "In the event of an attack—"

"In an attack, old friend," Conan said gruffly from the saddle, "you know what to do, as does every Aquilonian blade. Should you need me, look for me where the killing is thickest."

CHAPTER 19
Judgment

In the gray dawn, made grayer and tardier by mists rising between the Karpash peaks, the king and his dwarf circled the unquiet, half-empty camp. They rode forward to the defensive line; on the way they passed troopers shuffling groggily to battle, crouching in weeds to dine on hardtack and pemmican, and waiting with their heads pillowed against stones in the morning chill.

Discreet questions gave them a direction to follow—because Amlunia, as the most provocative, perilous, scandalous woman in the expeditionary column, went nowhere without being amply observed. An awed subaltern directed them toward the center of the host on the highest, broadest part of the plateau. A hulking Bossonian corporal nodded them quietly forward to where his company sat, honing and oiling their broad-bladed axes behind a stand of boulders. Where they rounded the pile, the scout crouching on duty, a half-Pict female, merely flicked her eyes contemptuously toward the open, uncontested ground.

There, some way off, could be seen the trim, powerful stallion Conan had given Amlunia. It grazed peacefully among the pale stone columns and pediments rising from the dewy grass.

A shout might have availed nothing; or it might have called forth retaliation from the enemy host that lurked—reportedly, at least—in the field just beyond. To bring along a squad of horsemen might have launched a small war with Amlunia as the prize; Conan was not ready to provoke his adversaries thus, at least not yet. So he and Delvyn, hoping to be overlooked by the enemy's sentries, spurred their mounts forward into no man's land, unescorted.

As they descended through damp, misty meadow their surroundings subtly changed. Slopes of dewy grass shouldered up around them to hide the outlines of the cold, barren Karpash tors. Slender stone pillars, ancient but unmarred by time, rose gradually taller and statelier on either hand—although, as Conan noted, they were shaped out of granite too hard for human tools to hew and polish. The paves of antique streets and plazas scuffed beneath their horses' hooves. Morning mists congealed and curled skyward in the depression, shrouding the view of the military line they had just left.

And so at last, the place took on a haunting familiarity redolent of dream. There before them stood the oft-glimpsed row of columns and entablatures, squarely linked against the sky; there the low-walled court, and there the stone-curbed pond of glossy black, whose ripples had spread so insidiously through so many nightmares. Conan had never trodden this elder courtyard, but had dreamt it. As he eyed the unnatural stirring of the water, the scene resonated dread and wonder in his soul.

Amlunia stood but a short walk beyond her tethered horse. She leaned against one of the low balustrades with her weapons sheathed and her bare arms folded across her breast. As Conan and Delvyn dismounted, she left off contemplating the dark water of the pond to turn and address them.

"So, you come at last! I know not what drew me here, but I sensed you would follow. There is something . . . thrilling about this spot, is there not, Conan?" Detaching herself from the balustrade, she moved sinuously toward the king and laid a black-gloved hand on his shoulder. The look on her upturned face was a seductive one.

Her overtures were interrupted by a clink of harness at the far side of the court. There, from behind the square corner of a pediment, emerged a lone warrior in brightly polished breast-armor, leading a horse—a fine beast, royally groomed and fitted out. Conan recognized the man and his imperial trappings instantly: the crested helm, the studded gauntlets, the shield striped with the bastard bar.

"Armiro!" The king's sword leaped into his hand as he spoke. "Bring on your ambush, Princeling! I am ready!" His eyes scoured the courtyard for signs of a trap. "Is dream-conjurement such as this now a part of your trickery?"

The low stone curbs and retaining walls before him, if not illusory, could hardly have concealed men, much less another horse. The silence that answered the king's echoing challenge might have made him seem foolish if the stench of the supernatural had not hung so heavily about the place.

Armiro, having looped the reins of his steed over a metal fixture in the stonework, took his time turning to face his rival. When he did so, he loosened his own sword in its sheath but did not draw it.

"Why, 'tis Conan, my impetuous foe!" The prince strode a few paces forward and halted near the center of the court. "If, as your leather harlot claims, you do not know why you are here—well then, you have even more rashness and obtuseness than I credited you with!"

"What is it I should know, stripling? Why am I here?" Conan strode forward, his blade raised in lethal readiness. Delvyn hurried after him, tugging at the king's empty scabbard and whispering restraining phrases; simultaneously, as if in answer to the king's question, a deeper roiling and rippling commenced in the murky pond. Bubbles began to froth at its surface; of a sudden the gurglings formed a cracked, rudimentary voice. This unwholesome phenomenon made the Aquilonian pause in his tracks.

"Hail, Mortal Kings! I extend a godly welcome to the two foremost champions of the human breed!" As the liquescent voice spoke, fires sprang alight in brackets and basins set around the courtyard. Lit by no visible hand, the greasy yellow flames had the odd effect of darkening the daylight; Conan fancied that the color of the sky overhead changed from dawn-pale to a deeper, more cosmic blue. "By my divine power," the voice proclaimed, "I, Kthantos, have guided you both here, that I may choose one of you to rule as sole lord of my earthly domain."

"What devilment is this?" Conan cried, glancing back at his friends to see if they had heard the same as he. "Armiro, I knew you for a a foul, murdering scamp! But now I find you a skulking sorcerer as well, requiring the help of a gargling night-demon to frighten your enemies!" He stalked farther forward, ignoring the bubbling pool. " 'Tis unmanly, just as I would have expected of you. . . ."

"Enough jabbering, barbarian!" Armiro lashed back. "I have a low opinion of imps and sorcerers myself, but here is no measly demon! Kthantos is a full-fledged god. . . ."

"Precisely. A god!"

The turbulence in the pool had grown frenzied as Conan spoke; the dark fluid now swirled in a near maelstrom, from which Kthantos' broken voice blasted forth powerfully. Near the edge of the pond, a black skeletal hand broke the surface, clutching a bent javelin. It drew back and hurled the weapon outward and upward.

In mid-flight, the javelin turned to a jagged lightning bolt. With a mighty crash the bolt struck the nearest, stoutest pillar, which stood on shoulder-high curbing just above the pond. The stone cracked audibly, and for a moment small lightnings shrouded the monolith like briary, luminous vines. When the glare subsided, the column stood split askew; blackened shards rattled down, and the smell of scorched granite filled the air.

"A small demonstration of my strength, which grows and multiplies by the hour." Kthantos' voice had fallen to a croaking calm even as the upheaval of the pond subsided to a steady lapping. "I will leave the pillar standing as a reminder to you. Both kingly champions are spiritual enough in nature, I should think, to see the virtue of faith in me, and the penalty for lack of it."

Conan, frozen in his tracks by the awesome display,

nevertheless shook off his supernatural dread and brandished his sword again, this time at the lapping pond. "I have slain gods before," he challenged. "Why should I league with one whom a rogue like Armiro claims as an ally?"

"Not as ally, but as supreme arbiter," Kthantos' voice spouted up from the center of the pond. "Only one of you will leave this place—that one the more worthy of the two, and he privileged to restore my worship by mortal men as sole god on earth."

"One of us chosen—by single combat, you mean." Conan nodded with frank anticipation. "Good then, I welcome my enemy with ready arms!" Reaching to his belt, he drew forth his dagger to brandish alongside his sword. "And yet," he continued with a note of doubt, "the whelp and I have met before at swordpoint. I bested him man to man and he answered me with betrayal. I am the better warrior"—Conan frowned with growing suspicion—"so why should he face me boldly, unless he has some unfair advantage hidden away—such as a private understanding with you, the appointed judge? He plainly knows more of this nefarious business than I do." Conan shook his dark mane stubbornly, the locks lashing free beneath the slim gold circlet of his crown. "Besides, even if by some trick he manages to slay me, my Aquilonian legions are more than a match for his!"

"Conan, King Jaw-cruncher"—Delvyn's voice piped up unexpectedly from beside him—"divine Kthantos has struck no bargains. He seeks only the best ruler to inaugurate his worship." Delvyn edged around the king's side to gaze solemnly up at him. "But I will second you in any test of arms or armies, O King! You are the finest warrior and the greatest monarch, as all men know."

"So, Delvyn, you too are a part of all this!" Conan eyed the jester with new understanding. "Likely Amlunia, as well—with her role in luring me here." He glanced over his shoulder at the leman, who looked back at him with an enigmatic smile. "I should have known that my ambitions would prove but a rattling cart to your brace of oxen."

"Nay, Sire, I am only a buffoon—" The dwarf blinked up at Conan with persuasive modesty. "—A mere foil to your greatness, which is all! But you know, King Ravager, 'twould be a great waste for you to slay Armiro the Koth, and for your legions then to spend their strength in wiping out his." He gestured with zeal to Armiro, who stood watching patiently. "Here at this ancient shrine are met, not just two mighty kings, but two vast armies whose power, combined, is capable of achieving either commander's wildest dreams of conquest." The jester's words obviously were meant for Armiro, too, although his every syllable was directed carefully at his liege lord.

"What is needed, as I see it," the dwarf continued, "is a compact between you two monarchs: an agreement that, whoever wins this duel—and it will be you, Conan, none could doubt that," he added in a low voice, "—whoever wins, both armies will join together under the command of the victor." The little man finally shot a frank glance across to Armiro, as if tossing out a challenge. "Furthermore, both empires, Kothian and Aquilonian alike, must bow to the winner's rule." Delvyn looked gravely from one king to the other. "It is in the power of both monarchs to decree this and be obeyed. Remember, 'twould enable the surviving one to unify all men, and therewith end their petty warring and spite. The aim of every great conqueror—to bring peace to the world—lies in the grasp of one here today! But to do it, you must risk all."

"Risk, aye," Conan answered, reflecting. "A wager of sorts. But to guarantee it, ranking second officers from both sides would have to be brought forward to hear the terms and witness the fight. Whether they would then abide by the result"—he shook his head uncertainly—"well, with a display of this godling's power, they might." Letting the point of his sword fall to rest on the gleaming pavement, he looked across at Armiro. "Even so, I cannot say I care for the stakes. This duel would either leave the world in the charge of a callow princeling, or leave me subject to the whims of a bubbling, puddle-dwelling hobble-de-god! If you ask me, there is little to choose between a matricide and the demon he worships."

"Matricide!" At this word Armiro suddenly flared. "A fine calumny to come from you, slayer of my mother! Take back the lie. . . ." For the first time, the prince's sword hissed out of its jewel-encrusted sheath. ". . . Or I will carve a niche in your black heart to shrine it forever, armies or none, empires be cursed!"

"Why would I lie to the son of lies?" Conan snarled back at him. "Pose as you may, rankle as you might, all men know it was you that had fair Yasmela cast down from her prison tower!" Raising his sword, he took a menacing step toward his foeman. "Her love for you was great, but even her loving memory will not keep me from dealing you the fate due an unnatural son!"

"Liar! Rogue!" Armiro started forward too, then halted abruptly and edged back to his place. "But stay, barbar-king, you cannot provoke me until all the stakes are on the table! I will have your tough, hairy hide and your ill-gotten holdings with it! What say you to your dwarf's proposal?''

"True enough, 'tis true,'' Conan muttered back. "I shall not fight until the fate of my empire is too well assured to be stolen away by treachery!'' He lowered his sword again and looked from Delvyn to the lapping, inscrutable pond. "As of now, I like not the terms of the contest, nor the temper of our self-proclaimed referee.''

As he spoke, letting his former rage ebb back to surliness, his gaze was drawn up toward the sky. Rather than dawning to full, bright day, the heavens seemed to have grown all the dimmer since their arrival. Behind the mists beyond the pillars, a sphere now hovered that looked too pallid to be the sun. Above and beside it a second, even paler orb glinted in the half light—too shrunken to be the moon, and hanging impossibly where no moon should hang. He glanced down to find neither orb reflected in the surface of the black pond. With a shiver, Conan again addressed the dark water.

"I know not what place this is, Kthantos—though it strikes me as being nearer hell than heaven. And I know nothing of you and your creed. Having seen your force of destruction—part of it, anyway—and your talent for lure and menace, I ask you, what is your power for good?'' He glanced suspiciously to the other humans. "And what, pray tell, is your true aspect? What form do you take when you rear up out of that black mire to impress your worshipers?''

"Down the course of history,'' Kthantos burbled back, "true gods, unlike paltry demons, grow ever more reluctant to show themselves to mortals. You, O

King, a worshiper of coy northern deities, should know this. The adherence of one's followers should be at best a matter of perfect faith.'' The spouting bubbles had grown calm and even. ''Therefore, it pleases me to remain in my pond; I but seldom leave it. Yet my powers, you will find, are near limitless—for good or evil either one, if you cling to the notion that the doings of a god may be measured by such quaint, outmoded concepts.'' The pond gouted and burbled in what may have been scorn.

''I can sway mortals through dream, as you have seen; my power over men's minds shall be, in time, quite complete. Already, by subtle means, I can change the course of human history—as evidenced by the epochal battle I have convened here, in this improbable place.'' The bubbling simmered complacently a moment, then resumed speech. ''The energy and ability of my disciples, I should add, are boundless . . . however stunted their mortal frames.'' Here the jester Delvyn stood carefully still, rendering no word or look, although the woman Amlunia was heard to laugh sharply. ''And further I have my messengers, extensions of my own hand, whom I can send across earth to perform any errand. So you see, mortal, a god is not a sprite or hobgoblin with one tawdry trick. A god is unopposable.''

''What mighty Kthantos says is true''—Amlunia's voice rang out abruptly from the edge of the courtyard—''especially of the willingness of his disciples.'' As she spoke, the leman strode boldly forward past Delvyn, into open space between Conan and Armiro. ''Long I sat here this morn, communing with the god's essence. Then, when I heard the holy one speak, his words struck to the deepest core of my being. I have seen the truth and so I proclaim myself Kthantos' disciple! Faithfully. Eternally.'' Her words echoed forth with seeming conviction.

''In furtherance of his ends,'' Amlunia continued, drawing a new and deeper breath, ''I mean to offer myself as a prize to the victor of this contest. Know you, Prince Armiro—'' She turned toward the Khorajan, meanwhile loosening the already slack laces of her leather suit to show off her womanly charms more favorably. ''—Know, O Tyrant, my talents are many. I am a savage fighter, a skilled courtesan, and a most eager concubine. Should you triumph, I promise you, my abilities would not be wasted . . . in whatever way you choose!''

Armiro barked out an astonished laugh. ''And what of your devotion to dour Conan, there? Will your faithfulness to Kthantos and me be no greater than to him?''

Amlunia sighed, settling her supple weight on one hip and resting her hand on her jutting sword-hilt. ''To tell the truth, I grow weary of Conan. I am tired of his scars and his battle stories. In you, O Prince, I see a more cunning fighter, and a better champion for Lord Kthantos.'' She sighed again, shifting her weight to her other hip. ''It matters not—I know Conan, and I can take what he deals out. But he is so slavish to tradition, I do not think he will ever make me his queen—at least not while prudish Zenobia lives!'' She shook her head in distaste. ''Nay, the world needs a free-spirited ruler. In this duel, Prince Armiro, my hopes rest on you.''

Armiro laughed heartily again. ''Boldly spoken, wench! I never formed the taste for such as you—but perhaps I am not too old to learn! Rest assured, if you are my prize, you will be used well and . . . completely.''

''A most sordid desertion, Amlunia!'' Delvyn declared from her side. As he did so he made a swift, wary glance at Conan's face, which had remained impassive. "This is a slight for which my own champion will savor his revenge later, once he is victorious! But for now, it may be convenient." The dwarf's voice levelled in amazingly swift resignation. "Now you can ride to Prince Armiro's camp and summon his lieutenants to witness our bargain—while I, with His Majesty's permission, go to fetch King Conan's. I suggest, Amlunia, that you take the prince's horse. Straddling such a fine beast, a comely wench like you will never be pricked with arrows by his sentries!" The dwarf gave the leman a pat on the rump, then turned and strode toward his own idle pony. "Now at last, the full power of conquerors is poised," he declared over his shoulder. "However it may fall out, the world is doomed."

"Hold, mannikin, I still do not think—"

Conan's protest was cut short by the stamp of hooves and the creak of travel-worn wheels. The mortals present all turned to see a splintered, mud-spattered chariot, a light trap with but two horses left in its team, rumbling toward them. Its course through the meadow was flanked by fully armored riders from the Aquilonian camp: Prospero, in his sable-blue livery, was among them, as were other high officers and, to Conan's surprise, Chancellor Publius, his white beard powdered gray with trail dust.

The chariot rattled up onto the pavement and wheeled to a halt. Conan saw its occupants then, and his jaw fell. Behind the haggard, half-dead charioteer knelt Zenobia, Queen of Aquilonia, bending over a prone figure wrapped in a filthy black travel-cloak.

A half-dozen elite guards, their uniforms soiled and rent by long, harsh travel, reined up around the chariot.

Dismounting, each fell to one knee in salute to the king. As Zenobia looked longingly at him, Prospero sprang down from the saddle and cried, "Sire, your royal wife brings you urgent news!" He glanced at the scene around them with an uneasy air. "I know not what dark spell hangs over this place, nor why morning itself seems blighted here, but thank Mitra we have found you!"

"Aye, milord," Publius panted from his saddle, "it is a matter of the utmost importance."

Conan went to join them, turning his back on Armiro, the mystic pool, and its invisible denizen. Striding up to the chariot, he seized Zenobia in a fierce embrace. She gave a faint cry, and her joyous tears plastered travel dust to his face and hair. But at once, she fought free of his arms and gasped up to him, "Conan, my husband, we have galloped all the way from Tarantia—we have run a dozen horses to death, my love, so that you may hear the truth!" Her eyes, red-rimmed with anguish, searched his deeply. "Hear it not from my lips," she said at last, "but from hers!" Looking down, he saw that her slim, dust-grimed hand pointed at the cloaked passenger lying in the bottom of the chariot.

It was an old woman, Conan saw as he knelt with his queen—vaguely familiar to him, though the side of her head was sore disfigured by a scar. She lay weak and ill from the journey, yet her rheumy eyes were open and her hand rose up from the copious sleeve of her black robe to beckon him. The hand was not withered and palsied, he noted. So perhaps she was not as old as she seemed.

Her voice issued from her dusty lips in forceful but irregular accents: "The truth is for Armiro, too."

Puzzled, Conan looked up at Zenobia, who gazed back into his eyes and nodded. He shrugged and looked around the court for the Khorajan. The prince stood watching the proceedings at a distance, waiting near Delvyn and Amlunia, who likewise seemed to watch with uncertainty.

"Princeling," the king called out, "come hither! This news is for both of us, so they tell me."

Armiro hooked a hand on the hilt of his sword and regarded the gathering of Aquilonians suspiciously. Scowling, he declared, "I do not fall so easily into a trap!"

Conan shook his head with an impatient jerk. "My word is worth its measure—unlike yours, villain!" Arising, he faced his officers and guards. "Listen all! I hereby command you to allow Prince Armiro safe conduct among us." He turned back to the Khorajan. "Now do you believe me?"

In answer, after further hesitation and fierce looks at his foemen, Armiro walked forward. As he drew near enough to see the face of the reclining woman, his step quickened. "Vateesa," he exclaimed, "my mother's bodyservant! An unintended victim of my fight against Aquilonian treachery." With more suspicious glances at the stricken maid's companions, he knelt at her side.

"Aye, so," Conan marvelled to himself, " 'tis she, Yasmela's maid! Vateesa, girl, I thought you dead!"

The king bent over her with freshened attention, and Prince Armiro's aspect was not unkind either as he reached down and clasped her hand. They did not need to lean so close, however; for her rough voice, impelled by dry sobs, spilled brokenly across the courtyard.

"My mistress died without telling it, Lords—but before I pass out of this world, I must!" Her hand impulsively tightened on that of the young prince. "Armiro, heed me—Conan is your father!" Her streaming eyes sought out the elder king's. "Conan, Armiro is your son!"

The shock that swept through both men was tangible to all present, and more powerful than the spell of a sorcerer of the third Khitan ring. Yet the two did not at first express any emotion. After staring frozen-faced at the gasping woman for a long heartbeat, they looked up at each other. Their gazes locked together and would not part.

"Armiro, is it possible . . . ?" Conan ventured.

"Why yes, it must be so." Armiro whispered the fact with amazement. "By Erlik, I have been a sorry fool!" He shook his head in pained fascination, though his eyes could not tear themselves away from Conan's. "I set inquiries afoot in the court of Khoraja, to no avail! Long I sought my true father, ever in vain. But now, at last . . ." He rose slowly to his feet, eyes still fixed on Conan's face. "Now, at last, I can kill you!" His sword, wrenched instantaneously from its sheath, swung savagely at Conan's head.

No weapon could have risen in time to meet the plunging blade. Instead a dive, swift and pantherine, saved Conan as the still-ringing metal swept past him. It passed an ear's-breadth over his head, to embed itself with a *chunk*! in the weathered wooden rail of the chariot. Armiro's miniscule delay in wrenching it loose gave the king time to dash erect and draw his own steel brand; then both fighters were clear of the chariot, stamping and whirling across the courtyard in a man-made storm of flashing, ringing steel.

Mindful of their monarch's previous order, and confident too of his skill, none of the Aquilonian warriors moved to interfere. Zenobia, overcome with fatigue and the horror of the spectacle, sank helpless to the platform of the chariot. Thence she looked on, propped up by the arm of elderly Publius. Beside them Vateesa lay senseless, mercifully unaware of the fury her words had caused.

The maid Amlunia, by contrast, capered with excitement as she watched the contest, issuing hoots and cries at the warriors' most skillful passes. Her applause favored the prince, but was balanced by that of Delvyn, who called out encouragement for his nominal master's strokes and parries.

Conan, for his part, found himself severely pressed. Before this, in Yasmela's bedchamber, the prince had fought with measured zeal and calculated skill against his armorless adversary until the tide of Conan's strength had surged against him. Now, facing a warrior girded as tightly as he, Armiro's rash ferocity made him a far more lethal threat. He drove fearlessly in at the king, landing a clashing stroke on the gold-chased hauberk followed by a fierce, ripping upswing that scored into the leather straps of Conan's harness. In a trice he planted a kick on the Aquilonian's hip armor that bode fair to stagger the larger man; then, whirling, he delivered a sidelong slash and struck sparks from the jewelled edge of the king's epaulier, an inch away from the throbbing veins of his neck. After a dozen more such passes of arms, Conan found himself easing back, hoarding his strength and waiting for the safe chance, which never seemed to come.

To complicate matters, he did not want to kill Armiro. He could no longer doubt that the lad was his son. An instinct older than honor and kingship, deeper than the roots of his tribal Cimmerian boyhood, told him that to slay his child would be impossible. He might disable the youth—fight him to a standstill, or offer up his own life for the sake of the bond. But alas, he sensed that the prince would be only too eager to seize on that.

"Armiro! Son!" he rasped, sidestepping a whistling slash. "It is not meet that we battle so. I offer you a truce!"

"Seducer! Bastard-maker!" Snarling, the prince renewed his attack. "Offer me your belly instead, that I may—" His words were dinned out by the noise of his blade clashing against Conan's greaves, and by Conan's sword driving the weapon up and aside. He finished breathlessly with: "Betrayer! You killed my mother, now kill me!"

"You accuse me falsely." The king, to make himself heard, had to give ground once again. "I never killed her, I swear it! If you can truly say the same, lad, there is no issue between us."

"No issue!" Armiro's voice rose suddenly to a shriek. "Vile deserter, I am your issue! What of your betrayal, your cowardly flight?" He drove in at Conan with a blind, furious thrust. "Why, knave, did you leave me fatherless, and my mother unprotected? *Where were you?*"

Conan parried the desperate thrust with all the strength in both his arms; then, for the first time, he saw his attacker's blade waver indecisively in air. Looking to his adversary's face, he was amazed to see Armiro's fierce, hawklike eyes blinded with streaming tears. A new surge of feeling welled up in him—or rather, a vacancy: a vast, aching abyss of misunderstanding and loss.

The emotions were disabling—dangerous, Conan knew. Yet he could not bring himself to drive in and exploit Armiro's weakness. And before steel could clash again—if, indeed, it would have—a fresh turmoil exploded nearby. The dark water in the pool had been seething and surging, ever more violently cascading and foaming. Strangely, though, the frothing dark liquid did not splash the onlookers; it stayed contained within the pond's stone rim. Now great bubbles surfaced and belched forth words in godly command.

"Fight and slay! Slash and kill! Strive mightily, O champions, for the winner shall win the world, and with it my divine favor!" As the gargantuan voice chanted its litany, gaunt skeletal arms thrust up from the waves to frolic and applaud. A long, compound appendage, formed of more than one black, dripping limb jointed together, jutted up and thumped a rusty sword against an antique shield held high aloft by a similar gruesome limb. Where the decaying metal clanked together, small, brilliant lightnings darted outward from the impacts.

Then a scream sounded from among the clustered watchers. Both royal fighters, standing distracted by the unholy spectacle, at once turned their eyes in the other direction.

Most of the newcomers gaped silent, appalled by the sudden horror in the fountain; it was the ailing servant-woman Vateesa who cried out. She had arisen from the chariot bed, and now she stumbled forward, drawing anxious Queen Zenobia and Publius after her with the urgency of her halting steps.

"There it is!" she cried. "The monster, it killed milady!" She raised a trembling hand toward Kthantos' heaving fountain and the upraised, frolicking arms. "That thing, that cursed thing, came to us in the night wearing this very robe"—she plucked distractedly at her own soiled, outsized garment—"and killed Princess-Regent Yasmela! I was lying near to death, but the dream awoke me—the nightmare that came true! It made me rise up and journey half across the world. . . ."

With a final, piteous gasp, Vateesa toppled forward and fell to the paves—as dead, seemingly, as her beloved queen. Zenobia, stricken by grief, knelt over her, and then cried out with an upraised, despairing face, " 'Tis true, Conan, 'tis true! When first she found her way to me in Tarantia, the poor wanderer, she told of a dark, eldritch thing that came to the tower to strangle her mistress! Yasmela died trying to escape it." The queen looked up imploringly at the two combatants. "Conan did not slay Yasmela, nor did Armiro!" She raised her hand to point an accusing finger. "It was that creature, that abomination—the evil thing in the pond!"

"Lies, all lies," the jester Delvyn proclaimed of a sudden. Waving hands to draw attention to himself, he moved in front of the still-pointing Zenobia. "Not lies of yours, milady! I beg your pardon, for I do not think you would seek to mislead your royal husband—but lies of the mad servant's making! Certainly Kthantos did not kill Yasmela! I know not who did, but not he! He is a noble god, an honorable god who would not stoop so low. To accuse him is sheer blasphemy. . . ." The dwarf, in his attempt to be earnest, began to seem more pathetically comic than ever he had in jest. None laughed at his blustering, but eyed him suspiciously, until the sullen-faced Amlunia flared up.

"What matters it anyway?" she cried, drawing her dagger and flourishing it overhead. "On with the combat, I say! We fight for the world, not for the honor of a dead mistress! Come, champions, fight and slay! — So that I may give the mercy stroke to the loser, and lavish myself upon the victor!"

"Yes, fight!" The most spirited urgings still came from the animated pool, whose heavings were violent as ever. "These interruptions stay the business at hand—which is no mere business, but a ritual sacred to me! Fight and slay, I adjure you, and cast the victim's body into the sacrificial pool! Finish quickly, if you do not wish to see my divine wrath visited on all present!"

The godly decrees the pool belched forth were wasted on the combatants. For it seemed that, in the last few soul-wrenching moments, some silent understanding had passed between king and prince. Resolutely Conan sheathed his sword, Armiro following suit. The prince muttered a curt word to Conan, and the king nodded and turned.

Both men strode to the nearest brazier, set in a low retaining wall a few paces from the pond's rim. Standing at either end and seizing the metal mesh of its rim in their gauntleted hands, they wrenched at it together and pulled it free of the stone. Facing one another, they shuffled its weight to the rim of the pond and, with a heave, cast it in.

The glowing, flaming coals seethed as they met the dark fluid; the metal itself frothed and steamed. It made a hissing sputtering mass as it sank out of sight in the pool, driving a gout of gray vapor skyward.

At this assault, the bubbling voice clamored forth afresh, expressing not pain or fear, but outrage. "So! You join together in mutiny against me, your rightful lord! Fools, you know not what fate you call upon yourselves! Do you really wish to set your eyes upon the face of the Living God?"

As the voice lathered forth, its timbre deepened and intensified, as if some change were taking place in its watery bed—as if, in fact, it was rising to the surface. The crowd of Aquilonians watched in dread uncertainty. But the two fighters, father and newly acknowledged son, paid no heed, intent as they were on a new exploit.

Conan, flanked closely by Armiro, clambered to the top of the breast-high retaining wall. Striding to the scorched, splintered pillar that had been struck by Kthantos' lightning, the king set his armored shoulder against it, while Armiro drew his sword. The prince began driving his blade into the gaping crack near the column's base, widening the fissure by prying out chunks of shattered granite. Before long he was hacking savagely with chiming steel at the brittle stone. Meanwhile Conan strained and battered at the monolith, his armor scraping and clashing against it in his efforts to topple it into the pool.

From the water below a monstrous birth commenced. A shape, which at first resembled a gnarled stump or a huge, knotted turban, broke the wave-tormented surface. Its color was the gleaming black of the pond, striated by glossy greenish veins; it continued to rise until it stood out of the water taller than a man, poised on a thick, pliant stem.

Then the tightly wrapped tentacles began to unfold. Aghast, the onlookers saw that its shape was that of a *fist*, which soon blossomed forth into a *hand*—an inhumanly tapering, sinuous one, it was true, but handlike in its gargantuan form.

In the tips of all five supple, boneless finges, large lidded eyes blinked open to survey the scene. Simultaneously, in the concave palm of the monstrous fistule gaped a mouth, circular in shape and ringed by pointed triangular teeth. The pulsations of this orifice, large enough to engorge a man whole, gave the thing a hideous, flesh-hungry look.

There was no knowing whether this was the god Kthantos' main part, or how much more of him might lurk beneath the surface; but its emergence brought shouts of terror from the watchers. It was enough, even, to overawe several of the Black Dragon guards; they froze in their tracks an unseemly time before rushing forward with Prospero to join their king's struggle with the pillar.

The earliest of them arrived too late, in any case . . . for, rocked by the efforts of king and prince, the column had already begun to topple. It gave way with a grinding rumble, twisting aside from the center of the pool as it gathered force. Meanwhile, the thing emerging from the water had found its voice again—a voice that smote their ears with its full volume, unmuffled by the inky fluid. "HERETICS!" it thundered more brutally than before—"FAITHLESS INFIDELS! NOW LEARN THE WAGES OF THOSE WHO LEAGUE AGAINST THEIR GOD—"

The quintet of eyes, peering from the tips of the waving black fingers, focused on the soldiers nearest the wall. The titanic hand stretched toward them; a moment later, the shadow of the pillar swept across the grasping thing. Then it was obscured entirely by the curtain of black water that flew skyward as the column struck the pond.

The pillar smote the curb of the pool with a deep, seismic impact, granite tolling against granite like massive bronze. It fell to one side, but once in the basin it rolled and settled toward the center, trundling to the place where Kthantos had been. There the god no longer was, having disappeared from the surface of the water.

At the sight, the warriors atop the ledge cheered and exulted. In the excitement Conan and Armiro even embraced, laughed together bright-eyed, and smote one another's armored backs in congratulation. Yet their gazes returned warily to the pool as they wondered what new horror might emerge. Part of the fluid had been splashed out, along with gouts of muck, foul-smelling bones, and rusted armor scraps which now smirched and littered the white granite of the court. A sizeable crack had also been made in the pond's curbing; it gaped darkly, extending beneath the black waterline.

"Look," a guardsman suddenly shouted, "the level is falling! The water is flowing into the crack—down, into the mountain below!"

And so it indisputably was. On the pond's surface, oily currents could be seen curling into the crack, and from the crevice a faint gurgling could be heard. Each moment more of the granite basin was exposed, with more of its reeking, bone-littered bottom muck. Nowhere in it could Kthantos' shape be seen.

"Fools, have you truly thrown away your chance?" This cry came from Amlunia, who ran to the edge of the pond and stared out across it in outraged disbelief. "With the help of Kthantos' power, the world could have been ours! But now . . . if you have killed him . . ."

"If they have killed him, harlot, they have killed one too few!" So shrieked Zenobia as she darted forward from beside Vateesa's fallen body. "If you love your grasping god Kthantos so—then join him, slut!" Overtaking the warrior woman beside the pool and striking before the leman could draw sword, she dealt out a shove followed by a vicious kick. Amlunia faltered an instant on the mud-slimed granite, then toppled over the curb to land with a splash in the retreating water and filth. Her fall was hailed with applause and delighted outcries from the watchers.

Amlunia was unhurt by the fall, through black-slimed from neck to toe. Cursing and threatening her attacker, she immediately started scrambling up the slippery side of the basin. Then something impeded her; there came a faint stirring in the water near her ankles, and all at once she began to slip backward toward the center of the pool.

Her face showed that something was terribly amiss. Thrashing and struggling in earnest, she gave a panicked cry. She clawed desperately at the hard granite and thin, yielding mud, but it availed nothing; screaming and sobbing as she went, she was drawn relentlessly back into the ebbing water. Near the pond's center where the fallen pillar tapered out of sight, the last splashes flurried, along with Amlunia's gargling, drowning cries. Then she was gone. It happened so swiftly the onlookers could scarcely credit it—and it transpired without any reappearance of the pool's sinister occupant.

"By Crom, a hideous death even for a traitor!" Conan sprang down from the wall to join Zenobia and draw her back from the pond's edge. "Can it mean we have not killed Kthantos?"

From the place where the last dregs of pond pooled down the fissure in the stone, amid a steaming waste of filth, a faint, familiar voice gurgled up.

"Killed a true god?" it demanded. "By a mere gaggle of thankless mortals? Delayed . . . yes, perhaps!

Vexed . . . indeed, most certainly! But killed? No, never!''

The voice was receding but seemed inclined to speak on. ''And do not fear for the life of the one called Amlunia. I rest now, but I do not go to my repose alone. I have been given a young, fresh soul to keep me company. Mortals, I accept your sacrifice—a warm spirit and supple body to amuse me for a millennium or two. Come, my dear, snuggle closer. . . .'' Here the god's accents were interrupted by a flurry of bubbles that seemed to indicate a struggle of some sort, along with shriller frothings that almost suggested screams.

Then, though it was broken and nearly inaudible, Kthantos' voice resumed: ''. . . My legacy to those on earth . . . my high priest who failed me. In consequence, he is removed from my protection . . . spell is ended. He must make his own way in his own form. My curse upon . . . fickle mortals. . . . Live in fear until my return.''

With those last conjurations and threats, Kthantos' gurgling dwindled to nothingness. Behind him was left a thin, foul film of sludge and debris in the hollow granite basin. No trace remained of his repellent physical shape, nor of luckless Amlunia.

Conan stood clasping Zenobia with one arm, frowning and mumbling over the last words of the vanished god. ''High priest? —In his own form—?'' Of a sudden, he relinquished his hold on the queen and stood gazing around the courtyard, his weapon again raised. ''Delvyn!'' he called out, ''dwarfish rogue, where are you fled to?''

His question was answered by several of his guards, who stood at the edge of the paved court. They called to him and pointed toward the tethered horses, where it seemed Delvyn had fled, possibly in hopes of escaping on his own undersized mount.

But now, it was evident, the dwarf had been overtaken by a bizarre sort of change. He lay on the ground, struggling in some strange way, and the stout-hearted guardsmen held back from him as if hesitant to approach or seize him. Indeed, Conan saw as he ran up, it would have been difficult for him to mount his small horse any longer—or even a full-sized one, because the dwarf was growing so rapidly in size.

His current difficulty was due to the increasing tightness of his custom-made armor—but that was only temporary, as leather stays snapped and metal plates buckled before the inexorable force of his growth. Having thrown off his helmet and kicked aside his boots, he let the rest of his armor and clothing split and slough away, except for a stretched, sundered kirtle that bound his waist and preserved his modesty. Thus was revealed a form far stouter and stronger than his former one, if no less ungainly or blocky-shaped. When he climbed ponderously to his feet, Conan saw that he was a giant, half again as tall as the king himself, with a huge, leering face, and hands thick enough to crush the life out of two men at once.

"What devil's trick is this?" Conan demanded of him. "How comes it I have befriended a shape-changer—and one who leagued with a swamp devil to steal my soul? Is that friendship?"

"Who ever spoke of friendship, King Knuckle-rapper?" Delvyn challenged him back in a thunderous voice. "You looted me from old King Balt in battle, remember? You were the master, I the knave! That may yet change."

"A knave you ever were," Conan shot back, "and

shall remain, methinks! But how comes this unseemly growth?"

"No great mystery in it," Delvyn said in his new-found stentorian voice. "A giant I was, strong as ten ordinary men and feared and hated by them in consequence. I faced a life of solitary toil and despair—for, whenever I sought the company of mortals, they called me monster, and banded together to slay me." Looming half-naked among the soldiers like one of Kthantos' granite monuments, he told his story unashamedly.

"So I broke open a temple library and throttled the holy hermits who tended it. I spent years teaching myself the ancient scripts and poring through forbidden scrolls. I sought a spell to reduce my accursed size. In time I conjured forth a demon, Kthantos, who swore to grant me that.

"I was clever, you see!" Delvyn grinned down at his listeners, though his expression showed little regard for what they truly thought. "Knowing that my former great size had been a curse," he explained, "I bade Kthantos spell me even smaller than a puny mortal. That way, 'twas easy to confront foolish men and work my way into their confidence—for just as every human hates anyone larger than himself, he loves having someone smaller to set off his own greatness—someone he can bully, ridicule, and outshine! With the knowledge I had gained, and with the help of Kthantos, I soon became a friend and advisor to great kings, steering them to my own secret purposes." Delvyn shook his head and laughed a mighty, roaring laugh. "In time I myself would have been king—King of the World, Delvyn the Great!"

"Wretch! Scoundrel!" Conan reproached him, shaking his sword, "I never scorned you, never dishonored you! Why choose me as the butt of your evil plan?"

The giant laughed ponderously again, staring around him to intimidate the soldiers as they tried to contain him in a circle of raised pikes. "I battened onto you because you were rich, well-beloved . . . and foolish! Imagine a king who loves himself so little that he thinks all others must hate him—who, great as he is, wants to believe himself ten times greater—and who does not know happiness when he holds it in his hand!" Delvyn shook his head with giant, leering contempt. "Of all the kings of Hyboria, none would have been easier to hoodwink than you! Your brat here, Armiro—I might have had to work at ensnaring him. But you, you would have given me the world on a platter! —except, alas, that your friends were too loyal in spite of all your bluffing and strutting!"

Conan glowered grimly up at him. "And so you had your demon kill Queen Yasmela! You baited me with Amlunia, and set me against Armiro!"

"Aye, indeed," Delvyn gloated, "because I knew that when the time came—when I had badgered you to mastery of the world—one final thing would destroy you totally and without question: the knowledge that you had killed your own son!"

"Devil! Schemer!" Conan raged. "Know you, I have slain greater monsters before! I have no fear of facing you alone!"

"Good, then," Delvyn sneered back. "Come at me, little man! I will tear you open and sup up your liver for lunch!" He made a lumbering step forward; it was menacing enough to make the two spearmen standing in front of him fall back, while others closed in from behind. "Then I'll take your buxom queen for my lap-doll and send your puny army scampering off through the hills, King Bunion-thumper!''

Livid with fury, Conan hefted his sword. Then he looked around the circle of watchers—Zenobia, Count Prospero, the aged Publius, Armiro standing ready, with steel once again drawn—and he lowered his own weapon. ''Traitor or no,'' he called up to Delvyn, ''you once were my friend. I would not slay you! And yet, Mitra knows, you cannot be allowed to live.''

Delvyn snarled back, a noise of rage and anguish. ''Mitra knows I would not want to!''

Conan nodded, turning away. ''Guards!'' he commanded harshly.

A rushing stamp of feet sounded, mingled with shouts and muffled curses.

In moments it was over. Delvyn lay dead on the ground, and none of Conan's guardsmen had taken a hurt more serious than a broken limb.

CHAPTER 20
Impasse

After most of the contention and revelation was past, King Conan set his men to build a cairn over Delvyn's giant remains. He and Armiro meanwhile saw fit to remain on the neutral ground of the once sacred courtyard. Word was sent back to their two armies, still poised for strife, that a parley of great moment was underway. A group of officers and guards finally came forward from the Kothian side to guarantee Armiro's well-being. At Zenobia's urging, young Prince Conn was brought from the Aquilonian camp, where he had been left by her for his safety.

Since their high-spirited defeat of Kthantos, feelings between Conan and Armiro had been left unexamined. So various were the possible outcomes between them, and so vital the national interests at stake, that their next exchange boded to be world-shaping. Therefore both rulers were coached intently by their advisors, and meanwhile forced to stand a great distance apart, eyeing one another uncertainly.

Publius, for one, had a proposal which he saw as a rare diplomatic coup for his kingdom. "Your Majesty, you can now establish a dynasty—nay, you already have done so! By publicly acknowledging your paternity of Armiro, you can claim a degree of kingly authority over Aquilonia and Koth together! And later," he added with a glance to Zenobia, "you can influence the division of that vast realm between Armiro and your other offspring by exercise of your royal will." The chancellor beamed at the elegant simplicity of it. " 'Twould be primarily a matter of form, of course, since Armiro would hold tenaciously to what power he already has. But it would serve your goal of uniting the world in a bloodless way—without war, without the power of our two great empires tragically cancelling one another out."

Conan shook his head, his eyes busy watching the Kothian prince converse amid the huddle of his officers. "Nay, Publius, I would not risk putting young Conn in a position of certain rivalry with his half brother; especially given Armiro's advantage in years and in . . . courtly guile." Looking to Zenobia and noting her nod of relief, the king spoke on. "Besides, can you imagine that young firebrand ceding parental authority to me?" He laughed, the toss of his head revealing more admiration than annoyance. "No, Chancellor, in such a prickly, uneasy alliance as that would be, I fear the real power would fall to you and your diplomatic ilk. You go-betweens would keep us always teetering on the brink of civil war."

"What then, Sire, is your plan, if I may ask?" Whether Publius was annoyed or merely crestfallen was a question his tact concealed any answer to. ''An abandonment of the war? Recognition of the current borders?''

''An alliance, grounded on mutual respect,'' Conan said with certainty. ''His for me, and mine for him.'' He nodded to Zenobia. ''And a strong defense, of course. Good fences make good neighbors.'' He bent closer to Publius and spoke in a lower voice. ''Most likely, old friend, our borders will have to return to the former ones. Nemedia and Ophir can be set up as buffer kingdoms under Halk and Lionnard, for the sake of keeping the young hothead at a safe distance.'' He frowned thoughtfully. '' 'Tis a sore price to pay. But my son is a sharp dealer, and we will have to sacrifice dearly if we expect him to do the same.''

Prospero, waiting close by, entered the conversation with an amazed smile. ''Does this mean, milord, that you have abandoned your hopes for world conquest?''

Conan laughed sharply and a little ruefully. ''I can think of only one thing that could have kept me from it—and Crom has seen fit to place that thing in my path. An obstacle I would not wish to destroy.''

Publius shook his head with cautious doubt. ''Milord, is such an acceptance of, ah, limited triumphs, consistent with the greatness of one who aspires to be a god?''

''A god?'' Conan guffawed sharply. ''I am no god! Believe me, I have seen enough puny would-be gods to last me for Kthantos' long lifetime!'' He blinked as if remembering something in the dim past. ''I have seen a real god, too—but I have far to go before I can match him.'' He made a casual gesture toward Armiro, who stood gazing back from among his officers. ''Besides, if I am a god, then yon prince is at least half a one . . . and he is no godling!''

Turning from Publius and Prospero, Conan went to Zenobia's side and kissed her. From her arms he took his young son Conn and held him up before his face. ''I tried to win the world for you,'' he told the boy, ''but now you will have to take as much of it as you need.''

Handing the lad back to his mother, he turned and strode out into the courtyard to meet Armiro. As he went, his troopers sent a cheer ringing skyward.

''Hail, Conan the Great!''